THE
RED QUEEN
DIES

ALSO BY FRANKIE Y. BAILEY

*Wicked Danville: Liquor and Lawlessness in a
Southside Virginia City (VA)* (with Alice P. Green)

Wicked Albany: Lawlessness and Liquor in the Prohibition Era
(with Alice P. Green)

African American Mystery Writers: A Historical and Thematic Study

*"Law Never Here": A Social History of African American Responses to
Issues of Crime and Justice* (with Alice P. Green)

Popular Culture, Crime, and Justice (with Donna C. Hale)

Out of the Woodpile: Black Characters in Crime and Detective Fiction

THE
RED QUEEN
DIES

Frankie Y. Bailey

MINOTAUR BOOKS
A Thomas Dunne Book
New York

A THOMAS DUNNE BOOK FOR MINOTAUR BOOKS.
An imprint of St. Martin's Publishing Group.

THE RED QUEEN DIES. Copyright © 2013 by Frankie Y. Bailey. All rights reserved. Printed in the United States of America. For information, address St. Martin's Press, 175 Fifth Avenue, New York, N.Y. 10010.

www.thomasdunnebooks.com
www.minotaurbooks.com

Library of Congress Cataloging-in-Publication Data

Bailey, Frankie Y.
    The Red Queen dies: a mystery / Frankie Y. Bailey.—1st ed.
        p. cm.
    "A Thomas Dunne Book."
    ISBN 978-0-312-64175-7 (hardcover)
    ISBN 978-1-250-03717-6 (e-book)
    1. African Americans—Fiction.   I. Title.
    PS3552.A368R44 2013
    813'.54—dc23

                                    2013013934

Minotaur books may be purchased for educational, business, or promotional use. For information on bulk purchases, please contact Macmillan Corporate and Premium Sales Department at 1-800-221-7945, extension 5442, or write specialmarkets@macmillan.com.

First Edition: September 2013

10 9 8 7 6 5 4 3 2 1

To my family, who always believe in my dreams

Acknowledgments

Let me begin by thanking and apologizing to anyone that I forget to acknowledge here. So many people contributed to the process of transforming an idea that occurred to me on a train bound for Albany into the book that you are about to read that I fear I am bound to forget to mention someone.

Thank you to the faculty and staff of the English Department at Virginia Tech. It has been my honor and privilege to serve on the Distinguished Alumni Advisory Board and to have the opportunity to come home to Tech for those board meetings. Thank you to the members of the advisory board, who have given me support and encouragement. A special thank-you to Ed Weathers for introducing me to Kathryn (Kaye) Graham, and to Kaye for answering my Lewis Carroll question with a suggestion about the Salvador Dalí edition of *Alice in Wonderland*. My thanks also to my professors in the English Department when I was a student. Let's hear it for Shakespeare and children's literature!

Thank you to my friends and first readers, Joanne, Angie, and Caroline. Your comments and suggestions were invaluable. I hope you enjoy your characters.

Thank you Rob Edelman and Audrey Kupferberg for inviting me to dinner. Rob, as you will notice, your collection inspired me.

Thank you to the members of the Great Dane rescue group with whom I chatted during the UAlbany Fall Festival and Book Fair.

Thank you to my friend Joy Pollock, who was not called on to read this one, but who should know she'll be hearing from me on the next one.

Thank you to my late parents and my brother for sharing hours of television watching and discussion. Those hours in front of the television set were not wasted. Not only did they prove useful in my future career, but, as you will notice, Wayne, discussions about giant insects and aliens are an excellent springboard for literary endeavors.

To my fabulous aunt Kitty, who is always there to laugh with and to provide support and encouragement.

Thank you to Dr. Doug Lyle, who answered my medical questions. Any mistake in the translation of your information, Doug, is solely my own.

Thank you to James Miller, former public information officer for the Albany Public Department. Although I ended up operating in a parallel universe in the near future, it was helpful to talk with a PIO about responses to crime scenes.

Thank you to the members of the Sisters in Crime—Upper Hudson Chapter (the Mavens of Mayhem) and the Capital Region Romance Writers of America. The support for writing that happens in both groups has made me a better writer.

Thank you to the faculty, staff, and students in the School of Criminal Justice for putting up with a sometimes eccentric mystery writer in your midst. A shout-out to fellow mystery readers Han Toch and David Bayley.

Thank you to Marcia Markland, my editor at St. Martin's, who could see the potential for a book in an e-mail. You don't know how much I appreciate your willingness to say, "Go for it, and let me know when you have something." My thanks, too, to Kat Brzozowski, associate editor. I appreciate not only your hard work on my behalf, but your enthusiasm about my book. Thank you to Lauren Hesse digital marketing; and Hector DeJean, publicity, for tips over lunch about how to plunge into social media. And, thank you to Helen Werner Cox, illustrator; John Hamilton Design; and David Rotstein for giving me a cover to die for. Thank you Carol Edwards and Amelie Littell for their copyediting expertise, and the other members of the production staff.

My thanks to Jonathan Lyons, who walked me through my contract for this book.

Finally, my special thanks to Josh Getzler, who is my first agent and with whom I am already thrilled to be working.

1

DATE: **Thursday, 24 October 2019**
TIME: **0700 hours**
WEATHER TODAY: **Mid 90s. Air quality poor. Evening storms.**
DISPLAY ON WALL: *Wake-up News*

"*Good morning, everyone. I'm Suzanne Price.*

"*First, the news from the nation. The federal government says, 'No hoax, no conspiracy, but still no definitive answers.'*

"*The administration denies suppressing portions of the commission report on the November 2012 close encounter between NORAD fighter jets and the black boomerang-shaped UFO that appeared over the Mojave Desert, creating worldwide awe and panic before disappearing in a blinding flash of light.*

"*In Las Vegas, preparations are under way for the now-annual spectacular celebration of that close encounter.*

"*However, a warning from alien invasion survivalists, who say this seventh anniversary will be the year the spacecraft returns leading an armada. Survivalists plan to retreat to their bunkers on November 2. Gun shop owners report sales of firearms are up, as they are every year as the anniversary approaches.*

"*Meanwhile, the National Weather Service says another eruption of solar flares could cause more communication and power disruptions early next week.*

"*Forest fires in both Canada and breakaway nation New France continue to burn out of control, sending smoke southward.*

"*Scientists taking part in a climate change conference in Philadelphia disagree about the explanation for the significant improvement in the acidity levels of the world's oceans. 'It shouldn't be happening,' an MIT oceanographer said. 'Nothing in anyone's data predicted this turnaround. But I think we can safely rule out divine intervention and UFO babies.'*

"*Out on the presidential campaign trail, a political firestorm erupts as Republican front-runner Janet Cortez accuses independent candidate Howard Miller of 'rallying angry, frightened people to commit hate crimes.' During an arena speech yesterday, Miller called on several thousand supporters to 'reclaim America for Americans' and 'restore our way of life.' Cortez says Miller is 'morally responsible' for the attacks that have been escalating since he announced his third-party candidacy.*

"*Now, here at home . . . a chilling scenario posed by a local crime beat threader. Is there an 'Albany Ripper' in our midst?*"

"Dammit!" Hannah McCabe jumped back as the grapefruit juice from her overturned glass splashed across the countertop, covering the still-visible display of the nutrition content of her father's breakfast.

"Bring up the sound," he said. "I want to hear this."

"Half a second, Pop. Hands full." McCabe shoved her holster out of the way and touched CLEAN UP before the stream of juice could run off the counter and onto the tile floor.

"*. . . Following last night's Common Council meeting, threader Clarence Redfield interrupted a statement by Detective Wayne Jacoby, the Albany Police Department spokesperson . . .*"

In the chief of police's office, Jacoby struggled to keep his expression neutral as the footage of the press conference and his exchange with Redfield began to roll.

"The Albany Police Department remains hopeful that the Common Council will approve both funding requests. The first to expand GRTYL, our Gang Reduction Through Youth Leadership program, and the second to enhance the surveillance—"

"Detective Jacoby, isn't it true that the Albany PD is engaged in a cover-up? Isn't it true that the Albany PD has failed to inform the citizens of this city of what they have a right to know?"

"I know you want to offer your usual observations, Mr. Redfield. But if you will hold your questions until I finish—"

"Isn't it true that we have a serial killer at work here in Albany, Detective? Isn't it true that a secret police task force has been created to try to track down a killer who has been preying on women here in this city?"

"That is . . . no, that is not true, Mr. Redfield. There is no secret task force, nor is there any cover-up. We . . . the Albany PD does not engage in . . ."

From his position by the window, Chief Egan said, "Stammering like a frigging schoolgirl makes it hard to believe you're telling the truth, Wayne."

"The little bastard caught me off guard," Jacoby said, his annoyance getting the better of him.

The others at the table avoided his glance, their gazes focused on the wall where his confrontation with Redfield was continuing.

"So, Detective, you're telling us that there aren't two dead women who—"

"I'm telling you, Mr. Redfield, that we have ongoing investigations into two cases involving female victims who—"

"Who were the victims of a serial killer?"

"We have two female homicide victims. Both deaths were drug-induced and both occurred within the past six weeks. On each occasion, we made available to the media, including yourself, information about—"

"But you didn't release the details that link the two cases. You didn't tell the media or the citizens of this city that both women were—"

"We do not release the details of ongoing homicide investigations, Mr. Redfield. And you are not aiding these investigations with your grandstanding."

"My grandstanding? Don't you think it's time someone told the women

of Albany that the police can't protect them? That they should stay off the streets after dark, get inside when the fog rolls in, and lock their doors? Shouldn't someone tell the taxpaying citizens of this city that in spite of all the hype about your Big Brother surveillance system, a killer is still moving like a phantom through the—"

"What the citizens of Albany should know is that the Albany PD is bringing all its resources and those of other law-enforcement agencies to bear to solve these two cases. Veteran detectives are following every lead. And the citywide surveillance system the department has implemented—"

"When it's working, Detective Jacoby. Isn't it true that the solar flares have been giving your system problems?"

One of the captains sitting at the conference table in Chief Egan's office groaned. "Is he just guessing?"

On the wall, Jacoby's jaw was noticeably clinched.

"As I was about to say, Mr. Redfield, before we began this back-and-forth, the DePloy surveillance system has been effective both in reducing crime and solving the crimes that have occurred. That is the end of this discussion."

"You mean 'Shut up or I'm out of here'?"

"Ladies and gentlemen of the press, I am now going to finish the official statement regarding funding. I will only respond to questions on that subject. . . ."

Chief Egan said, "Not one of your better performances, Wayne. You let him rattle you." He walked over and sat down at the head of the table. "Her Royal Highness, the mayor, was not pleased when she called me last night."

On the wall, the anchorwoman took over.

"Detective Jacoby then completed his statement about the proposals before the Common Council. When a reporter tried to return to the allegation made by crime beat threader Clarence Redfield that a serial killer is at work in Albany, Detective Jacoby ended the press conference and left the podium. Mr. Redfield himself declined to respond to questions from reporters about the source of his information. We'll have more for you on this story as details become available.

"In another matter before the Common Council, a proposed emergency

*expansion of the existing no masks or face-covering ordinance to include
Halloween night. The new ordinance would apply to everyone over eight
years of age. The recent outbreak of crimes involving juveniles . . ."*

"Now, they're even trying to take away Halloween," Angus McCabe
said from his place at the kitchen table. "Well? Any truth to it? Do we
have ourselves a serial killer on the loose?"

McCabe put her empty juice glass on the shelf inside the dish-
washer. "Since when do you consider Clarence Redfield a reliable
source, Pop?"

"He ain't. But I've spent more than half my life grilling official
mouthpieces, and the way Jacoby was squirming—"

"Jacoby can't stand Redfield. You know that." McCabe snagged
her thermo jacket from the back of her chair and bent to kiss his
forehead. "And you're retired now, remember?"

"I may be retired, but I'm not dead yet. What's going on?"

"Got to run, Pop. Have a good day."

"Have a good day nothing." He rose to follow her into the hall.
"Hank McCabe, you tell me what's—"

"Can't discuss it. I'll pick us up some dinner on the way home.
Chinese okay?"

He scowled at her, his eyes the same electric blue they had always
been, the bristling brows gone gray.

"No, Chinese ain't okay. I'm tired of Chinese. I'll cook dinner tonight. I've got all day to twiddle my thumbs. What else do I have to
do but make dinner?"

"I thought you might intend to work on your book. You do have
that deadline coming up in a couple of months."

"Book, hell. There ain't no book. I'm giving the advance back."

"If that's what you want to do," McCabe said. "On the other
hand, you could just sit down and write the book."

"You try writing a damn book, Ms. Detective."

"Not my area of expertise. But you've done it a few times before.
Even won an award or two."

"This one's different. Nobody would read it even if I wrote it. And don't 'If that's what you want to do' me. We were talking about this serial killer that Redfield claims—"

"Sorry, Pop, I really do have to go. I want to get in a few minutes early this morning."

"Why? What are you—"

She closed the door on his demand that she get herself back there and tell him what was going on.

Striding to her car, McCabe tried to ignore the whiff of smoke that she could taste in the back of her throat and the sticky air, which made her want to step back into the shower.

The heat was due to break tonight. That would clear the air.

And Pop would pull himself out of his funk. He always did.

Of course, the other times, he'd had an office to go to . . . and no restrictions on his alcohol consumption.

"I have every confidence in your ability to get what we need, Mike boy."

"Right." Baxter flashed his best cocky grin. "You know you can count on me."

His caller nodded. "I know I can." He pointed his finger at Baxter. "Watch your back out there, you hear me?"

He disconnected, his image fading from the screen.

Baxter closed his ORB and leaned back on his cream leather sofa. He stretched his arms over his head, fingers clasped. His gaze fell on the framed photograph on his desk. Himself in dress blues. Graduation day from the Academy.

Baxter grunted, then laughed. "You should have seen this one coming, Mike boy."

He rubbed his hand across his mouth, whistled. "Well hell."

Baxter reached for his ORB again. He pulled up a file and began to update his notes.

When he was done, he grabbed his thermo jacket and headed for the door.

His mind on other things, he left the apartment on cooldown and the lights on in the bathroom, but the condo's environmental system had gone into energy-saver mode by the time he reached the lobby.

In the garage, Baxter paused for his usual morning ritual, admiring the burgundy sheen of his vintage 1967 Mustang convertible. Then he got into his three-year-old hybrid and headed in to work.

McCabe was stuck in traffic on Central Avenue, waiting for an opening to maneuver around a florist van.

In Albany, double parking had always been considered a civic right. With more traffic each year and the narrow lanes that had been carved out for Zip cars and tri-bikes, Central Avenue in the morning was like it must have been when Albany was a terminus for slaughterhouses, with cattle driven along Central Avenue Turnpike. Stop, start, nose, and try not to trample one another as they moved toward their destinations.

McCabe tilted her head from side to side and shrugged her shoulders. What she needed, yearned for, was a long run. Even with geo-simulators, five miles on a machine was never as good as running outside.

McCabe's attention was caught by a flash of color. On the sidewalk in front of Los Amigos, a young black woman in a patchwork summer skirt laughed as an older man, suave and mustachioed, swirled her in a samba move. Still laughing, she disengaged herself and scooped up her straw handbag from the sidewalk. Hand over his heart, the man called out to his impromptu dance partner. Giggling, she went on her way.

Stopped by the traffic light at the intersection, McCabe lowered her window enough to hear the music coming from the open doorway of the restaurant. Before it was Mexican, the place had been Caribbean, and before that, Indian. The owners of the hair salon on one side and the discount store on the other had complained about this latest example of ethnic succession. Loud music, spicy smells—in other words, the threat posed by "Mexs" moving into this block as they had others. Some legal, some American citizens, some neither, arriving in Albany in greater numbers during the years when the convention center was going up. Now the resentment was more vocal, the sense of being in competition greater. Even the imagined threat of an interplanetary invasion hadn't changed that dynamic. Earthlings still distrusted other earthlings. They defended what they thought of as their turf.

Since the UFO, old episodes of Rod Serling's *Twilight Zone* had become a cult favorite with teen "space zombies." According to Pop, the zombies weren't the only ones who should be watching the series. He claimed that in the event of another close encounter, Rod Serling had left instructions. Rule number one: Even if the spacecraft looks flashy, check to make sure it isn't a balloon from a Thanksgiving Day parade. Rule number two: Even if the lights do start going on and off, don't turn on your neighbors, assuming they must be the aliens. Rule number three: Even if the "visitors" introduce themselves and seem friendly, ask for additional information about how they plan "to serve" mankind before hopping on their spaceship.

Meanwhile, daily life continued on Central Avenue, where Zoe James, the black female owner of the beauty shop, refused to patronize the Mexican restaurant next door.

At least she and Sung Chang, the Korean-American owner of the discount store, had stopped calling the cops every time the music and dancing overflowed onto the sidewalk. Of course, the JANET CORTEZ PARA PRESIDENTE sign now on proud display in Los Amigos's front window might set them off again. Both James and Chang had signs supporting the current vice president, who was male, black (biracial, actually), and likely to be the Democratic nominee.

But according to Pop, the candidate they all needed to be worried about, should be scared to death of, actually, was Howard Miller, that smiling "man of the people." Howard Miller, who was as smooth as the churned butter from that family-owned farm he boasted about having grown up on.

McCabe stared hard at the traffic light that was supposed to adjust for traffic flow and right now was doing nothing at all. She decided to give it another thirty seconds before she reported a problem.

Howard Miller.

They hadn't looked at that kind of hate crime because they had two white female victims. But the murder weapon . . . What if one of Miller's crazy followers . . .

Horns blared.

McCabe was reaching for her ORB when the traffic light flickered and went from red to green.

More horns blared.

Three women, pushing metal shopping carts, had decided to make a last-minute dash across the busy intersection. White with a hint of a tan, clad in light-colored shorts and T-shirts, they were too clean to be homeless.

The women were almost to the other side when a bike messenger zipped around a double-parked produce truck.

The women darted out of his way. He skidded and went down hard. Sunlight sparkled on his blue helmet, but his work-tanned legs were bare and vulnerable.

One of the women looked back, peering over her designer sunglasses. She called out something. Maybe it was "Sorry about that." Then she and her fellow scavenger hunters sprinted away in the direction of Washington Park, where Radio KZAC must be holding today's meet-up.

The taxi driver behind McCabe leaned on his horn. She waved for him to go around her.

She watched the bike messenger get up on wobbly legs. He looked down at his knee and grimaced. But the next moment, he was checking his bike. Then he grabbed for his leather satchel before a car could run over it. Hopping back on his bike, he pedaled off.

A car pulled away from the curb, opening up a spot a few feet away from Cambrini's Bakery. McCabe shot forward and did a quick parallel park.

She got out and headed toward the intertwined aromas of fresh-baked muffins and black coffee. Maybe the day wasn't going to be so bad after all.

The line wound back to the door, but it seemed to be moving fast. McCabe glanced at the old-fashioned chalkboard that always had the morning's "featured muffin." Not in the mood for pumpkin, she found what she wanted on the menu and sent her order from her ORB to checkout before joining the queue.

"Good morning, sister. Is God blessing you this fine day?"

She turned toward the deep voice and beaming smile of the man in the black New York Yankees baseball cap and the white suit and white shirt, which contrasted with his chocolate brown skin.

"Good morning, Reverend Deke."

"I said, sister, 'Is God blessing you this fine day?'"

"Yes, thank you, He is," McCabe said.

"I'm pleased to hear that."

Reverend Deke went out the door carrying his steaming coffee cup. By high noon, he would be bringing "the message" to any of the office workers who decided to leave the climate-controlled Empire State Plaza complex to patronize the lunch wagons lined up along the street. Some of the workers would pause to listen as Reverend Deke broke into one of the spirituals that he had learned on his Georgia-born grandmother's knee.

McCabe watched him go, greeting the people he passed.

Ten minutes later, she was jammed in sideways at the counter by the window, munching on a lemon-blueberry-pecan muffin. Half a day's supply of antioxidants, and it even tasted like it was made with real sugar.

The police frequency on her ORB lit up. She touched the screen to see the message that Comm Center had sent out to patrol cars.

McCabe swallowed the last bite of her muffin and grabbed her iced coffee container from the counter.

Out of the sidewalk, she spoke into her transmitter. "Dispatch, Detective McCabe also responding to that call. En route."

"Copy, McCabe. Will advise," the dispatcher responded.

Mike Baxter picked up the same dispatch as he was pulling out of the fast-food drive-thru. He shoved his coffee cup into the holder and reached for his siren.

"Dispatch, Detective Baxter also responding."

"Copy, Baxter. McCabe's headed that way, too."

"Thought she would be. This could be our guy."

"Happy hunting."

McCabe pulled herself to the top of the fence and paused to look down into the alley. She jumped and landed on the other side, one foot slipping in dog shit. The man she was chasing darted a glance behind him and kept running.

In a half squat, McCabe drew her weapon and fired. Her bola wrapped around the man's legs. He sprawled forward, entangled in the cords, crashing into moldering cardboard boxes and other garbage.

McCabe ran toward him. He twisted onto his side, trying to sit up and free himself.

"Get these ropes off me, bitch!"

"Stay down," she said, training the weapon, now set to stun, on the perp's scrawny torso. "Roll over on your belly."

He looked up at her face, then at the gun. Either he was convinced she would use it or deterred by the minicam that was attached to the weapon and was recording their encounter. He sagged back to the ground and rolled over.

She stepped to the side, about to order him to raise his arm behind his back so that she could slip on the first handcuff.

"You got him!" Mike Baxter said, running up. He was sweating, cheeks flushed, eyes bright with excitement. "That was great."

"Cuff him," McCabe said, trying not to let Baxter see that she was breathing hard.

She was thirty-four to Baxter's twenty-nine, and, yes, she had outrun him. But she should be in better shape than this. Today's air-quality reading was no excuse.

Baxter snapped the cuffs into place and McCabe retracted her bola.

Baxter hauled the perp to his feet.

"Hey, man, this is police brutality, you hear me?" the perp said. "I'm gonna sue both of you."

"That all you got to say?" Baxter said.

"Say? You're supposed to read me my rights, man."

"You got it, man," Baxter said. "You have the right to remain silent. Anything you say can be used against you . . ." He recited the words with the controlled irony of a cop who had been saying them for several decades. But he looked like a college kid. That was why he had been recruited from patrol to work undercover vice. But word was that he had wanted out of that and played a commendably discrete game of departmental politics, involving his godfather, the assistant chief, to get reassigned.

Sirens screeching, two police cruisers pulled into the alley.

Baxter grinned at McCabe. "Great way to start the day, huh, partner?"

"Absolutely," she said, scraping her shoe on the edge of a mildewed cardboard box.

She hoped he realized that the likelihood that this was the guy they were looking for was about zilch.

2

Outside the station house, two uniforms were hauling a drunk hooker out of the back of their cruiser. Hands cuffed behind her, purple wig askew, the hooker kicked one of the uniforms in the shin with her pointed-toe stiletto. Her momentum sent her sprawling.

The perp McCabe and Baxter were bringing in laughed. "Bitch down on her—"

"Shut up," McCabe said.

The perp glanced at her and closed his mouth.

The uniform who'd been kicked dragged the hooker up from the ground by the handcuffs. The hooker's colorful complaints filled the air.

Baxter greeted the two detectives coming out of the station house. "Hey, guys, what've you got?"

"Two thugs in an alley," Sean Pettigrew said. "The vic's at St. Pete's."

"Looked like a professional job from the cam," Walter Yin, his partner, said.

Yin squinted up at the sun, then at the gray fedora in his hand.

"New hat?" McCabe asked.

"Casey bought it for me," Yin said, referring to his wife. "She said my old one was too dirty to clean and too hot to wear anyway."

"That one's nice," Baxter said.

"Very nice," McCabe agreed.

"It's made of some kind of new material," Yin said. He stared at the hat, squinted again at the sun.

He put the hat on his head and tugged at it to give it a tilt. "Let's move, Sean."

Pettigrew, his own head hatless, waved his hand in farewell. "Off to the war, fellow gumshoes. Crime's breaking out all over this fine day."

Baxter and McCabe headed into the station house with their perp.

"If the weather report's right," Sid Wallace, the desk sergeant, was saying to a uniform, "a big storm's supposed to come through tonight. That'll clear the streets. But then tomorrow, we got a full moon. The loony tunes are going to be out—" He broke off when he saw McCabe. "Hey, McCabe, you got a visitor. That old lady from the droogie boys' case. I put her in Interview A."

"Thanks, Sarge," She glanced at Baxter. "Mike, can you handle—"

"Got it under control," he said. "I'll make sure our guest here gets checked into our best accommodations."

"I'm still going to sue," the perp said.

"Go for it," Baxter told him

"Wait for me to start questioning him," McCabe said.

He nodded, but McCabe didn't want to leave him on his own too long. Baxter was eager to prove himself.

She opened the door of Interview Room A. The room had no windows. Someone had turned on scenery. Clear, sparkling morning sunlight dappled a meadow of wildflowers. Birds chirped and butterflies fluttered. McCabe touched the console, replacing the dewy meadow with white walls and silencing the sound effects.

She smiled at the woman. "I can do without a spring meadow this morning. Seems a little silly when you walk out of the building and it's already eighty-five degrees, with the air smelling of smoke from north of the border."

Mrs. Givens, who had been sitting rigid, her face blank, nodded. "Scenery's pretty to look at. But sometimes it can wear on your nerves."

McCabe sat down across from her. "I'm sorry you had to wait for me. I had to make a stop on the way to the station."

Mrs. Givens was in her late seventies. Bifocals that were not a retro statement perched on her nose. "It wasn't like you knew I was coming by. I just decided I'd better come on down here."

"Now that we're both here, what can I do for you, ma'am?"

Mrs. Givens pushed at her glasses. She sucked her bottom lip between her teeth.

McCabe reached across the conference table to touch her hand. "What is it, Mrs. Givens? Has something happened?"

The woman glanced down at McCabe's pale brown hand covering her darker one. "Honey, how'd you hurt yourself like that?"

The scratch from the fence was red and jagged. "I was chasing someone," McCabe said. She drew back her hand, covering the gesture by reaching for her ORB.

Mrs. Givens said, "Well, I guess if you like your job. . . ."

"Yes, ma'am, I do. I think it's important work. But let's talk about why you came in. Do you have questions about the call you received from the DA's office?"

"No, I understand what they want me to do. That's why I needed to come in and tell you in person."

"Tell me what?"

"I feel real bad about this. But there's no point in me meeting with that assistant district attorney. No point at all, because I can't testify."

"Has someone threatened you? If someone has, we can provide protection for you and—"

"No, it ain't that. I can't testify because I don't remember that night like it happened."

McCabe sighed inwardly, afraid she knew what was coming.

"How can you not remember, ma'am? It was only a couple of weeks ago. You made a statement at the time."

"I know I did. But since then . . ." The woman pushed up her glasses. "I'm going to tell you the way it is, Detective McCabe, because I appreciate how you handle yourself with people in the community."

"Thank you, Mrs. Givens. Now, why can't you testify?"

"It's like I said. I can't testify because I don't remember about that night. I can still see some of it if I think about it real hard, but it's like I'm not there."

"Like you're not there?"

Mrs. Givens cleared her throat.

"What do you mean it's like you're not there?" McCabe said again.

"I . . . my niece, she's studying to be a medical technician. She told me about this stuff you could take. . . ." Mrs. Givens's gaze held McCabe's. "You know about it, don't you? About the stuff that they been using with the soldiers who get hurt fighting in the war? They call it 'lullaby.' "

"I know about it. Lullaby is the street name for the version that's available on the black market. It's an illegal drug."

"I know you can't buy it in no store. But I couldn't eat, and I couldn't sleep. I was about crazy with what I was seeing in my head."

"I know your memories of what happened must have been upsetting, Mrs. Givens. But, ma'am, you—"

"My niece said you didn't need me to testify. She said you had them boys right there on your cameras. One of them got his mask yanked down when they was fighting with that other boy. And you got their DNA, don't you?"

"That's true, Mrs. Givens. But you are our most important witness. Your testimony about the attack—"

"I told you I can't do that now. My niece said there won't no reason for me to keep on suffering. 'Being traumatized,' she called it."

"So your niece got you some lullaby?"

"No, she didn't. She just told me about it. Then somebody else gave me the name of somebody who could get me some. But I ain't going to say who."

"Did your niece tell you that this drug can be dangerous? That the black-market version is sometimes laced with—"

"I got it from somebody who guaranteed his batch was okay. He said he knew the man who made it."

"The effects of the drug don't always last, especially when it isn't taken within the first few hours after the event. You may start to have flashbacks again, nightmares that are worse than—"

"Then I'll take some more."

"You don't want to do that, Mrs. Givens. You don't want to get addicted to a drug that messes with your mind."

"My niece will make sure I'm okay."

"Your niece isn't a doctor. If you're having problems, you should see a doctor and get help with—"

"I'm not having problems no more. My niece told me that the drug would work better than talking to somebody, and she was right. I ain't had one bad dream since I took it. I'm sleeping fine now. Don't dream at all. But I feel bad about not being able to testify, and I wanted to come in and explain."

The door of the interview room slammed back against the wall. Jack Dole, all six four of him, loomed in the doorway.

"Lieutenant Dole," McCabe said. "Did you need something, sir?"

Dole glared at her witness. "That's nice of you to come in to explain. You want to explain to the family of that kid who got himself killed helping you? You want to explain how you couldn't testify and those little savages who bashed his head in and stomped on his dead body ended up back out on the street?"

Mrs. Givens blinked at him. "My niece said I . . . I don't—"

"You don't what, lady? Explain it to me."

A tear trickled down the woman's cheek, making a trail beneath her glasses. "I was having dreams. Awful dreams. And you ain't got no call to speak to me like that. I know you got what you need. I can't be no help to you."

McCabe scraped her chair across the floor and stood up.

"Lieutenant Dole? Sir, the DA's office may be able to make its case without Mrs. Givens's testimony. We have the forensics—"

"I know what we have, Detective." The flush that temper brought to his ruddy brown face was still visible when Dole turned back to Mrs. Givens. "Who did you buy the lullaby from?"

"I didn't know him. He was . . . he was just a man I went to meet in the park."

"Which park?"

"Why you want to know that?"

McCabe tapped her fingers against her pant leg, uneasy, on the verge of reminding the lieutenant that Mrs. Givens had the right to a lawyer if this was about to turn into an interrogation about a drug buy.

But she had opened it up by asking the woman if her niece had been her supplier.

"Haven't you seen the billboards?" Dole said to Mrs. Givens. " 'Keeping Watch to Keep You Safe'? The surveillance cameras we've got all over the city? The ones that caught the droogie boys' attack on you? If you bought lullaby in the park, one of our cameras would have picked up—"

"I'm an honest citizen. You ain't got no right to harass me because I don't want to remember being hurt and frightened. My niece said—"

"I don't give a rat's . . . I don't care what your niece said. You were a witness in a homicide case. You aren't any use to us now." Dole stepped aside and gestured toward the door. "Don't let us keep you."

Mrs. Givens stood up. She was trembling. She glanced at McCabe.

McCabe said, "Take care of yourself, ma'am."

Mrs. Givens nodded, then made her way out, her head bowed.

In the silence that followed, McCabe said. "You were pretty rough on her, weren't you, Lou?"

"I'm getting fed up, McCabe. I'm getting fed up with victims who decide they don't want to be victims, and witnesses who decide they don't want to be witnesses."

"Maybe the ADA can get around the problem by giving Mrs. Givens immunity on the drug charge. Then he can put her on the stand to explain why she can't remember clearly what happened. She's an elderly woman. A jury would understand how upset she was about being attacked and then seeing her rescuer killed in front of her. And with the court ruling about overwhelming forensic evidence—"

"You think the bozos on the jury are going to care about that? All we need is one bleeding-heart juror who looks at our droogie boys' sweet little faces . . . We've even got diversity, a black one, a white one, and two Hispanics. Wanna bet their public defender claims the cops profiled them because we don't like that kind of race mixing. Before their PD's done, the jury will want us on trial for using our technology to frame the little darlings. Why the hell couldn't the woman put up with a few nightmares until after she'd testified?"

"I think she was already scared about testifying." McCabe reached for her ORB on the conference table. "And then came the nightmares. That can be hard to deal with."

Dole touched the console, shutting down the camera and recording equipment in the room.

He turned and looked at McCabe. "You ever think of going that route, McCabe? You ever think of swallowing some lullaby and forgetting?"

McCabe stared back at him, her gaze holding his. "Have I ever given you cause to think that, sir? Have I ever given you cause to think that I would take an illegal drug?"

"You must be dealing with some memories now that your brother's back in Albany." He squinted at her. "You look tired, McCabe. Bad dreams keeping you awake?"

McCabe took a deep breath. She had known "Big Jack" Dole since she was nine years old and he was a patrol cop in uniform. He knew what he was asking. She knew why he was asking. But the questions still made her mad.

She kept her voice even. "I don't break the law by taking illegal drugs, sir."

"I'm glad to hear that, because I understand your brother's going to be staying around."

"Yes, sir," McCabe said. "He was invited to join a research team at UAlbany."

"Smart guy, your brother."

"Brilliant, sir."

Dole studied her face. "You know where my door is if you need to talk . . . off the record."

"Thank you for the offer. But there's nothing to talk about. With Adam and me, it is what it is."

Dole ducked his head and smoothed his hand over his freckled, shaved scalp. "What's the story on that perp you brought in?"

"We haven't had a chance to question him yet."

"I know that, Detective. I'm asking for your gut reaction."

"That maybe he knew the girl who'd lived in that house had been murdered. And he decided to break in and see what he could see. I don't think he's our guy."

"Then he'll keep. I need you back out in the field."

"Yes, sir. We saw Pettigrew and Yin heading out as we were coming in. Pettigrew said it was a busy morning."

"It just got busier. We've got another corpse."

McCabe took in the twist of the lieutenant's mouth. "Is it a woman, Lou?"

"A white female. Appearing right now on camera."

He gestured for McCabe to precede him out the door.

3

A scream greeted them as they walked into the emergency room at St. Peter's Hospital.

Pettigrew and Yin stopped, saw the woman who had screamed was clutching a limp child, saw a nurse was rushing toward her.

Yin picked up the conversation that they were having, pushing the image of the child out of his head before it could settle there. "So, are you going to ask her out?" he said.

They had been discussing the cooking class Pettigrew was taking. Or more specifically, the woman who was teaching the class that Pettigrew was taking. She was the only woman in whom Pettigrew had expressed interest in recent memory.

Yin, married for twelve years, was always interested in his divorced partner's social life, or lack thereof.

"I'm not sure that would be appropriate," Pettigrew said. "She's the teacher, and I'm a student in her class."

"Sean, it's a cooking class at a nutrition center. She's probably glad even to see a man in the class."

"That doesn't mean she wants to date the one she sees. Anyway, there's another man, an older guy who's taking the class with his wife. He used to work for—"

"Sean, the teacher. The pretty, really nice teacher who didn't get mad when you set the kitchen on fire."

"I didn't set the whole kitchen on fire. Only my unit."

"Sean, are you—"

"I'm thinking about it, Walter. The class meets two more times."

Pettigrew held up his badge for the nurse at the admitting desk.

The vic they'd come to see was dozing when they stepped into the curtained cubicle. He opened his swollen eyes and blinked up at them.

Looking at his face, Pettigrew was reminded of raw meat. "Mr. Jorgensen," he said. "Sorry to disturb you, sir. I'm Detective—"

"Get lost." The sheer antibacterial mask that had been applied to Jorgensen's face rippled as his swollen lips moved, "I got nothing to say."

Yin said, "You should rethink that. If you know who—"

"I got nothing to say to the cops."

Pettigrew rubbed at his chin with the back of his hand. "You're 'Swede' Jorgensen."

"Used to be him," Jorgensen said, and closed his eyes again.

Pettigrew glanced at Yin. Yin shrugged and said aloud, "If the guy's busted up by thugs and he doesn't want to talk to us, it's his funeral."

Pettigrew looked again at the man's battered face, the muscular body gone to fat outlined beneath the sheet. "You were a terrific baseball player, Mr. Jorgensen. We'll get back to you if we come up with anything."

On the way back to the station house, Yin took out his ORB and pulled up the information on Jorgensen. "His current address is a boardinghouse."

"How does that happen?" Pettigrew said. "How does a guy who was one of the greatest pitchers in the league end up like that?"

"He played for the Yankees for a while, didn't he?" Yin said. "Maybe he got zapped by that curse you're always telling me about."

"They almost broke it in 2014. This year, we're back in the series. All they have to do is hold on and—"

"And the champagne will flow and Yankee fans will dance in the streets."

"It's got to happen," Pettigrew said. "Sooner or later, it's got to happen."

"Keep the faith, partner," Yin said. "Getting back to Jorgensen, curse or no curse, he pissed somebody off."

"So what could a broken-down ex–baseball player do to piss someone off enough to get a visit from two thugs?"

4

McCabe and Lieutenant Dole had joined Pete Sullivan in the Communications Center. The center was home to the 911 system. It also housed the interfaces for the surveillance cameras that watched what was happening in the city twenty-four hours a day, seven days a week and for the sensors that registered the sounds of gunfire or explosions and pinpointed the locations.

Pete Sullivan was in charge of the Comm Center day shift. His handlebar mustache twitched as he glanced up from his monitor. "This definitely falls into the category of 'not good.'"

McCabe looked at the camera-eye view of the crime scene. "This vic looks a lot older than the other two. Maybe this isn't our guy's work."

Sullivan said, "That's not what I meant. Look at her face." He panned in, giving them a close-up of the dead woman's face. "Recognize her?"

McCabe leaned forward. "She looks like . . . that can't be who I think it is."

"Unless she has a clone," Sullivan said. "I think we have a match."

Behind them, Dole said, "Wanna share it with me? Who do you think she is?"

"She looks a whole lot like Vivian Jessup," McCabe said.

"In the now-deceased flesh," Sullivan said.

"Vivian who?" Dole asked.

"Jessup. She's an actress," McCabe said. "She won a Tony last year. I think it was her second or third."

"See that pendant around her neck?" Sullivan zoomed in.

Dole said. "What is that? A rabbit wearing a jacket? Standing on its hind legs?"

"The White Rabbit from *Alice in Wonderland*," McCabe said. "That was Jessup's first role as a child actress."

"She played a rabbit?" Dole said.

McCabe smiled. "No, sir, sorry. She played Alice. In a movie musical. Then later, as an adult, she played the Red Queen, one of the other characters, on Broadway."

"That's what they call her," Sullivan said. "The Red Queen. Not just because of that role but because of the red hair. That hair's one of her trademarks."

"It could be her," McCabe said. "She was here in July. She was interviewed about a play that she's writing, set here in Albany. She was working with one of the theater profs at UAlbany on some kind of lab for students."

"That would explain why she's back," Sullivan said.

Dole cursed. "If we've got a dead Broadway actress, we're going to have press from the City all over this. As soon as it goes out over the wires, they're going to be on the next fast train."

McCabe looked again at the monitor. "Do we already have officers at the scene?"

"A couple," Sullivan said. He panned away from the body to a boat ramp and then to two uniformed cops standing on the bank of the rushing stream, backs turned to the camera. They seemed to be deep in conversation.

"Were they the ones who called it in?" McCabe asked.

Sullivan shook his head. "The call came from an emergency box." He cued the playback.

"Hey, listen, you'd better get some cops out here." The voice was male, juvenile, and frightened. *"There's a dead woman down by the creek."*

"I'll dispatch a car immediately. May I have your name and—"

"No way! I'm not getting mixed up in this shit. I'm supposed to be in school."

"That's it?" Dole said.

"Afraid so," Sullivan replied.

"Got cam on that box?"

"Not in that location."

"Okay," Dole said. "Review the surveillance and give us whatever you have on the crime scene."

Sullivan leaned back in his chair. "I can tell you what we have right now. Nothing."

"Nothing?" Dole said. "How could you have nothing?

"The area under that bridge is a blind spot."

"Then what the hell are we looking at now?"

"Footage from the mobile cam the uniforms set up when they located the body."

"All right," Dole said. "But what about the cameras on the traffic lights? On the bridge itself?"

"We have cameras in both places. But they went down a couple of weeks ago, after the solar flares."

"And they haven't been fixed?" McCabe asked.

"The techs have the ones on the inhabited portion of Delaware and the side streets back online. The others on the bridge are on the list," Sullivan said. "In case you missed it, the budget increase we asked for hasn't been approved yet."

"Sorry," McCabe said. "I didn't mean—"

"We're going to get all kinds of blowback on this one." Sullivan tugged at his mustache. "Vivian Jessup, and the damn cameras are out. Nobody's going to take into account that we've got equipment all over the city to keep functioning. Priority goes to maintaining and enhancing coverage of those areas where we've got people and property to protect. We're supposed to make sure Joe Elk from Buffalo doesn't get mugged when he's walking back to his hotel from the convention center."

"I'm all for protecting tourists," McCabe said. "But this is one of those times when I wish our surveillance system really did live up to the hype."

"If I had known Vivian Jessup was going to wind up dead on that boat ramp, McCabe, I sure as hell would have moved those cams to the top of the list."

"I know that, Pete. I know we're dealing with budget and solar flares."

Dole, who had been listening with his ORB in his hand, said, "So what it comes down to is that either our perp got lucky or he knew somehow that the cameras on the bridge were out."

Sullivan shook his head. "No way he could have known that for sure unless he's one of our techs or a cop in that zone. The cameras are still in place. It looks like they're on. They're just not transmitting."

"I need to alert the commander. We'd better get Jacoby in on this, too."

He stepped away from them and started making his calls.

McCabe said. "Pete, this location . . . the K-9 training facility is out there. Where's the crime scene in relation to that?"

"You've got the farm with the community garden and the dog park—"

"And the horse patrol has stables there," McCabe said. "But where is—"

Sullivan tapped the screen. "The road down to this ramp was put in last spring. Compliments of Ted Thornton. He wanted a convenient boat ramp on the Albany side of the bridge. He paid, and the city approved."

"I must have missed that."

"Most people did. They put it in while some construction was going on up on Delaware. They put a couple of picnic tables down there and stuck up a sign about it being a public ramp, in case anyone noticed and asked questions."

McCabe nodded. "Okay. So you're the killer and you're driving around with a body in your car and you see a side road—"

"No problem about the dog park being nearby," Sullivan said. "Nobody likely to be down there walking their dog at night. No hikers following the 'yellow brick road' through the woods and over the old bridge. And probably no cops hanging around at the facilities."

"The 'yellow brick road,'" McCabe said, her head coming up.

"The bricks . . . when they were building the old turnpike road, the bricks they used had a yellow hue—"

"I know about that. When I was a kid, a teacher told us that Albany once had its own yellow brick road and that a portion of it was still visible. . . . If the victim is Vivian Jessup—"

"Wrong movie. She was in *Alice*."

"I know that. But both *Alice* and *The Wizard of Oz* were stories about little girls who—"

"But what do the first two victims have to do with the stories? They were in their early twenties, not little girls. The first vic was found beside her car after she left a club. The second vic got a flat tire on her way home from work. And if this is Jessup, even if the killer knew about the yellow brick road, he didn't dump her body there, either. He left her on the—"

McCabe held up her hands. "Okay. You're right. I'm having a wacky brainstorm. So the killer manages to find Ted Thornton's new road down to a boat ramp. But if it is our guy, why did he move the body in the first place? He didn't move the other two."

Lieutenant Dole spoke behind her. "McCabe, you're assuming he killed her somewhere else." He held up his ORB. "Jacoby put me on hold. Get moving and take that kid Baxter with you. The CO was in a meeting, but he's on his way. As soon as he gets here, we'll be over there."

Sullivan said, "I hope Jacoby can keep Clarence Redfield away from this. That's all we need, to have Redfield threading about this."

"See you at the scene, Lou," McCabe said.

She was already going over what she had seen on-camera as she started down the hall in search of Baxter. If it was Vivian Jessup . . . if she was the third victim . . . then a Broadway actress had become the victim of a serial killer while visiting Albany.

That was not going to thrill the mayor.

Even with the fast train—ninety minutes instead of the two and a half hours it used to take—cosmopolitan types from Manhattan had not been making Albany their destination of choice. City dwellers had not rushed to relocate to Albany to take advantage of the cheaper real estate market. Most of them seemed uninterested in even coming up to spend a day or a weekend in the capital. The mayor had been spending serious money—much of it from corporate benefactors like Ted Thornton—on a campaign to sell the attractions of Albany to the rest of the Northeast, particularly the residents of the Big Apple. She was determined to convince tourists from downstate that Albany was New York's "vibrant, historic capital" and should be more than a station stop on the way to Montreal.

Having Vivian Jessup die here was not going to do much for either tourism or promoting Albany as a bedroom community. Especially since, as McCabe recalled from the bit she'd heard on the news, the mayor had planned to tie Jessup's play into her "It Happened Here" ad campaign about Albany history and culture.

Not that some people—including Clarence Redfield in one of his more inflammatory threads—thought it was desirable to have people from the City coming to Albany. According to him—and some cops agreed—enough prostitutes, drug dealers, gang members, and other assorted troublemakers were already taking the train or the Northway up to Albany.

McCabe opened the door to the third interview room. Baxter was standing there, arms folded, a disgusted expression on his face. He was staring down at their suspect from that morning.

Mouth open, snorting, the perp was managing to both drool and snore.

Baxter said, "Ready for me to wake Pigpen up so we can talk to him?"

McCabe shook her head. "Get someone to put him in holding. We just caught another call."

"What's up?"

"Female vic. She could be number three."

"I thought this was way too easy. Pigpen here walks right into our arms by breaking into the first vic's house."

"It happens," McCabe said. "Stupid perps. Drug addicts. Except nothing our killer's done so far would suggest he's either. And now, if this one's his, it looks like he's gone for extra points."

"How? What'd he do?"

"I'll tell you in the car. I'm going to grab my field bag while you're getting our friend here stored away."

Baxter met her at the entrance to the garage.

McCabe pressed her thumb to the ID slot.

"Detective Hannah McCabe," the Voice said. "Please drive carefully."

The detectives in the squad room had never agreed on who the Voice sounded like. But someone had decided that the Voice should give his automated safety reminder when they checked out a car. Call them by name just so they knew he knew who they were.

The turbolift descended from the third-floor parking deck. A blue sedan came into view in its stall. The barrier slid back and the car rolled out.

"Hey, we got one of the new ones," Baxter said. "How'd you pull that off?"

"Luck of the draw," McCabe said.

"Want me to drive?"

"Sure, if you want to."

In the car, McCabe shrugged off her thermo jacket, tucked her field bag by her feet, and strapped herself into the passenger seat. Then she looked over to see why they were still sitting there.

Baxter was studying the console.

"Mike, it should already be programmed with the location."

"I know." He pointed. "See that? This baby has superenhanced night vision. The guys working vice were really pumped about getting Prowl Vision 240 on the new cars."

"I'm sure they were. But we're the dull cops with the dead body waiting, remember?"

He grinned. "Right. Let's roll, Hank."

They shot out of the garage enclosure and down the street, merging into traffic.

"Hannah," she said.

Baxter glanced at her. "What'd you say?"

The collision warning signal on the console beeped. Baxter was driving on manual control. He had to swerve around the commuter shuttle bus that had stopped to pick up passengers.

McCabe glanced over her shoulder at the car they'd cut off with their lane change. "With an inch or two to spare," she said.

"Maybe we should turn on the siren and plow the road."

"We don't want to attract too much attention. The press will probably beat us there as it is."

"You mean after what happened last night with Redfield sticking it to Jacoby? I was going to ask if you saw that."

"On the news this morning."

"Think we've got a leak in the department?"

"Either that or Clarence Redfield is clairvoyant."

Baxter laughed. "Nobody I hear talking about it gives the asshole that much credit. Hey, what were you saying about your name?"

"That I prefer to be called Hannah."

"Sorry. I thought I heard your dad call you Hank that day he stopped by."

"Yeah, he did. But it's a family nickname. Hannah's for general consumption."

"Got it," Baxter said as they reached Lark Street. "Are you sure we don't want to use the siren? We're hitting traffic."

"Let's just beep the siren if we get stuck. We have officers at the scene." McCabe reached for her ORB. "While you're getting us there, I want to have a look at the terrain around the crime scene. The CO will decide how we deploy to search the area, but it's always a good idea to be prepared for his questions. He tends to shoot them out and expect answers." She pulled up the search engine. "And I'd better see what I can find about Vivian Jessup while I'm at it."

"Vivian Jessup? That actress with the red hair? British accent? I saw her on one of the talk shows. What does she have to do with this?"

"It looks like she may be our victim."

"Vivian Jessup? You're kidding me, right?"

"Completely serious."

McCabe filled him in on what they'd seen on the crime-scene cam and about Vivian Jessup's use of Albany as a setting for her play.

"What's this play about?" Baxter asked.

"I didn't catch it all. Something about John Wilkes Booth and an actress. They—the actress and Booth—performed here in Albany on the eve of the Civil War."

"So she's writing this play about the guy who assassinated Lincoln and she gets murdered."

"If it is her. As Pete said, she could have a clone. A look-alike."

Baxter beeped the siren and went around a car waiting to turn. They beat the red light onto Delaware.

"Would you ever do that?" he asked.

"Do what?" McCabe said, looking up from her ORB.

"Get yourself cloned?"

McCabe was silent for a moment, scanning Vivian Jessup's bio on her screen. "I've never really thought about it. I suppose if I were dying or something."

"Yeah, it'd be really handy to have a spare organ or two then," Baxter said.

"Except the clone would be another real person and you might have to kill him or her to harvest the organs."

"Thought you said you hadn't thought about it."

"I haven't. I happened to see a science show where they were debating the ethical issues about approving the process." She glanced over at him. "Why'd you ask about that anyway?"

"I know this guy who has cancer. My age, but he's dead if they don't find him a lung. I went to visit him and he was joking about how convenient it would be if we all had a clone stashed in a room somewhere."

"I'm sorry about your friend. That's tough."

"Yeah. But he's still hoping." Baxter cleared his throat. "Not that

I'm wishing Vivian Jessup dead, you understand. But if she is, this could be really big. Can you imagine the press we'll get on this?"

McCabe stared at him as what he had said began to sink in.

Even with Jacoby, the public information officer, who was in charge of all police department communications, if the case went cosmic and New York City and national media covered it . . . Reporters always wrote about the cops on big cases. Did background pieces . . .

Baxter said, "Hey, sorry if that sounded cold. But I don't mind admitting that I want to be chief someday."

"Nothing wrong with a little ambition," McCabe said. "Actually, I was just wondering if the CO will keep me on the case."

"Why wouldn't he? We caught it. And if it's big, a serial killer and Vivian Jessup, they'll assign as many detectives as they can to it. We'll have everybody on this. State Police. FBI. That task force Redfield was talking about."

McCabe glanced down at the scratch on her hand, which she had forgotten to cleanse with disinfectant. "Safety in numbers," she said. "So hopefully I won't find a camera pointed in my direction."

"Why are you worried about that anyway?" Baxter said. "Don't tell me you're camera-shy."

He was grinning at her, like he was teasing. Did he expect her to believe no one had told him her story?

Even if the rest of the cops had managed to restrain themselves, Baxter's godfather was Assistant Chief Danvers. No way Danvers hadn't filled his godson in on every detective in the unit.

Her new partner seemed to be trying to blow serious smoke up her ass. "Since I was a kid. Everyone in my family is camera-shy."

"Then I'll jump in front of you whenever a camera turns in our direction. No problem, partner."

"Thanks," McCabe said.

She turned back to her ORB. "Looks like this terrain is going to be tricky to search with the wooded area and the water. Be interesting to see how the commander handles it."

5

"Airship captain, you are cleared to land."

"Roger, tower. Over and out."

Captain Chuck Kessler turned to the man who had joined him in the cockpit shortly after their departure from JFK but who was only now taking off his headset. Even when he wasn't listening to classical music, or whatever he'd been listening to, Ashby wasn't much for conversation. After five years of flying for Ted Thornton, first the plane and now the airship, Kessler still wondered why a man like the boss would pick Ashby to take along when he went adventuring. Even if they had been roommates in college.

The only thing Kessler could figure was that Ashby was loyal and discreet, and he didn't mind going into caves or climbing mountains or forging through jungles or doing whatever else it was the boss took it into his head to do. Ashby had even gone along on the maiden voyage of this airship, when people were calling it "Thornton's Folly." And he seemed pretty good at the business stuff the boss had him handle, too.

"The boss tell you if we're going back down to the City today?" Kessler asked.

"That depends on Lisa. She may want to attend an exhibit at one of the local galleries."

"Never thought I'd see the day when the boss would let a woman make his plans," Kessler said.

"Lisa is an unusual woman."

"Roger that. She's really something all right."

Bruce Ashby slid out of his seat. "I'd better go back and make sure they're ready to land."

"You might want to use the intercom," Kessler said. "They could be busy."

Ashby hesitated. Then he sat back down and reached for the intercom.

"Ted? We're going to be landing in about ten minutes. Do you need anything?"

A woman's soft laughter.

"Got everything we need, Bruce, old man," Thornton said. He sounded distracted. "Give us another . . . five minutes or so after we touch down."

"Right," Ashby said.

From his place behind the controls of the airship, Kessler glanced over at Ashby and put a big smirk on his face.

Deadpan as always, Ashby reached for his headset.

6

A police cruiser was parked at the top of the road that led from Delaware Avenue down to the boat ramp where the body had been found. The officer standing by the cruiser watched as they pulled up. Young and solemn, she strode toward them with an e-board in her hand.

"Good morning, Detectives. If I could see ID and if you would please sign in."

McCabe nodded her silent approval.

Baxter fished out his badge and signed his name. He passed the e-board to McCabe.

"Thank you, Detectives," the officer said.

McCabe glanced at the name tag on the woman's shirt. "Thank you, Officer Lawrence. Looks like you've been keeping out everyone who doesn't have business here."

"Yes, ma'am. I know I'm supposed to do that." Lawrence's grin was quick and infectious. "The instructor for that class at the Academy hit hard on that one. Check all IDs and make sure everyone who goes in signs in and signs back out again. No matter who they are."

"Keep up the good work," McCabe said. "The PIO's on his way, but we're depending on you if the media beat him here."

Lawrence nodded. "Yes, ma'am. Another officer should be here in a few minutes. We won't let anyone get by us."

Baxter drove down the hill on the road leading to the boat ramp. The paved road had been cut out among the trees that stood sentry on each side. The tires crunched over bits of broken branches from the last windstorm.

"If you didn't know this road was down here, you could drive right by without noticing it," McCabe said. "It's not that obvious from up above."

"And even if you saw it," Baxter said, "would you drive down here?"

"If you had a body to get rid of, at least it would get you off the street, away from prying eyes."

"Unless someone saw you turning down here. Then you're screwed if they could give a description."

"There is that," McCabe said. "Of course, for all you know, you're already dealing with the possibility that you've been caught on a surveillance cam somewhere along the way."

"But maybe you've got that body and the most important thing is to get it out of your car."

"As the lou pointed out to me, it could be a mistake to assume she was killed somewhere else and dumped here."

"Either way, you've got a live woman or a dead body and you need to get off the street and finish what you started. So why here? Was this road the perp's destination, or did he just stumble on it?"

Whatever Baxter is, he isn't stupid, McCabe thought.

He brought the car to a stop in the graveled parking area and they got out.

McCabe shifted her field bag to her shoulder and glanced around. Nearby there was a cement platform with the picnic tables that Pete had mentioned when they were looking at the crime scene on the cam. Beyond the picnic area, lay the ramp for launching canoes or other small craft into the Normanskill. Sparkling in the sunlight, the creek surged over boulders and pushed at its banks. After the flooding all summer, they had been lucky that September, and the first couple of weeks of October had been drier than predicted.

McCabe glanced from the creek up toward the bridge where the killer might, if he'd been willing to risk being seen, have stopped his car and looked down here. The nonfunctioning cameras were up there on that bridge. For all he could have known, he might have been on-camera if he had stopped to look. And he would have been blocking one of the two lanes of traffic in each direction.

The uniforms who had been first at the scene had been occupying themselves walking to the end of the landing and back. Now they were headed toward her and Baxter.

"So how do we get started?" Baxter asked.

"We could tramp on into the crime scene and start poking at the body," McCabe said. "Except that wouldn't make us popular with FIU." She took a closer look at his face. "Are you okay?"

He nodded. "But this would probably be the time to mention my gag reflex. Ever since I was a kid. I know it's a liability for a cop."

Baxter hadn't been there for the first two victims. She and Jay O'Connell, who was in court this week testifying in another case, had been the lead detectives.

"So this is your first dead body?" she said.

"No. I saw an accident victim or two when I was on patrol. And a woman whose husband had carved her up . . . a dead junkie when I was working vice. But I was always able to keep my distance." He gave a pained grin. "You know, not get close enough to actually embarrass myself."

McCabe opened her field bag and took out two portable masks and a folded plastic-lined white paper bag. "This mask should help. But barf into the bag if your gag reflex kicks in. We don't want to contaminate the crime scene."

He took both. "Thanks, partner."

"We've all been there. Think of this as practice for the autopsy we're going to have to attend."

"Oh shit."

"So you didn't do that . . . attend an autopsy in the Academy?"

"We watched on satellite. No smells."

"I'm afraid this is going to be up close and in living color."

The two uniformed officers reached them.

McCabe held out her hand to the older of the two. "Officer Curtis? I think we worked a robbery together last year."

"Yes, ma'am. Good to see you again. This is Officer Walker."

"Officer Walker," McCabe said, extending her hand. "And this is Detective Baxter."

Baxter shook hands with the two officers. So he understood the need to establish rapport.

McCabe said, "Officer Curtis, would you walk us through this? The usual. What you found when you arrived, how you approached the body."

Curtis, an old hand at crime scenes, pulled out his ORB and began to read his notes.

"Too bad there's no ID," McCabe said when he concluded with the notation that no personal identification had been found with the victim. No purse in sight.

"That would have made it easier," Curtis said. "We did find some bike tracks."

"Where?"

Curtis pointed toward a patch of dirt. "If the kid who called it in made them, looks like he stopped right over there. Then he must have seen her and turned around and gotten out of here."

"I don't blame him," McCabe said.

Baxter said, "The question is, how long had she been down here before the kid stumbled on the body?"

McCabe glanced up at the sky. "In this kind of heat, it doesn't take long for a body to begin to break down. But in the close-up we saw on the cam, she didn't look like she'd been out in the sun for a whole day. Besides, if that kid was down here, this could be a hangout."

Baxter said, "What you're saying is that if she had been here during the day yesterday, someone might have found her. As hot as it is, you have to think some grown-ups are probably coming down here, too, to get to the water."

McCabe said, "Yeah, I noticed some beer cans and food wrappers in the trash barrel back there."

"Wonder how often garbage is collected down here. Makes it harder for the forensic guys."

"Not too hard if she hasn't been here long. We're interested in the fresh stuff," McCabe said. "But they'll collect it all and take it back to the lab."

"Here they come now," Curtis said.

They all turned to watch as the FIU van came down the hill and drew to a stop. The medical examiner's car was right behind the van.

"We got a regular parade," Baxter said. "The lou and the commander are bringing up the rear."

"I hope Jacoby's in place, too." McCabe said. "We aren't going to have too much time before the media onslaught."

With the team in place, Commander Paul Osgood and Ray Delgardo, the FIU crime-scene coordinator, discussed the search pattern that they wanted to use. When McCabe passed on Officer Curtis's observation about the bike tracks, Delgardo went over to have a look. When he nodded, Osgood ordered the last patrol car to arrive to go back up on Delaware Avenue and start looking for kids on bikes.

They waited while the assistant ME, who was there subbing for Dr. Singh, the chief medical examiner, had a look at the body and made the official pronouncement of death. Then they waited again until the FIU tech had entered the coordinates of the crime scene into his ORB and made a preliminary video.

Then McCabe motioned to Baxter that they could walk up to the body.

Halfway there, Baxter jumped back. "Geez, what's that?"

Trying to keep the revulsion from her own voice, McCabe said, "Nothing to worry about. Looks like what's left of a dead snake after the insects and other animals got to it. We'll assume for now that it died of natural causes."

Baxter said, "Sorry. For a moment I thought it was a piece of . . . that it was from our vic."

"You okay?"

"Fine. Let's get to work."

The women kneeling beside the vic looked up and nodded at McCabe. "Caught this one, too, huh?"

"It's getting to be a habit," McCabe said.

She introduced Baxter to Rachel Malone, the assistant ME, who was finishing up her work prior to transport of the body.

McCabe watched Baxter look down at the dead woman. His eyes widened above the mask he had donned. He blanched and stared off into the distance. But, to McCabe's relief, he managed to keep his breakfast down.

The victim's face was pale, more waxen than it had looked on the cam.

This one wasn't bad compared to some McCabe had seen. No battered face, no blood, no mutilation.

The killer had unbuttoned the short-sleeved white cotton blouse but had left the plain white bra underneath in place. If this vic was like the other two, she had died almost instantaneously when a needle containing poison was plunged into her heart. The ME would be able to tell them if that had been the means of death and what had been in the syringe, whether it was phenol, like the others. He also could tell them if this victim, like the other two, had been rendered helpless with a stunner.

McCabe hunkered down to get a better look at the body without leaning over it. There was a bruise on the victim's right arm. Had she gotten that when she fell?

"How do you think she got the bruise?" she asked Malone.

"Looks like she was struck with something," Malone said, passing her scanner over the area.

Baxter, who had stepped away, said, "Where's the flower? Didn't

I read in the master file that the perp left a flower beside the bodies at the other two crime scenes?"

McCabe nodded. "Silk flowers. A red poppy at the first scene, a tiger lily at the second."

"But there's no flower beside this body," Baxter said. "Would a serial killer change his pattern?"

"That's a question for the profiler. But I'd say no."

"So maybe this isn't one of his," Baxter said.

"Maybe not," McCabe said. "It's too soon to know."

"McCabe and Baxter, see you a moment."

They turned at the sound of the CO's voice.

Osgood motioned them over to where he was standing with Lieutenant Dole. Unlike some of the brass, he was careful not to trample through his detectives' crime scenes. If the case was important enough, he showed up to coordinate, but he stayed out of the way of the work that was being done.

Osgood wiped his handkerchief across his sun-pinked forehead. "I'm leaving you in charge here, McCabe. As soon as you and your partner get done, get back to the station. I'll have the State Police and FBI on board by then."

"Yes, sir," McCabe said.

Osgood scowled at his lieutenant. "Jack, we need to get on this before that idiot Clarence Redfield has the story all over his thread. If we've got a leak, we need to shut it down. Now."

"Yes, sir," Dole said.

He flashed McCabe and Baxter a glance that said, Don't screw this up. Then he followed in Osgood's wake, matching his steps to those of the shorter, bulkier man.

"Big Jack" Dole respected Osgood. They had both come up through the ranks when politics were more openly rough-and-tumble than they were now. Osgood, a cop's cop, was in line for assistant chief, and probably chief after that.

.   .   .

The wagon took the body away at a little before noon. By then, it had been photographed and sketched and examined from every angle. At that point, they were looking at it as if it had never been human. Now it was evidence in their investigation.

McCabe watched the medical examiner's assistant drive away. By the time they got back to the station, the ME might have the identification. If the victim had ever had dental work done or gotten a print ID or been arrested and had her DNA entered into the data bank that New York State maintained, they would soon know for sure who she was. Know more quickly than they might have otherwise, because time was precious on this one. Not only because they might have a serial killer who had murdered a third woman but also because they needed to deal with the fallout if the third victim had been famous.

There would be people to notify no matter who she was. People to talk to about the last days and hours of her life as they tried to figure out how she had ended up dead on a boat ramp by the Normanskill.

"We have confirmation that Vivian Jessup was in Albany yesterday," the lieutenant said when he reached McCabe on her ORB. "Her publicist has been trying to contact her since around seven-thirty yesterday evening. Left a bunch of tags that Jessup didn't return. The publicist was able to put us in contact with Jessup's dentist. Jessup's dental records have been sent to the ME."

"That should answer our first question," McCabe said.

"Since Jessup hasn't been heard from in over twenty-four hours, it isn't looking good. The commander has alerted the mayor. How's it going there, McCabe?"

McCabe glanced around her at the search that was under way. "Slow. You know how meticulous Delgardo is about collecting anything that could be evidence."

"I'm glad he's handling this one personally. I'm going to pull a couple more detectives and get them busy helping out with the canvass."

"Thank you, sir. We—" McCabe began, then broke off. "How did he—Mike, we've got—"

"See him." Baxter took off at a sprint.

"What is it?" Dole asked. "What's going on?"

"Clarence Redfield, Lou. You aren't going to believe this, but he's out in the creek in a canoe. He's got a cam."

Dole cursed. "If we're lucky, he'll drown. Get him out of there."

"Baxter's trying to talk him in, sir. But it's going to be tricky for anyone to swim out to him with the rocks. Water Patrol hasn't gotten here yet with their boats for the search."

"Tell Baxter to wait. Water Patrol's en route. They were tied up with a drowning in the river. And tell that son of a bitch Redfield that he'll be under arrest as soon as he sets foot on dry land if he doesn't paddle his canoe away from our crime scene."

"Yes, sir," McCabe said. "But I'd be willing to bet he's already called his lawyer."

The Water Patrol Unit arrived a few minutes later. When they went out after him, Redfield informed them that they were violating his First Amendment rights as a reporter.

"Exactly what school of journalism did that asshole attend?" Baxter asked when they were watching a cruiser drive away with Redfield inside.

"None," McCabe said. "We looked it up a while ago. He has a degree in chemical engineering. He used to work for the oil companies until he came back here when his mother was ill. She died, but he stayed around and did some consulting."

"And somewhere along the way he became a crime beat threader?"

"That happened when his neighbor's dog was killed by a hit-and-run driver. His threads about now the callous APD couldn't care less when the victim was a beloved pet went over well. After that, he was off and running."

"And now he's a damn pain."

McCabe said, "I feel a little sorry for him. He was married, but his wife died in childbirth. The baby, too."

"That's tough," Baxter said. "But does it give him the right to make our lives miserable?"

McCabe said, "Nope. But it was the mayor who thought he'd be defanged if he were given a press pass."

"Bright idea, if it had worked," Baxter said.

"That's how it goes with bright ideas," McCabe replied. She tugged at the visor of her APD baseball cap and glanced sideways through her dark glasses at the sun that had been beating down on them for the past three hours. "Speaking of bright, a few passing clouds would be welcome about now."

"I love this weather. The hotter the better, as far as I'm concerned."

"Then you have nothing at all to worry about when you die. Either way, you're good."

Baxter laughed. "What now? Do we hang around, or can we go up on Delaware and help with the canvassing?"

"Let's check in with Delgardo and see what else we need to cover. I'm wondering if we want more people searching along the road leading down here. The perp might have had the victim's purse in his car and tossed it out as he was driving away."

Delgardo nodded when she suggested that. "Yeah, that occurred to me, too. As soon as we finish down here, we'll work our way back up to the road." He flashed her a grin. "Hope you're wearing your tick repellent."

"I came prepared. I've got the latest version in my bag."

Delgardo told Baxter, "She has more stuff in that bag than a deranged Girl Scout."

"Says he who carries around an even larger bag," McCabe said.

"Ah, we're two of a kind, McCabe, *querida*."

She liked Delgardo. He was happily married, and everyone knew it. That was why he was safe to flirt with—something she rarely did with cops. But FIU detectives were in a different category. The science guys of the police department.

7

They knew by two o'clock that afternoon that the victim was Vivian Jessup. But Wayne Jacoby had given the press the usual line. Name of victim withheld until next of kin have been contacted.

Jessup's publicist had supplied them with next of kin. Vivian Jessup's daughter from the first of two marriages lived in Colorado with her husband and infant daughter.

By 3:30, the daughter had been informed that her mother was dead. Her husband called back to say that he had booked her on an early-morning flight to Albany.

By four o'clock, Wayne Jacoby was ready to announce the name of the victim from his mobile command post on Delaware Avenue. He was timing the announcement to give the search team time to wrap up. They needed to get to Jessup's hotel before the press found out she was the victim and started trying to find out where she had been staying. Police officers were posted on the door of her room, but it would be better if they got to the hotel before the camera crews arrived.

The search team made a quiet exit while the reporters were focused on the MCP vehicle, parked in the lot of a hamburger place. McCabe and Baxter followed the FIU van out onto Delaware Avenue.

McCabe nodded to Officer Lawrence, who was still on duty

McCabe watched the feed of Jacoby's press conference on her ORB. Questions came at Jacoby from left and right. This was only the Capital Region press. When the story went national . . . McCabe thought. Maybe she should ask the lieutenant to take her off the case. Adam was not fond of the tabloid press. Her brother would not be pleased if their own family saga ended up as a juicy tidbit amid the feeding frenzy about a serial killer in Albany.

But, damn it, this was her job. Her career.

Vivian Jessup had been tidy. Her clothes—two pairs of slacks, a dress, and a couple of skirts, in neutral colors and travel-friendly fabrics—hung in the closet. Her empty suitcase sat on the luggage rack beside the dresser. Underwear—sensible, if expensive, natural-fiber panties and bras—was in the top drawer of the dresser. Blouses, T-shirts, shorts, and tops in the second. Her nightgown and robe in the bottom drawer.

Nothing that screamed, This is the room of a Tony Award–winning Broadway actress.

McCabe closed the last drawer with her gloved hands and turned to Ray Delgado, who was coming out of the bathroom.

"Find anything yet?"

"Not yet," he said. "Usual grooming products on the counter."

"Notice what's missing?" she said.

"What?" Baxter asked, turning from his observation of one of Ray's technicians scanning the bedcover for fluids.

"Nothing here but her clothes," Ray said. "She was here to work. How was she doing that without an ORB? How was she staying in touch with people?"

"So," McCabe said. "Jessup's ORB is probably with her missing purse. Still in the killer's possession, pawned, or tossed somewhere."

"First vic," Delgardo said. "The killer took her ORB but emptied her purse on the ground and left it beside her body. Second vic's ORB was also missing, but her backpack was left behind."

"But this time," Baxter said, "he took everything."

"If it's the same guy," McCabe said.

"Don't let Clarence Redfield hear you say that," Baxter said. "Can you imagine what he'd do with two killers murdering women?"

8

Clarence Redfield was still being detained when McCabe and Baxter got back to the station house.

McCabe went into Lieutenant Dole's office. "Is Redfield going to be charged?"

"The legal eagles are debating what we can charge him with. Technically, he didn't cross the police line. He got a canoe and came down the creek. He shot the crime scene from there."

"And he's about to be sprung," the commander's gravelly voice said from the doorway.

Dole said, "We're releasing him, sir?"

"That's what I said. Never mind that the son of a bitch streamed to his thread as he was filming. The ADA is trying to get a court order now to get it down."

"How much of the crime scene can you see?" McCabe asked.

"Take a look." The commander touched the wall, bringing up the Web and then Redfield's node.

Detectives and uniformed cops had been captured on-camera as they went about their jobs. The details of the crime scene stood out in stark detail.

McCabe said, "I guess we should be grateful he didn't get there before the body was taken away. That would have been tough on the family."

Osgood glared at the images. "I thought stationing a cruiser up on the bridge would be sufficient to keep anyone with a cam away. We even managed to get agreement from the TV stations not to fly over in helicopters."

Dole said, "Nobody but that asshole Redfield would have gotten a canoe and come down the creek."

"Is there any concern that he'll try to sell what he shot to the tabloids?" McCabe asked. "He's never done that before. But when he finds out who the victim is, he might be tempted."

The commander scowled. "He claims he did this because the public has the right to know how the APD is conducting its investigation into murders that are being carried out by a serial killer." He looked at McCabe. "You'll be pleased to know that he gave your team a B plus for procedure."

McCabe shook her head. "Why didn't we deserve an A?"

"He would have preferred all the cops be 'properly attired.' Only the FIU detectives were in what he considered appropriate crime-scene gear. Everyone else was wearing only gloves. He also questioned the number of officers present."

"Too many?" McCabe said.

"Not enough," the commander said. "He wanted the State Police, FBI, Water Patrol, and the canine unit."

"Well, he got two out of four right," McCabe said. "The Water Patrol arrived just in time to haul him out of the water. And, as you know, sir, Delgardo requested assistance from the canine unit when we were doing the search of the wooded area along the road."

"Did the dogs come up with anything?" the commander asked.

"No, sir."

Dole was scanning Redfield's node. "Look at this garbage. Redfield says he wanted to share his arrest with his audience so that they can see the APD in action, police suppression of information."

The commander said, "One member of his audience has rushed to his rescue."

"His attorney?" McCabe said.

"And a second attorney who's joining his legal team. Wendell Graves."

"That showboat?" Dole said. "Jeez, what did we do to deserve this?"

"Graves describes himself as a defender of the oppressed," McCabe said, and then regretted she had mentioned that when the commander fixed his stare on her.

"He might have been in the early days, McCabe. But now it's all about him." The commander rubbed the side of his nose and shoved up his horn-rimmed glasses. "Graves has been in touch with the mayor, threatening a press conference. The mayor has directed—let me rephrase that—has 'strongly suggested' to the chief that Mr. Redfield be released."

McCabe waited to see if Lieutenant Dole would mumble his opinion of the mayor under his breath. He managed to contain his disdain.

McCabe happened to be in the lobby, talking to Angie Hogancamp, the second-watch desk sergeant, when Clarence Redfield and his defense team, old lawyer and new, left the station house.

Redfield looked about like she remembered him from the other couple of times she'd seen him in person: five ten or so; around 165 pounds, sandy hair cut short, but not a crew cut; short-sleeved blue T-shirt, khaki shorts, and canvas sandals. Nothing off-putting about his appearance. Nothing about the way he looked to suggest he had become a royal pain in the city's and the police department's butts.

He saw McCabe and nodded in acknowledgment of her presence. He didn't look as if he was gloating, but she didn't doubt that he was.

As they went out the door, McCabe heard attorney Graves suggest dinner at Jack's Oyster House. That makes sense, she thought. They would have an excellent dinner. And if the mayor happened to drop in, as she sometimes did, they would be there to annoy her. Undoubtedly, that was what Graves had in mind. McCabe wondered if Graves intended to try to parlay his media exposure during the investigation into a run for mayor.

Mayor Beverly Stark was an anomaly in the history of Albany's four-hundred-year-long old boys' club. She'd been able to rise to power because of the departure of the former mayor to a federal post in Washington. And she had undoubtedly benefitted from the euphoria three years ago, when a woman had become president of the United States. That euphoria had long since faded, and after a hellish first term that had left her severely wounded politically, the president was probably going to yield the nomination to her vice president.

Meanwhile, in Albany, Stark's survival as mayor was always in question.

"Catch you later, Angie," McCabe said to the desk sergeant.

"Eating my spicy tofu sub," Hogancamp said. "Since nobody invited us to go along to Jack's."

McCabe laughed. "You know how that goes. Nobody wants to hang out with cops."

McCabe headed back down the hall to collect her ORB with her notes from the first two crime scenes. The profiler from the FBI office in Albany was due within the next half hour. The State Police was sending someone, too. That meant they had at least another couple of hours in store of reviewing the evidence and the meager leads from the first two cases and what they knew so far about what had happened to Vivian Jessup.

The Jessup autopsy was tomorrow morning, and then they would have confirmation that she had died of a lethal dose of phenol and was probably the killer's third victim. In the meantime, they were operating on that strong probability.

But if this was their guy, Baxter had asked a pertinent question. Why hadn't the killer left a flower at the scene? Why the change in pattern, including taking Jessup's purse?

The commander had been called in for another meeting with the chief. The lieutenant was chairing the gathering of Albany PD detectives and the representatives from the other agencies. As the only detective who had worked all three cases, McCabe went over the interviews with family members and associates of the victims. She walked the newly established task force members through the crime scenes and summarized the autopsy reports on the first two victims.

The FBI profiler was up next. They listened as she offered her interpretation of the evidence.

When she was done, McCabe said, "I understand your theory about this, Agent Francisco. But could we go back for a moment to the killer's choice of weapon? The phenol—"

"I heard what you said, Detective. Phenol was used by the Nazis during World War Two to execute Jewish prisoners. But there is nothing to indicate that the killer is targeting women because of their religion." Francisco adjusted the cuff of her jacket. "As you reported, victim one was from a Protestant family, even though she had stopped attending church. Victim two was a lapsed Catholic."

"Yes," McCabe said, determined not to be intimidated by Francisco's cool brunette self-confidence. "But the point I had intended to make when I mentioned the Nazis was not about the victims' religion. What I was noting is that information about the Nazis' use of phenol in the death camps is available on the Web. The articles I found provided a description of how the executions were carried out and even the amount of phenol used."

"And?" Agent Francisco said. "Where does that take us in your opinion?"

"In my opinion, where it takes us is not to focus too quickly on the killer's possible medical background."

"I didn't say the killer was a doctor or nurse, Detective. I was simply pointing out that a hypodermic is different from a gun or a knife. The killer didn't strangle his victims. He stabbed them in the heart with a hypodermic filled with a deadly substance."

"Phenol. Carbolic acid. A substance that is available to people who are not medical professionals," McCabe said. "I'm not arguing with your reasoning, Agent Francisco. I just want to make sure we keep an open mind about other possible types of suspects."

Whitman, the State Police investigator, spoke up. "I agree with that. And I'm not sure we should rush to rule out the Nazi aspect of this. Even if neither of the first two victims was Jewish, we could still have some kind of neo-Nazi tie-in. With Howard Miller out there holding his rallies, we could have a lone wolf on our hands. Someone who's targeting women he's decided aren't fit to live."

McCabe cast a glance in Lieutenant Dole's direction. He nodded, apparently agreeing that she had been right not to allow Agent Francisco to hijack the theory-building process.

Agencies might cooperate, but their own turf wars always lurked beneath the surface. Especially when the representative from one agency came in arrogant.

Baxter caught her eye and winked.

McCabe sat back to listen to what Whitman was saying about hate crimes.

The storm was sweeping in when she left the station house at nine. Driving along, Central Avenue, McCabe caught glimpses of homeless men who had taken shelter in the doorways of shuttered stores. Overhead, against a flash of lightning, she saw the question streaming across Radio KZAC's bulletin board: ARE YOU AFRAID OF THE DARK?

"What now?" McCabe mumbled to herself. "Radio on. KZAC."

KZAC was known for its provocative stunts, from scavenger hunts for lists of highly unusual objects to sending listeners out with KICK THE RASCALS OUT signs in front of the legislative offices during the most recent state budget deadlock.

"Okay, I get that," Larry Coffman, the radio host, was saying. "But come on, Clarence. Do you really believe we have a serial killer out there? I mean you've been telling us about Jack the Ripper in London in 1888. This is Albany, New York, in 2019. And we may have three dead women. But only two of them seem to have anything in common. And we don't even know yet how Vivian Jessup died."

"But we do know she was murdered."

"Yeah, but that doesn't mean it was the same killer. I mean, the first two victims, maybe. Both in their twenties. They could have both hooked up with the same crazy guy. But then we've got a third victim. A Tony Award–winning actress who was in her forties. Born in England, not Albany. Don't serial killers always choose the same type of victim? And if the same guy killed the first two women but the third was done in by someone else, then by definition we don't have a serial killer, right? A serial killer requires three or more victims."

"And would that be any better? That we have two killers? We still have three women butchered. And according to the Albany PD, that should not be happening. According to the police, there are surveillance cameras on every corner, at every stoplight, on many of the buildings that we walk past, keeping us safe."

"And that's your real point, right? That's this whole 'Watching Albany to Keep You Safe' surveillance program isn't working. It isn't keeping us safe."

"That's exactly my point, Larry. If this surveillance program were functioning as the police claim, it would be difficult, if not impossible, for a killer or killers to prey on women without being seen and apprehended."

"As I recall, you said in your thread that there are technical problems, that with the solar flares, the system has been malfunctioning and isn't being properly maintained."

"That's right, Larry. After investing money the city didn't have in a system that isn't working, the police department is understaffed. There aren't enough officers out on patrol. What it comes down to is that the APD and the mayor have given citizens a false sense of security. Every citizen in this city, particularly women, should be afraid to be out in the dark at night. We should stay home at night with our doors locked."

"Isn't that giving the streets at night over to the criminals?"

"Yes. I'm afraid it is. But what choice do we have? It's the best we can do until we can find a way to fix a criminal justice system that's broken."

"Clarence, as always, it's been enlightening. Thank you for joining us. What about it, citizens of Albany? Are you afraid of the dark? KZAC Rangers, why don't we make that your assignment for tomorrow. Stop your fellow citizens on the sidewalk and in stores, talk to your neighbors. Ask them if they feel safe going out on the streets of Albany at night. Ask them, 'Are you afraid of the dark?' Then let us know what kind of responses you got."

"Radio off," McCabe said, leaning forward to see through the rain. The street lights overhead swung and swayed in the wind. "Thanks so much, Larry. And thank you once again, Clarence Redfield."

She was exhausted. Ready for food, a shower, and bed.

But when she saw her brother's van in the driveway, McCabe almost kept driving. She wasn't sure she had the energy left to deal with Adam tonight.

She listened for a moment to the rain pounding against the roof of her car. Thought again about the broken umbrella she had forgotten to replace. Then she opened her car door and made a dash for the house.

She shoved the front door shut against a gust of wind.

"That you, Hank?" her father called from the living room.

"It's me," McCabe called back.

"Come in here. Your brother's here."

"Be there as soon as I dry off. It's pouring out there."

In the half bath, McCabe used a hand towel to scrub at her face and hair. She hung her wet jacket on a hook on the door.

Her father was sitting on the sofa, slippered feet up on the coffee table and a bowl of popcorn in his lap. Her brother had pulled his wheelchair up beside him. They were watching a soccer game.

"Hi, you two," she said. "Sorry I missed dinner."

"We saw the news," Angus said. "I guess that answers my question about whether we've got a killer on the loose. First those two girls. Now Vivian Jessup. You got your hands full with this one."

Adam turned his head toward her and smiled slightly. "We heard that interview with the crime beat threader, too. Are we safe in our own beds tonight, sis?"

The black patch over his left eye stood out, rakish, against his café au lait skin. Eight years her senior, Adam had inherited a biracial variation on their father's Scots-Irish coloring and hawkish good looks. He'd also inherited their mother's ability to deliver subtle verbal jabs.

"Safe enough, bro. Cool Jolly Roger," she said, indicating the tiny white emblem on his eye patch.

Adam tilted his head. "A gift from a friend."

"Female, of course."

"Of course."

She went behind the sofa and kissed her father's bald spot. "Something smells good, Pop. I hope you saved me a plate."

"Jerk chicken and rice in the oven. Salad in the refrigerator," he said. "Bring a tray in here. I want to hear about this serial killer."

"I'm too tired to talk about it, Pop," McCabe glanced at her brother. "Why don't you tell him all about your latest breakthrough in your lab?"

"Already have," Adam said. "We've been waiting to hear about your adventures, Sherlock."

"Sorry, I really am too beat to talk," McCabe said. "First, I'm going to have a bite to eat, and then I'm going to drag my weary body upstairs and . . ."

When she turned, Adam was watching her from his turbocharged state-of-the-art wheelchair. A brain wave–controllable product of his work in his lab.

He seemed to prefer the chair rather than the exoskeleton that allowed him to walk on legs he could not feel.

He said, "Yeah, you look done in, sis. You should go on up and sack out."

"But not before you tell us what's going on," Angus said.

"In the morning, Pop," McCabe said. "You can interrogate me during breakfast."

"Guess I'm going to miss that," Adam said.

McCabe paused. "You could stay over and join us for pancakes."

"Thanks, but we'll have to make it another time. A lady's expecting me."

"In that case, I guess you're going to have to rely on Pop for any details he can pry out of me. Carry on with your soccer game, guys. I'm going to go find sustenance."

9

Walter Yin stood in the hallway, listening to his wife Casey's soft voice soothing their seven-year-old son. Yin was no good at coping with a child's fears. But she always knew what to say.

"Okay?" she said.

Todd giggled the way he did when she tickled his neck.

"Okay?" she said again.

"Okay, Mommy."

"Sleep tight, June bug."

She came out, lowering the light in Todd's room but leaving the door ajar.

"What are you doing out here?" she asked.

In a flash of lightning, Yin saw her smile.

"Waiting for you," he said. "I need tucking in, too."

She tucked her arm in his and they went down the hall together. He breathed in the floral scent coming from her hair.

"Tired?" she asked. "Interesting day or all paperwork?"

"One of those offbeat cases that Sean loves. An ex–major-league baseball player. Used to be big-time, nobody important now. But a couple of professional thugs paid him a visit."

"Why did they do that?"

"He's not talking. But Sean's determined to find out what happened, even if the victim won't cooperate."

"Sean cares."

"Too much sometimes. So what did the school shrink say about that picture Todd drew?"

Casey's hand squeezed his arm. "She said he seems to be having some issues with being a cop's kid."

"Since when?"

"Since a couple of months ago, when he heard in a special bulletin that two cops had been shot during a traffic stop."

Yin sighed. "So what are we supposed to do?"

"Talk to him."

"And say what? That detectives don't get shot at?"

"Well, that's what you always tell me."

Pettigrew picked up one of the action figures from the table in his living room: Swede Jorgensen with a baseball in his hand. Pettigrew had been collecting since he was a kid and he and his dad used to go to ball games together. Walk out through the tunnel and come out into the daylight of the stadium, green field and blue sky, the players warming up.

Until today, he had never seen Swede Jorgensen in the flesh. Only watched him on television or listened to the game on the radio.

Pettigrew put the Jorgensen action figure down beside the one of Pete Rose.

He padded out to the kitchen in his leather bedroom slippers and opened the refrigerator. It was stocked with the food that he had picked up from the shopping list that Willow had given them after the last cooking class, but he didn't feel like tackling any of the recipes tonight.

Milk, a little nutmeg, a little whiskey, and he'd be good to go.

Carrying his drink into the living room, Pettigrew stretched out on the sofa.

The fourth game in the series had been rained out.

Sighing, Pettigrew shuffled through his music files and settled on Vivaldi. Volume low.

He knew he should count his blessings. At least he wasn't the primary on the serial killer case. Hannah was beginning to show the strain from that one. Too early to tell if Baxter was going to be any help.

Pettigrew took a long sip of his milk and whiskey punch and set his mug on the coffee table. He settled into a more comfortable position, spine sinking into the cushions.

He was almost asleep when his ORB buzzed. He picked it up and said hello, heard her voice say, "Sean? Did I wake you up?"

He touched the screen, bringing it into view mode.

She was smiling at him.

He sat up on the sofa, rubbed at his eyes. "Ellie, what . . ." He cleared his throat. "Elaine, why are you calling?"

His ex-wife, sitting in a hotel room somewhere, said, "I've been thinking about you. I'm going to be in the City in a couple of weeks. I thought I might take the train up to Albany and maybe we could have lunch or dinner or whatever—"

"Sorry," Pettigrew said. "I'm going to be busy."

"Sean, I—"

He closed his ORB, cutting her off. He stretched out on the sofa again.

"Better," he said to himself. "That was better." Of course, she would probably still show up. But he was doing better. At least this time, she hadn't been quite so sure of her welcome.

Pettigrew saw a flash of lightning. Thunder cracked overhead, echoed and vibrated around the high-rise apartment building.

Might as well stay on the sofa. No point in having to get out of bed and find his pants if there was a tornado warning and he needed to evacuate to the basement.

10

DATE: **Friday, 25 October 2019**
TIME: **0745 hours**
WEATHER TODAY: **Mid 70s and sunshine. Air quality fair.**

McCabe parked in the hospital garage and walked across the pedestrian bridge. She took the elevator downstairs to the basement, where the morgue was located.

The worst part about the morgue was the chill that was intended to stop the decay of the bodies stacked in their individual drawers. Stepping off the elevator was like arriving at the entrance of a bright, well-scrubbed tomb.

Baxter was out in the hall, pacing.

"Good morning," she said. "Did we beat the ME here?"

Baxter shook his head. "He went upstairs to get some breakfast."

"Have yours already?" McCabe asked.

Baxter gave her a doubtful glance. "You eat before these?"

McCabe nodded. "Believe it or not, having a little food in your stomach actually helps."

"I think I'll wait for lunch. Or maybe dinner next week."

The elevator doors opened.

"Hannah McCabe, you have arrived." Dr. Ranjit Singh strode toward them, white coat flapping, glazed doughnut in one hand, cup of coffee in the other. "Let me gulp this down and we'll get to work."

"Take your time, Doc," Baxter said.

Dr. Singh stood on one side of the aluminum table. McCabe and Baxter, also wearing surgical gear, stood on the other. Vivian Jessup lay on the table between them.

Baxter had glanced at the body, then looked away.

Dr. Singh said, "As you know, Hannah McCabe, we use CT scans and MRI's as much as possible." He brought up the monitor on the wall. "These are the images we have already taken of the body."

Full-length 3-D images of Vivian Jessup's body appeared. Dr. Singh maneuvered them on the screen, providing them with different views. He explained what they were seeing.

Baxter said, "Wow!"

"I told you it was interesting," McCabe said.

"We only saw the old-style autopsy at the Academy."

Dr. Singh said, "We still make use of the traditional autopsy. To do this for every case would be both time-consuming and expensive. However, because of the circumstances, we need all of the information that our victim's body can yield." He shook his head. "It is too bad I was out of town each time and we don't have similar information on our other two women." He looked up from his visual examination of the body on the table. "Not to say my colleague did not do what he should have. The autopsies performed on the other two women were well done."

McCabe said, "And, of course, we didn't know until the second victim that there was a pattern. By then, the first victim had been long buried."

"And there is no need to dig her or the second victim up," Dr. Singh said. "Unless we should find something unexpected here. Shall we begin?"

McCabe glanced at Baxter. She couldn't make out his expression behind his plastic face mask and visor, but he gave her a thumbs-up with his gloved hand.

Singh said, "As with the first two young women, the killer took no chances with locating the heart."

"What do you mean?" Baxter asked.

"It is difficult to wedge a needle between two ribs and go directly into the heart. The killer wisely went in from below, angling the needle upward and toward the left shoulder from the soft pit of the stomach. The needle traveled through the diaphragm and directly into the heart. If you look closely, you can see the injection site."

"Yeah, I see it," Baxter said.

"But you'll have to do the tox screen to confirm the phenol, right?" McCabe said.

"That is correct. And we will need to confirm that these two small circular marks were caused by a stunner, as with the other two women."

When they were done, McCabe called Lieutenant Dole. "We won't have the toxicological report until tomorrow, but Dr. Singh says that what we have so far puts Vivian Jessup in line for victim number three. Same pattern as with the first two victims. Stunner followed by injection to the heart. The only difference is that bruise on her arm. Dr. Singh says she was hit on the arm with a lug wrench or something similar."

Dole said, "What came first? The blow to the arm or the stun?"

"Blow to the arm first." McCabe said. "Dr. Singh says the blow to the arm would have been sufficient to make her stumble and fall, but she wouldn't have been immobile. She was on the ground when the killer used the stunner on her."

"And that kept her immobile long enough for the perp to jam the syringe into her heart," Dole said. "Same as the other two."

"Dr. Singh also confirms that the body was moved immediately after her death. He says she was probably dumped ten to twelve hours before the nine-one-one call came in at eight seventeen hours."

"That puts time of death between eight and ten P.M. on Wednesday evening."

"Except," McCabe said, "Dr. Singh warns we have to take into account the intense heat and the possible impact of whatever she was injected with on body tissues."

"But he's pretty sure of time of death?"

"Assuming that she was injected with phenol, Lou. He says if it turns out to be something else, he may need to amend his time line. So he's not willing to go on record yet, but he's going to send you and the commander his initial report."

"Okay. Are you and Baxter on your way back in?"

McCabe glanced over at Baxter, who had walked down the hall. He was on his ORB. Talking to a girlfriend?

She said to the lieutenant, "Baxter and I were thinking of heading over to UAlbany to try to catch up with the theater professor that Vivian Jessup was working with. Has anyone been able to reach her yet?"

"No luck getting hold of her at home," Dole said. "But we know she hasn't skipped town. Her chairperson says she was in early this morning, then left again. He says he doesn't think she's avoiding us, just too upset to talk."

"So she knew Vivian Jessup well?" McCabe asked.

"Her chairperson didn't say. Just said she's taking it hard," Dole said. "Okay, head over to the university and try to find her. Tomorrow, I want you and Baxter to go down to the City. We've been in touch with NYPD. They're going to provide you with your own personal escort."

"Helpful of them. We'll check in after our interview with the professor."

"The police chief at UAlbany already knows we're going to be on campus. But give him a heads-up when you get there."

"Will do," McCabe said.

The young woman behind the desk in the Department of Theatre Productions office looked like a work-study student. Her attention was focused on the hologram she'd projected on the desktop: a court jester in Renaissance foolscap with bells.

"Good morning." McCabe held out her badge. "I'm Detective McCabe. This is Detective Baxter. We're looking for Professor Meredith—"

"Oh, you're here about Vivian Jessup." The young woman shot up and sent the desk chair skittering. "Excuse me, I have to let Professor Carmichael . . . excuse me."

She scurried across to the room, knocked on a closed office door, and darted inside when a man's voice called "Come in."

"Are we that scary?" Baxter said.

"Must be," McCabe said.

The office door opened. A man came out, followed by the skittish young woman.

He looked cautious but calm. Slender, curly blond hair, wearing blue jeans and a retro MAKE LOVE NOT WAR T-shirt.

"Hello, Detectives, I'm Ian Carmichael, chair of the department,"

McCabe identified herself and Baxter. "Sorry to disturb you, Professor Carmichael. We were inquiring about Professor Noel. She isn't at home or in her office, and we'd like to speak to her about Vivian Jessup."

Carmichael stuck his hands into his pockets. "She tagged me a few minutes ago. She said if you came by to ask you to come over to the Performing Arts Center. She's over there reviewing some footage."

"Reviewing some footage?" Baxter said. "So she had some work she thought she'd get done? We could just catch up with her whenever?"

Carmichael's gaze narrowed. "Actually, Detective Baxter, the footage is of Vivian Jessup. Professor Noel remembered that she had it and thought you would be interested in seeing it."

"Yes, we would be very interested in seeing that footage," McCabe said. "We'll go over and meet with Professor Noel now. And, thank you, Professor Carmichael, for taking the time to talk to us."

"No problem," Carmichael said. "Anything we can do."

Out in the hall, out of earshot of the office, McCabe turned to her new partner. "Mike, getting people's backs up going in—"

"Sorry," he said. "I guess I spent too much time hanging out with the guys in vice."

"They like to break down doors and throw people against walls. I prefer not to have to exert myself that much to get people to cooperate."

Baxter grinned. "But I hear you can be mean when the circumstances call for it."

"My legend precedes me?" McCabe said.

"Just kidding. You've got to learn to take a joke. What I heard was that you're a good cop. That's why I was looking forward to working with you."

"I'll try to make sure you learn a thing or two," McCabe said.

"Ouch."

"Let's get over to PAC before Professor Noel departs for some other location."

They were crossing the square to the Performance Arts Center when a male voice called out, "Hey, McCabe!"

McCabe turned. She smiled as she saw the short, muscular man coming toward them with a leashed dog that must have weighed as much as he did.

"Saul!" McCabe said, going to meet him. "Hi, Duke." She patted the giant dog on his head and leaned around him to hug his master. "What are you two doing on campus?"

"They've having a rally for the football team. When the mascot's a Great Dane, it's always fun to have some of the real dogs walking around. So they let our rescue group set up a table."

"That is some animal," Baxter said as he joined them and looked down at Duke's massive head and jaw.

"Great Dane-mastiff mix," Saul said.

"Saul Jacobs, this is Mike Baxter," McCabe said. "He just joined our unit. Mike, Saul was my first partner when I was on patrol. Now he's retired and living the good life."

The two men fell into shop talk, getting a fix on each other.

McCabe gave it a few minutes, then said, "Saul, we'll catch you for a beer at O'Malley's sometime soon. We're on our way to an interview."

"Don't let me keep you. Hey, you give any more thought to that puppy?"

"Still thinking," McCabe said. "Catch you later."

"What puppy?" Baxter said as they walked away.

"Saul's trying to get me to take a rescue dog."

"Great Danes must eat like linebackers."

"There is that." McCabe glanced at the simulated ivy climbing the white-and-gray granite sides of the nearest building. "I know it's green, but solar panel arrays don't quite say hallowed halls, do they?"

"Only if you're a science geek."

"Did you go to school here in the area?"

"I headed down to Houston," Baxter said. "I wanted to get away from home. And the girl I was dating in high school was going there. We broke up two months into our freshman year."

"But you stayed in Texas?"

"Liked the weather and the cowboy boots. So you majored in CJ here—"

"And psychology. Double major."

"I was prelaw. CJ and public policy."

"What changed your mind about becoming a lawyer?"

"I didn't change my mind, just decided to get some real-world experience first. Then I'll do Albany Law and become a prosecutor."

"If you don't become police chief?"

"That's my other option."

"Always helps to have a plan, huh?"

"Always," Baxter said. "Gotta know where you're going if you want to get there."

"So I've heard."

"Professor Noel's in the studio lab," the woman in the PAC office told them. "She said you were on the way and to send you in."

"Carmichael gave Noel a heads-up," Baxter said as they started down the corridor to the lab.

"Seems like," McCabe agreed. She stepped back out of the path of a student carrying a giant plastic ham with an opening in the bottom. "Let me guess. *To Kill a Mockingbird*?"

The student nodded and stepped sideways. "We're cleaning out the costume room."

Baxter said, "I must have seen that movie about a hundred times."

"The reason you wanted to be a lawyer?" McCabe said.

"Nah, I just thought it was a cool movie. I like movies set in the South."

"The hot weather thing, huh?" McCabe said. "This looks like the place."

Meredith Noel, petite, fortyish, with spiky blond hair, paused the footage she was watching when they walked in. Up on the wall, Vivian Jessup's hand froze in the gesture of brushing back her famous red hair. She was looking toward the camera, a book that looked like a journal or diary open on the desk in front of her.

"Sorry we've had such a hard time touching base," Noel said. "I was just so devastated when I heard about Vivian. I couldn't believe it."

They sat down at the conference table, McCabe and Baxter on one side, Noel across from them.

"Did you know Vivian Jessup well?" McCabe asked.

Noel shoved her fingers through her spiky hair and grimaced. "That's the crazy part. The reason I feel almost to blame for what happened."

From the corner of her eye, McCabe saw Baxter tense. Before he could blurt out something, she said, "To blame? Why do you feel that way?"

Tears appeared in Noel's eyes. "Because if Vivian and I hadn't met at that conference, and I hadn't mentioned John Wilkes Booth, she never would have come to Albany."

"I can see you're upset, Professor Noel," McCabe said. "But let's start at the beginning. What conference?"

Noel sniffed and dug into the pocket of her smock. She came up with a tissue and blew her nose. "A drama conference at NYU about a year and a half ago. Vivian was one of the actors who took part. She was interviewed and then there was a reception. And I had a chance to talk with her." Noel wiped at her nose again. "I mentioned I was at UAlbany, and she smiled and said she'd never been at all inclined to go to Albany. And I laughed and agreed that Albany isn't New York City. But I was thinking how incredible it would be if I could get her to do something with the department here. And so I went into the spiel we've been using to recruit grad students, about all of the famous writers, actors, and other performers who lived in Albany at various times or came here to perform."

"And that was when you mentioned John Wilkes Booth?" McCabe said.

Noel nodded. "I told her how he had been performing in Albany on the night that Abraham Lincoln stopped en route to his presidential inauguration. She was really intrigued by that. It always gives me chills, too."

"Yes, it is that kind of story," McCabe said.

"But what really intrigued Vivian was what might have been different if Henrietta Irving had killed Booth."

"Who?"

"An actress who was Booth's lover. It happened two months after Booth and Lincoln had both been in Albany. That April of 1861, Booth came back for a return engagement at the Gayety Theatre. Irving had performed with him in Rochester, and they were together again in Albany. They had a drunken quarrel when she realized he had no intention of marrying her. She tried to stab him, but he deflected the knife. His face was slashed, but not enough to do permanent damage to his classic profile. He left town the next day."

"What happened to Irving?" Baxter asked.

"She thought she had killed Booth. She went back to her room and tried to commit suicide. Luckily, she survived."

McCabe said, "If she had killed Booth that evening in April 1861—"

Noel nodded. "Then Booth and Lincoln would never have had

that final encounter in Ford's Theatre. Booth's madness would have ended here in Albany."

Baxter said, "That's what the play she was writing was about?"

"The story as told by an elderly Henrietta Irving. A play about Lincoln and Booth here in Albany, but also about Irving and who she was. Irving is one of those nineteenth-century actresses who is almost forgotten today."

Baxter said, "Was she charged with trying to kill Booth?"

"No," Noel said. "Not after she told them that he had seduced her and then refused to do the honorable thing. Apparently, she wasn't the first or last woman to make a fool of herself over Booth."

"But the only one who tried to kill him?" McCabe said.

"As far as we know. But the man was accident-prone. While he was in Albany, he also fell on the dagger he was using doing a performance. He was just returning to the stage after that injury on the night Lincoln stopped in Albany. Booth did his performance with one arm strapped to his body. The papers praised the passion of his performance."

"Probably pissed as hell that Old Abe was in town," Baxter said.

"I don't doubt he was," Noel agreed. "Albany was a Democratic town, but they turned out for the president-elect, even thought he was a Republican." She smiled. "Not to say that Booth didn't get better reviews in one of the newspapers. But he had been warned by the theater manager that he couldn't go around making inflammatory pro-South declarations."

"Not to say there were no pro-slavery Southern sympathizers here in Albany," McCabe said.

"Definitely not to say that, Detective McCabe. The North has never been pure in its ideology."

"But getting back to Vivian Jessup's reaction to the story you told her," McCabe said. "You said she was 'intrigued.'"

"Yes. And a few months later, she contacted me because she had this idea for a play and she wanted to know if I would be interested in doing a theater lab here in Albany."

"What's a theater lab?" Baxter asked.

"That's when a play is tried out, often with student actors. It gives the playwright and the director an opportunity to work through any problems. Since this was going to be Vivian's first attempt to write a play and the encounter had happened here in Albany, she thought UAlbany would be the perfect place to do the lab."

McCabe said, "Speaking of the 'it happened here' aspect, didn't I hear on the news that the mayor intended to feature the play as a part of the yearlong events?"

"Yes, she did. She and Vivian met at a UAlbany reception. The mayor was really excited about the idea of having a Tony Award–winning actress involved in her PR campaign."

"Now that we have the background, could you tell us what we're going to see in the footage?" McCabe said.

Noel glanced at the wall. "This is a 'work-in-progress' session that Vivian did for the Theatre Department. We post these for the students and anyone else who is interested. She's talking here about her inspiration for the play and what she wanted to achieve with it. And about her creative process."

"Okay," McCabe said. "Could we watch now? And then we'll follow up if we have more questions."

Noel waved her hand toward the wall, and Vivian Jessup completed the gesture of brushing back a strand of her shoulder-length red hair. The gesture seemed unconscious, made as she was focused on conveying what it was about Booth, Lincoln, and Henrietta Irving that had made her go home and start to jot down notes. And when she'd read more about Lincoln and his assassination, learned that the young couple who had joined the president and his wife in their box at Ford's Theatre had been a major and his fiancee from Albany, that the soldier who had shot Booth when he was trapped also had been from Albany, or close enough, from nearby Troy, she had gotten more and more excited about telling the story. Not just Albany's recurring role in the Lincoln-Booth saga but also Irving's story. She had imagined Henrietta Irving looking back and realizing that she had shared her bed with a future assassin, that if she had killed Booth that night in Albany . . .

Vivian Jessup pushed back her hair again and said, her British accent stronger, "There are moments when our lives intertwine and connect. Moments when we encounter each other, when a gesture, a word, a decision to do one thing rather than another changes everything. And we move through our lives, unaware of how what we did or didn't do affected other lives . . . unless something happens, as with Booth and Lincoln, and then we go back and we try to reconstruct. And we think, What if. What if I had done that or this? Or been able to do that? In my play, Henrietta Irving imagines, looks back. . . ." Jessup shook her head, smiled, and pointed to the open journal in front of her. "I was no more coherent when I tried to muddle through this in my writing log. But I hope the play captures the essence of what I want to convey."

"That's all," Noel said. "She planned to record a longer version later."

McCabe said, "Where was she in the production process? Had the play been performed in the theater lab?"

"Not yet. Vivian had a couple of months before beginning rehearsals for her next play—sorry . . . the play she was starring in, not the one she had written. Having that hiatus, she intended to spend two or three days a week here in Albany, working on 'John and Henrietta.'"

"That was the name of the play?"

"The working title. She wanted to work it through, see it onstage. . . ." Noel's eyes filled with tears. "She was so excited about getting started. We had scheduled the first public performance for November twenty-third. The mayor was going to be here to introduce . . ." Noel lowered her head into her hands. Voice muffled, she said. "I saw Vivian on Wednesday. We met here that morning and talked about what we wanted to do next Monday, with the students."

"What time did she leave?" Baxter asked. "Did she mention her plans?"

Noel raised her head. "She got here at a few minutes after nine. We were here until just before eleven, when I had to leave for my eleven o'clock class. She said she was going back to the hotel and work. And later, she was going to have dinner with Ted Thornton and his fiancée."

"She knew Ted Thornton?" Baxter said.

"Yes. She and Thornton are—were old friends. She had told him about the play. If it did well here and in repertory theaters, she thought she might persuade him to back it on Broadway."

Baxter shot McCabe a glance.

She was pretty sure he was thinking that this was even bigger than they'd thought, not only a Broadway actress but a billionaire businessman/adventurer to boot.

And Ted Thornton's name did keep popping up.

McCabe said, "Is there anything else you can tell us, Professor Noel?"

Noel frowned. "I'm not sure this is important. But Vivian mentioned that she had been talking to a collector about a Dalí edition of *Alice*."

"A what?" Baxter said before McCabe had to reveal her ignorance.

"Salvador Dalí," Noel said. "The Surrealist artist. He did the illustrations for a limited edition of *Alice in Wonderland*."

"So these editions are rare?" McCabe asked.

"From what Vivian told me, a mint edition is hard to come by. The one she had was stolen when the apartment she used to live in was burglarized. She had it in a glass case, which must have suggested it was valuable."

"When did this burglary happen?" McCabe asked.

"Years ago. She had just moved to New York City and was sharing a flat with two roommates."

"And she could afford a Dalí edition?" Baxter said.

Noel wrinkled her nose. "I think it was a gift from a friend."

McCabe said, "This friend wouldn't happen to have been Ted Thornton?"

"Oh, no, she hasn't known Thornton that long. I mean not as long ago as when she first moved to New York. She mentioned meeting him at a Hollywood party when she was out there for her role as Lady Macbeth. That movie came out about ten years ago."

"Okay," McCabe said. "If we could go back to the collector who contacted her. Did she mention a name?"

Noel shook her head. "Only that he lived here in Albany and he said he had both a Dalí edition and one of the stamp cases that Lewis Carroll designed."

Baxter said. "And was she planning to meet this collector to get a look at the book and the stamp case?"

"She said he was being cagey. She wasn't sure he actually had what he claimed to have." Noel pushed her fingers through her hair. "She said he contacted her after the interview she did the last time she was in Albany. It was a Public Radio interview, and the interviewer had asked about her *Alice* collection."

"How did this collector contact her?" McCabe asked.

"I think he contacted her through her publicist, who forwarded his tag to Vivian. That was after she had gotten back to the City. He offered to show her the book and stamp case the next time she came to Albany."

"But she wasn't sure he was for real?" Baxter said.

"He had this story about a distant cousin who'd been a huge *Alice* fan and how he'd been thrilled to inherit the items when the cousin died. Vivian thought that if he was for real, he was going to try to get as much money out of her as he could. She told him she'd rather they meet in the City and have the items authenticated. He was balking about going down there when she was going to be right here in Albany. She offered to pay for a hotel overnight. She was waiting to hear back from him."

"And that was where things stood on Wednesday when you spoke to her?" McCabe said.

Noel nodded. "Yes. She mentioned it because she was going back to the City on Thursday and she hadn't heard from him. She really wanted that Dalí edition."

Baxter said, "Did she want it enough to agree to meet the collector here?"

"I don't know." Noel looked from McCabe to Baxter. "But I thought I should mention it, in case . . . I mean, the man may be perfectly legitimate, but . . ."

"But we need to find him and confirm that," McCabe said. "Professor, when we searched Ms. Jessup's hotel room, there was no sign of any type of communication device. No ORB."

Noel said, "She had her ORB with her when I saw her on Wednesday. She . . . Do you think the person who killed her took it?"

"That's possible," McCabe said. "Did Ms. Jessup also have a purse or handbag with her on Wednesday?"

"Yes, a beautiful bag. Red leather in the shape of a rose. She said she'd bought it the last time she was home in London."

McCabe said, "The clothes we saw in Ms. Jessup's hotel closet were rather plain. Expensive, but not—"

"Vivian preferred classic lines in her clothes. But she loved one-of-a-kind accessories."

McCabe took her card from her own plain black shoulder bag. "If you should think of anything else, will you contact us?"

"Yes, absolutely," Noel said. "Vivian's daughter—"

"We're expecting her in this afternoon."

"Vivian adored her daughter and her grandchild. She even adored her son-in-law. Something that many mothers-in-law can't say."

McCabe didn't ask if Noel had a son-in-law, but from her tone, she suspected she did. "Thank you again, Professor Noel. You've been a great help."

"I will call if anything else occurs to me. It's so awful that Vivian should die . . . be murdered . . . here in Albany."

McCabe said, "But not your fault."

"Yes. I know that logically. But right now, it doesn't help."

They left her sitting there at the conference table.

Outside, Baxter said, "Didn't I hear your brother works here on campus? You want to stop in and say hello?"

McCabe shook her head. "He's probably busy, and so are we. We'd better let the lieutenant know about Vivian Jessup's dinner engagement with Ted Thornton and see how he wants to handle the interview."

"Discreetly?" Baxter said.

11

Go have lunch. I'll get back to you as soon as I hear from the commander." Dole ended his call with McCabe and turned back to the detective standing in front of his desk.

"Pettigrew, you've got at least four other cases from last week alone that you ought to be working on. Cases where you have a co-operative victim, or a witness, or a lead. Something. Anything."

"I know that, Lou," Pettigrew said. "But even if the victim isn't cooperating, we know a crime was committed. We have the attack on-cam—"

"We have two unidentified men wearing masks and gloves. We have a stolen car that they left in another alley. That's it." Dole rubbed his hand over his head. "In case you missed the memo, we're supposed to be focusing where we can get results."

"Just give us another forty-eight hours on this one, Lou."

"You've got twenty-four. Now, get out of my office and get back to work."

"Thanks, Lou," Pettigrew said.

Yin looked up from his ORB when Pettigrew sat down at the desk across from his. "We still on it?"

"Until tomorrow. Got anything?"

"Research came back with more on Jorgensen. Details of his rise and fall. Nothing we didn't already know. A phenom by the time he was twenty. Women, wine, and riding high. Then the gambling and getting kicked out of baseball."

"It was probably the gambling again," Pettigrew said.

"Where does a guy who went bankrupt and was on serious hook to the IRS come up with the kind of money for bets that would bring two professionals looking for him?"

"Maybe they were making an example of him." Pettigrew reached for his mug.

Yin grimaced. "I don't know how you can drink that stuff."

"It's better than the brand they were trying a couple of weeks ago. If you don't think about it, it tastes almost like real coffee."

"I'll take your word for it. Want to ride over to Jorgensen's address?"

"Yeah. The guy lives in a boardinghouse. Maybe his landlady can tell us something."

Yin reached for his new hat. "Bachelors in the city. When my great-grandfather first arrived in this country, he lived in a boardinghouse down in the City, on Mott Street. Now boardinghouses are back again."

"Did they ever go away?"

"Maybe not. Maybe they just called them something else for a while."

Pettigrew grimaced at the sour taste rising from his esophagus. He opened his desk drawer to find an antacid tablet. His ORB beeped.

"Detective Pettigrew," he said, putting it on voice only.

"Detective Pettigrew, this is Nurse Woods at St. Peter's."

Relieved that it wasn't his ex-wife calling back, Pettigrew went to visual and a blond woman in a white uniform appeared. "Yes, Nurse Woods?"

"It's about the patient you came to see yesterday. Mr. Jorgensen. I'm afraid he died this morning."

"Died?" Pettigrew said. "I'm going to put you on speaker so that my partner can hear this."

He clicked the ORB into the holder on his desk.

"What happened?" Pettigrew said to the nurse. "He seemed all right when we interviewed him. Battered from the beating, but not that serious."

"Mr. Jorgensen suffered an aneurysm. He died before he could be taken into surgery," Nurse Woods said. "Because you were investigating the attack on him, the doctor thought you should be informed."

"Yes, we should be."

"We have some personal items that belonged to Mr. Jorgensen. Apparently, he had no next of kin. Unless the young woman from this morning was a relative."

"What young woman?"

"A young woman called on an old-style cell phone. There was a great deal of static on the line, but she wanted to know how Mr. Jorgensen was doing. When she was asked if she was a relative, she hung up."

"Thank you, Nurse Woods. We'll want to listen to that playback when we stop by to pick up Mr. Jorgensen's personal items."

Pettigrew closed his ORB.

Yin said, "So now we have a dead ex–baseball player."

Pettigrew shook his head. "We'd better let the lou know."

"Cheer up," Yin said. "Maybe he'll give us more than twenty-four hours on this one now that the vic's dead."

"I wonder who she was," Pettigrew said. "The young woman who called."

12

To get to Ted Thornton's house on the hill, McCabe and Baxter drove past the homes of several other members of Albany's very well to do. Including the Tudor-style mansion owned by a former corporate attorney named Joanne Barker-Channing, who had made her fortune and then founded a monthly "literary salon" in her home. McCabe's father had sometimes been known to attend, drawn by the highbrow conversation and what he described as the hostess's "graciousness."

"If you got it, flaunt it," Baxter said as they drove up the landscaped driveway to the home that Thornton had built when he started doing business in Albany.

"Apparently, the key is to 'flaunt it' in good taste," McCabe said.

She parked the city-issue sedan they had picked up from the garage after lunch behind the only other car in the circular drive.

The other car's hinged upper body had been left up. It lifted on each side from the center to allow the exit of passengers and packages.

Baxter stood there staring at the car. Then he walked over and circled around it slowly, with reverence.

McCabe laughed. "Wipe the drool off your chin, Mike, and let's go in."

"Do you know how fast this baby can go?"

"Fast enough to flap its wings and take off from the ground?"

"I guess I'm not going to impress you with my collection of classic automobile magazines."

"Probably not," McCabe said. She walked over to the car. "And this looks more futuristic than classic."

"A futuristic take on a classic," Baxter said.

"Ah, now, I understand, sensei. Ready?"

"Yeah, let's get to it."

They went up the three steps to the door and McCabe knocked.

"Hello," she said as the door swung open. And then she realized no one was there.

"Mike," she said, drawing his attention from the car to the empty foyer in front of them and the empty stairway winding up to the balcony above.

He said, "The guard at the gate called—"

"Yeah," McCabe said.

"Hello," she said, pitching her voice louder. "Detectives McCabe and Baxter, APD. May we come in?"

From around the corner, a melodic female voice said, "Please come in, Detectives McCabe and Baxter."

A moment later, the speaker glided into view.

Baxter whispered to McCabe, "Ever see *The Jetsons*? Rosie, the robot."

"I am Rosalind," the maid said, focusing her metallic gaze on Baxter.

He coughed. "Sorry. Wrong robot."

Rosalind held out her arm in a gesture of welcome. "Please come in."

"Thank you," McCabe said.

They stepped into the foyer with the two-story ceiling, and Rosalind closed the front door.

"Please follow me."

The maid, clad in trim black uniform and white apron, glided off toward the back of the house. They followed.

McCabe caught glimpses of expanses of glass and airy rooms with modern furniture in white, black, and brown, with scattered animal prints. Lots of green plants.

A cat jumped down in front of them, springing from the back of a chair by the door of the room they were about to pass. Gold and brown, tail raised straight up, he stared at them. The cat weighed at least twenty pounds.

Both McCabe and Baxter stopped in their tracks.

Rosalind, the robotic maid, said, "The cat is named Horatio. He is a Maine coon cat and a fine fellow. He will not bite or scratch unless threatened. Please let me know if you are allergic and require medication."

McCabe said, "Thank you, Rosalind. I don't require medication." She looked at Baxter. "You okay, Mike?"

He shook his head, mouth twitching with laughter. "I'm just fine and dandy."

McCabe held her hand down to the cat. "Hello, Horatio."

Horatio strolled over, sniffed her hand, and then nudged her leg. She patted his head. He meowed and strolled off back into what seemed to be a library, where he jumped up onto an armchair and looked out at them from his golden eyes.

Rosalind said, "Please follow me."

A rainbow of colors played along her metallic legs as they passed the cathedral windows in an empty stretch of hallway.

They reached their destination: Ted Thornton's own private gallery.

McCabe turned to the left and right, looking around her. Thornton's taste was eclectic, but the theme seemed to be transportation—from toy trains on an elevated track to a miniature balloon about to take off from a field. From sketches of flying machines that might have been done by da Vinci to scale models of spaceships, if it moved, Thornton seemed to have cataloged it, including a replica of the UFO from 2012.

Rosalind said, "Mr. Thornton will be with you shortly." She gestured toward the rear of the room. "Please help yourself to refreshments from the bar. Wine, beer, and nonalcoholic beverages, including coffee and tea, are available."

"Do we get a movie on this flight?" Baxter asked.

"Movies are not shown in this room. However, I can activate a slide show of photographs."

"That's okay. I was only—"

He was too late. Rosalind had glided to a blank white wall. She waved her metallic hand and the slide show began. "Is there anything else you require?"

McCabe said, "No, thank you, Rosalind. We'll be fine until Mr. Thornton joins us."

"Please press the buzzer by the door if you should require my presence."

They watched her glide away, back the way they had come.

"I wonder if she cooks and does laundry," Baxter said. "I'd sure like to have one of those if she does."

"I don't think you can afford her," McCabe said. "Look at these photographs. They're incredible."

The slide show on the wall moved from one image to another, shifting, changing shapes, zooming in and out. The photos were of people in action, caught at the moment of danger: a parachutist falling through the sky; a bungee jumper flinging himself from a bridge; a man scaling a skyscraper using only his bare hands and feet; a bullfighter facing a charging bull.

"Amazing, aren't they?"

McCabe and Baxter turned at the sound of the voice that had become familiar to most Albany residents. It was deep, with a hint of amusement, a slight catch, sometimes a bit of a stammer.

As McCabe had expected, Ted Thornton was wearing blue jeans, sneakers, and his most disarming smile—his "Oh shucks" smile, as one editorial writer had described it. The smile that his opponents had come to recognize before he pounced.

In those few seconds before she had to respond, McCabe wondered if her superiors had reached the right conclusion during the meeting they'd held to discuss this interview. After considering the other options, once the commander had conferred with the chief and the chief had made a "courtesy call" to the mayor, it had been decided that she and Baxter should handle the initial interview. The reasoning had been that if anyone higher up in the food chain came to call, it would look as if too much was being made of the dinner plans Thornton and his fiancée had had with the victim. Better the primary investigators drop by for a routine visit. Better, too, in case the media got hold of it and declared Thornton had received special treatment by dealing with the brass instead of the lowly detectives working the case.

So here they were. And personally, McCabe thought she and Baxter had been sent in first to see if they survived.

"Yes, these photos really are amazing, Mr. Thornton," McCabe said, smiling back. "Did you take them?"

One of Ted Thornton's dark, devilish brows went up, slanting over a wide brown eye. "Me? Oh, not me, Detective, I'm not a photographer. These were taken by Lisa Nichols, my . . . my very talented fiancée."

"What I particularly like is how she caught each subject in motion," McCabe said, glancing a last time at the shifting display. Then she dug into her bag for her badge. "I'm sorry, I should introduce myself. I'm Detective Hannah McCabe, and this is my partner, Detective Mike Baxter."

Tall and gangly, Thornton stepped forward, his long-fingered hand extended. "Pleasure to meet you." He grimaced, accentuating the brackets on each side of his mouth. "Although the circumstances are horrible, aren't they? Vivian was a good friend. A dear friend."

McCabe shook his hand, noting the strength of his grip. "Yes, it is horrible. You have our sympathy, Mr. Thornton. We will do our best to find the person who killed Ms. Jessup."

"I'm sure you will. Sure of that," Thornton said, moving on to shake Baxter's hand. "Let's sit. . . . Can I get you something from the bar? Or you can just go help yourselves. And then let's sit down and talk."

"Thank you, we're fine," McCabe said.

"No, no, please. Rosalind invited you to have something, didn't she? What did you think of Rosalind?" That smile again. "But let's get our drinks. Detective Baxter, please, help yourself. And would you bring me back a beer. Bottle's fine. Detective McCabe?"

"Just a water, please," McCabe said.

"Great. Got that, Detective Baxter? Need a hand?"

"No, I'm good."

"Then let's sit right over here, Detective McCabe."

He gestured toward the sofa and chairs in one corner of the room.

McCabe, stalling for time, paused to look at a framed cartoon of a sheep, a duck, and a rooster in the basket of an ascending hot-air balloon.

Thornton said, "September 1783, the first balloon flight. It lasted fifteen minutes and the . . . passengers survived."

McCabe nodded. "I saw your airship landing at the airport once. It's really quite impressive."

"A fantasy I've had since I was a boy." A flash of his smile. "The really cool part about having lots of money, Detective McCabe, is being able to spend it on anything you damn well please. Including things other people think are nuts."

"Since your airship flies, I guess it wasn't as nutty an idea as some people thought." McCabe sat down.

Thornton sat down in a chair at an angle to hers.

Mike, coming back with the drinks, was left to occupy the sofa.

"Cheers," Thornton said, tipping his beer bottle toward them.

McCabe echoed his toast with her glass bottle of water. Mike did the same with his cola.

"Getting to why we are here, Mr. Thornton—"

"Ted, please, Hannah. Let's not stand on formality. I want to do all I can to help."

"Then . . . and forgive me for being formal. We're trained to do that. Cop thing. Then, Mr. Thornton, first, if we could ask you about Wednesday evening. Ms. Jessup mentioned to someone she spoke to that morning that she was planning to have dinner with you and your fiancée."

"Oh, now you see if I had known that was what you wanted to know about . . . You talked to Bruce, right?"

"Yes, and he said if we wanted to drop by, you would be able to see us."

"Umm, and you . . . you didn't ask him about the dinner on Wednesday evening?"

"No, we thought it best to speak to you directly. We have some other questions, as well."

"I see. Well, about the dinner, Hannah—you don't mind if I call you Hannah even if you won't call me Ted?"

"I actually prefer to be called Detective McCabe, Mr. Thornton."

"Pretty and feisty," Ted Thornton said.

McCabe decided to let that go. "About the dinner. You were—"

"Yes, I'm afraid we didn't. . . . I mean, it didn't come off. Something came up and I had to get back down to the City. I spoke to Vivian around noon and asked if we could reschedule for the next evening."

"And did she agree?" McCabe asked.

"She said that if I intended to come back to Albany, we would be crossing paths. She was planning to take the train down to the City on Thursday morning."

Confirming what she told Meredith Noel about her plans, McCabe thought.

"So you went down to the City on Wednesday afternoon and came back—"

"The next morning. Took the train down and then my fiancée and Bruce and I came back in the airship."

"So you all . . . your fiancée, Ms. Nichols, Mr. Ashby, and yourself . . . were here in Albany until what time on Wednesday?"

"Oh, Bruce wasn't here. He had some things to do for me down in the City. He alerted me to a situation that I needed to handle in person."

"And you went down to handle it?"

"On the one-twenty train. We were on the way to the station when I spoke to Vivian."

"Was Ms. Jessup upset that you had to cancel dinner?"

"We're old friends. She understood." Thornton took a sip of his beer. "Actually, she said she had some business of her own that she could get taken care of that evening."

"Business?" Baxter said. "Did she mention what this business was?"

Thornton shook his head. "I wish to God she had. But someone knocked on her door."

"The door of her hotel room?" Baxter said.

"Yes, that's where she was when I reached her. She said, 'That must be room service. I ordered lunch in so that I could get some work done.' And I said, 'Then go have your lunch. See you soon.'" He sighed. "That was the last time we spoke."

"The work Ms. Jessup mentioned," McCabe said, sliding back into the conversation. "Do you know what she was working on?"

"Her play. She was doing a rewrite of some dialogue between Henrietta and Booth. The argument before . . . before she tried to stab him. That was a pivotal scene in the play."

"So you had discussed the play quite a bit?"

"Yes." Another sip of beer. "She was excited about writing her first play. And I was interested because I have a deep and abiding love of the theater." He smiled. "Been hooked ever since college, when I played Richard the Third." He hunched his shoulders, raising one higher than the other. "'Now is the winter of our discontent/Made glorious summer by this sun of York.'" His brows rose. "How could you not love a villain like that?"

"He's always been one of my favorite villains," McCabe said.

Thornton's gaze fastened on her. "But you come from a literary family, don't you, Detective McCabe? I understand . . . understand that your father is Angus McCabe, the journalist and editor. And your mother was the poet Odell Vincent."

McCabe felt her stomach muscles tighten. "Do you normally investigate your visitors' backgrounds, Mr. Thornton?"

"Only the visitors who are investigating me," he said.

Baxter cleared his throat. "I'm feeling a little neglected over here, Mr. Thornton. Did you check me out, too?"

"My people are thorough, Detective Baxter. You have a solid background, some family connections. But nothing as interesting as Detective McCabe."

Baxter grinned. "Gee, sorry to hear I'm so dull. But getting back to the reason we're here . . ."

Baxter flicked a glance in McCabe's direction.

"Yes, getting back to that," McCabe said. "We understand Ms. Jessup hoped to eventually take her play to Broadway. This business she wanted to take care of, Mr. Thornton . . . do you think it could have had anything to do with that?"

Thornton smiled. "Obviously, you already know that Vivian was hoping I would be her backer."

"We did hear that. Was it supposed to be a secret?"

"Not at all. I wanted to wait until I saw the play in theater lab to commit. But this was Vivian Jessup."

"Meaning there was no reason Ms. Jessup would have felt she should be looking for another backer?"

"None."

"Did Ms. Jessup happen to mention to you a collector who had contacted her?"

Thornton took a sip from his beer bottle. "A collector of what?"

"Now, that's a good question. What we know is that this person claimed to have in his collection a Dalí edition of *Alice in Wonderland* and a stamp case designed by Lewis Carroll. Did she happen to mention that to you?"

"No . . . I can't recall that she did."

"Thank you, Mr. Thornton. While we're here, could we speak to your fiancée, Ms. Nichols?"

"Just routine, Mr. Thornton," Baxter said.

"No problem, Detectives. I understand. Let me see if Lisa is available."

A man walked in. Blond, wearing a tan sports jacket and slacks, he was as polished as Thornton was casual. "Ted, did I hear you mention Lisa? I was just coming to give you a message from her. She didn't want to interrupt your meeting."

So she sent him to interrupt it? McCabe thought.

"Bruce, I believe you spoke to Detective McCabe," Thornton said.

"Yes, I did. Excuse my abrupt entrance." He came forward with his hand extended. "Bruce Ashby, Ted's aide-de-camp."

Interesting description, McCabe thought as she stood to shake Ashby's hand. Thornton had never been in the military. Had Ashby?

She introduced Baxter, and the two exchanged handshakes.

"What was the message from Lisa?" Thornton asked his aide.

"That she decided to go out. She had some errands to run." Ashby turned back to McCabe and Baxter. "I'm sure if she had known you might want to speak to her, she would have delayed her errands."

Thornton shrugged, hunching his shoulders. "Sorry. Afraid you'll have to speak to Lisa some other time, Detective McCabe."

Ashby said, "It's my fault, Ted." Turning back to McCabe and Baxter he said, "I told Lisa that you had arrived. But it didn't occur to me until she dashed off that I should have suggested she stay in case she was wanted."

"No problem." McCabe said. "But we would like to speak to Ms. Nichols at her earliest convenience." She took her card from her shoulder bag. "Would you ask her to give us a call, Mr. Thornton?"

"Of course," he said. He took the card, glanced at it, and tucked it in his shirt pocket. "By the way, I've invited Vivian's daughter, Greer, to stay here. Much easier on her than running a media gauntlet at a hotel. You can talk to Lisa when you come to talk to Greer." He raised an eyebrow. "I assume you will want to talk to Greer."

"Yes," McCabe said. "She is going to contact us when she arrives. We'll make arrangements for an interview then."

Thornton nodded. "Please consider my house your house. Anytime you need to pop by. I'll leave those instructions with the guards."

"And with Rosalind?" Baxter said.

Thornton laughed. "You liked Rosalind, did you? She's a marvel of technology. Let me . . . let me call her to show you out."

He pressed the buzzer, then turned to Ashby. "Bruce, would you save the detectives some time and send over a copy of Lisa's and my train reservations from Wednesday. And, of course, the flight plan for the airship on Thursday morning."

"I'll see you receive both," Ashby said to McCabe.

"Thank you. We understand you were in the City on Wednesday, Mr. Ashby. Did you have appointments?"

"Back-to-back all day until Ted arrived that afternoon. Later, we had a working dinner. Would you like that information, as well?"

"If it wouldn't be too much trouble," Baxter said.

Rosalind glided in. "You called, sir," she said, fixing her metallic gaze on her "boss."

"Yes, Rosalind. Would you show our guests out?"

"This way, please."

McCabe turned in the doorway. "By the way, Mr. Thornton, the boat ramp where Ms. Jessup's body was found. Would you happen to have used it recently?"

Thornton raised an eyebrow. "That ramp . . . Let me see now. . . . I've only used it twice. The day that it opened . . . and the second time was . . ." He turned to Ashby. "Do you have that date, Bruce?"

Ashby checked his calendar. "That would have been on Monday, September sixteenth." Ashby turned to McCabe. "The mayor joined Ted for a short canoe excursion while they discussed her Albany initiative."

McCabe said, "That would be the 'It Happened Here' initiative?"

Thornton said, "I'm a real supporter of that campaign. Albany's history hasn't been highlighted enough. The Dutch, the British, the Revolution." He waved his hand. "The fur trade, the steamboat, the railroad. Everyone from Benjamin Franklin to Joseph Henry, the first secretary of the Smithsonian, had connections to this city. Vladimir Nabokov, the author of *Lolita* . . . the man stopped here to hunt butterflies in the Pine Bush. We've got to get that history out there and get more people interested in coming here and spending money." He smiled. "Don't you agree, Detective?"

"I'm sure that would be good for the city's economy," McCabe said. "Thank you for your time, Mr. Thornton."

"Anything I can do . . . anything to help find Vivian's killer. Just call on me."

Rosalind said, "If you have concluded your conversation, please follow me."

McCabe and Baxter followed the maid back the way they had come.

She opened the front door for them. "Good-bye."

"Good-bye," McCabe said.

"See you later, Roz," Baxter said.

"My name is Rosalind," she said, and closed the door.

Baxter grinned at McCabe. "Damn robot's as touchy about the name thing as you are."

McCabe glanced at him as they walked toward their car. "Thanks for stepping in back there when he threw me by mentioning my family."

"Always got your back, partner."

"Looks like your favorite sports car is out doing errands."

Baxter stared at the empty space where the car had been when they arrived. "I just hope she doesn't park it in a mall somewhere."

They got into their city-issue sedan. As McCabe was buckling her seat belt, she said, "Mike, did you get the sense Lisa Nichols may not be Ashby's favorite person?"

"You mean the way he tried to subtly suggest she might have ducked out on the interview?"

"Yeah, that."

"Maybe he's got the hots for his boss and isn't thrilled because the fiancée has come between them."

"It wouldn't hurt to check a little bit more on both Ashby and the fiancée."

"Just to see if anything turns up?"

"Never hurts to be thorough," McCabe said. "As I'm sure Ted Thornton would agree."

13

The trim gray-haired woman who had answered the door at the house in Pine Hills called back over her shoulder, "Thelma, don't forget to put parsley in the stew."

She turned to Pettigrew and Yin. Pettigrew noted that her eyes were red-rimmed under her glasses.

"I'm Caroline Young," she said. "You must be the detectives about poor Nils."

She used Jorgensen's given name rather than the name he had been known by on the baseball field.

"Detectives Pettigrew and Yin, Ms. Young," Pettigrew said

She glanced at their badges. "Please come in. I have to go out, but Thelma, who helps me here in the house, will show you up to Nils's room."

"Thank you, ma'am," Yin said. "But if we could speak to you for just a few minutes before you leave."

Ms. Young glanced at the watch on her wrist. "I can give you a few minutes, but I'm due at the community center. We have to finish putting together the care packages we're shipping out to the soldiers." She sighed. "I remember my mother doing that when I was a child. We're still doing it."

"Yes, ma'am, we won't keep you," Pettigrew said, "Is there anything you can tell us about Swede . . . Nils?"

Ms. Young nodded her head, "He came here to live three years ago. I explained at the time that I run a respectable boardinghouse. He always followed my rules." She frowned slightly. "At least he did until last Friday evening, when I caught him sneaking down the back stairs with a young woman."

Yin said, "So when you saw them, they were on their way out?'

"Yes, and Nils claimed they'd needed to speak in private and that was the reason he'd taken her up to his room."

Pettigrew said, "I don't suppose he introduced the young woman?"

"Introduced her? She ran past me and out the door." Ms. Young's lips tightened. "She was barely out of her teens, from what I saw of her."

"Did Jorgensen go after her?" Yin asked.

"He stayed for a few minutes to try to explain himself to me. And then he went out, whether after her or not, I can't say."

"When did he come back in?"

"To the best of my knowledge, he didn't return until the next morning. He came in as Thelma and I were getting breakfast set out."

"Did he mention where he'd been?" Pettigrew asked.

"No, and I didn't ask. It was not my business."

"How many other boarders do you have, Ms. Young?" Yin asked.

"Three others. Two of them travel with their jobs. Roy, who has the room across from Nils, is usually here. He's retired."

"Is he here now?"

"He said he was going out for a walk, but I expect he'll be back soon." She glanced at her watch. "And now I do have to leave." She picked up her wide-brimmed straw hat from the table by the door. "I am very sorry about Nils. In spite of the recent incident involving the young woman, I found him a good boarder." She sniffed and blinked behind her glasses. "And a good man." She called out, "Thelma, please show the detectives up to Mr. Jorgensen's room."

Thelma bustled in from the kitchen as Ms. Young was going out the door. She looked to be in her forties, perhaps a couple of decades younger than her employer, plump, with rosy cheeks. She said nothing other than "His room is upstairs."

They followed her up to the second floor. She pointed at a closed door halfway down the hall. Then she turned and went back down the stairs.

"Guess it's not locked," Yin said.

They opened the door of Swede Jorgensen's room and went in.

"Maybe he had to sell everything to pay off the IRS," Pettigrew said as they glanced from bed to dresser to armchair and lamp table by the window.

"Maybe he was practicing to be a monk," Yin said.

Pettigrew opened the closet door. "Clothes, but not too many of them."

Yin walked over to the dresser. "Well, maybe we'll find something in a pocket or in his sock drawer."

After he was done with the closet, Pettigrew got down on his knees to look under the bed. "Not even dust."

He lifted the edge of the mattress, then the pillows.

Yin dropped the chair cushion that he had been looking under. "I guess we should have expected this after we saw what the hospital called his 'possessions.' The clothes he had on when he was brought in, a bus pass, and a pack of energy gum."

"Yeah, but I still think the thugs might have gone through his pockets and taken whatever—"

"Sean, there's no record the guy even had an ORB. It looks like he was trying to live off the grid."

From the doorway, a squeaky voice said, "You the cops?"

The man in the doorway was no more than five feet tall, a shriveled little man with a full gray beard and bowlegs in his overalls. He was holding a bug-eyed Chihuahua.

Pettigrew said, "Your landlady allows pets?"

"She's okay with Max. Max doesn't yip unless something's wrong."

"Has he been yipping lately?"

"Nah. It's been quiet around here. Except for when Swede's little friend dropped by and Caroline caught them."

"So you were here when that happened?" Yin said.

"Yeah, but I was asleep until Swede and Caroline started arguing on the back stairs."

"So you didn't see the girl?" Pettigrew asked.

"Nope. Just heard the yelling about her."

"Did Swede say anything to you about what happened?" Yin asked.

"Swede wasn't much of a sharer. Or a talker, for that matter."

"So," Yin said, "I guess there's nothing you can tell us, Mr.—"

"LeBlanc. LeRoy LeBlanc. And I didn't say that." He nodded his head toward the hall. "Come over to my room. I got something to show you."

Pettigrew and Yin crossed the hall and stood in the doorway of LeBlanc's room, staring. "You collect locks and keys?" Pettigrew said.

"Used to be a locksmith," LeBlanc said. "Like to keep my hand in."

He found what he was looking for in the one clear space on his desk. Something wrapped in a wad of paper.

"I found this out in the yard after Swede and the girl were here. I was going to give it to him to return to his girlfriend."

Pettigrew unwrapped the paper. It was a lipstick case and mirror.

"Looks like real gold," Yin said.

LeBlanc laughed. "Yeah. So what does a girl with money and looks want with old Swede?"

Pettigrew opened the tube and rolled it up to make sure it did contain lipstick. "Pink," he said. "We should ask if she was a blonde."

Yin said, "Casey wears pink lipstick sometimes. She's a redhead."

"Got anything else for us?" Pettigrew asked LeBlanc.

"Nope, that's it. But you might want to talk to Thelma, if you haven't already. She saw the girl and Swede come in."

Thelma was in the small greenhouse off the kitchen. Pettigrew glanced around and thought again of trying to grow a few things on the terrace of his apartment.

In answer to Yin's question, Thelma said her last name was Wilson.

"Yes, I saw them. I was going to tell Caroline when she came back. But she caught them herself."

"Did you hear any of the conversation?" Yin asked. "Between the girl and Jorgensen, I mean."

"They weren't talking. Just trying to sneak up the stairs."

"So they were in a hurry?" Pettigrew said.

Wilson turned and gave him a look. "Yes, but I don't think it was for what you're thinking. That girl looked scared. He looked upset, too."

Yin said, "But she was going with him willingly?"

"She seemed to be. If she hadn't, I would have said something to him right then and there."

Pettigrew said, "Did you get a good look at the girl?"

Wilson nodded. "Long blond hair, big blue eyes, skinny but pretty. She was wearing a white dress, looked like it cost a lot of money. Little sandals on her feet."

"You seem to be a very observant woman," Pettigrew said. "What did you think of Swede?"

She considered that for a moment. "He was all right. Never gave me or Caroline any trouble. Worked down at the docks, but he never made a mess when he came in. Never had much to say, but polite when he asked for something."

Pettigrew said, "Ms. Wilson, would you be willing to come down to the station and give a sketch artist a description of the girl? That might help us locate her."

"I'll come. But you might be too late to help her if those same men who beat him up got hold of her."

14

"No, I don't want to go with you," Angus said. "I want to stay here with my shoes off, watching Bette Davis go blind and die. Then I'm going to start reading that new book about what might have happened if Truman really had beaten Dewey. Probably a lot of academic gibberish, but I might want to write a review." He waved his hand at her. "I got myself a full evening planned. Get out of here and go spend some time with your friends. Tell 'em I said hello."

McCabe kissed her father's forehead and left him to watch Davis's *Dark Victory*.

She intended to take the evening off. The toxicology report had confirmed that Vivian Jessup had died of a lethal phenol injection. The same way that Bethany Clark and Sharon Giovanni, the first two victims, had died.

Tomorrow, she and Baxter would go down to the City to meet an NYPD detective and go to Jessup's condo. Then they would come back and meet with the other members of the task force that the commander had put together. They would go over what they had and try to figure out what, if anything, the three victims, two Albany girls, one twenty-two, the other twenty-one, and a Broadway actress, British-born, age forty-seven, had had in common.

Tonight, McCabe didn't want to think about it. She had exchanged her workday blouse and slacks for a silk top and skirt and she was going to sit in her friend Chelsea's café restaurant and listen to whoever was playing the piano.

On Friday night, Chelsea's Place got busy. Reservations required.

As McCabe slid past the people waiting to be shown to tables, she heard a woman tell her male companion, "You have to try the zucchini pasta. I had it when I was here for lunch last week and . . ."

Somehow, Chelsea and her husband, Stan, managed to combine concepts like healthy, locally grown, vegetarian-based cuisine with cool vibes and live jazz on weekends, and make it work.

"Hi, slugger," Stan said when McCabe waved to him from the double kitchen doors. "Come on in and talk to me."

McCabe made her way into the heart of the kitchen. She perched on her usual stool in the corner, out of the flow of the controlled chaos of the kitchen staff, but within chatting distance of Stan's workstation. "Looks busy out there," she said. "Did Chelsea desert you?"

"She'll be back in a few minutes. She's on an emergency run to the supermarket."

"The supermarket? Chelsea?"

Stan laughed. "I offered to send someone, but she said we needed all of the staff here working on a Friday evening."

"What emergency could make Chelsea walk into a supermarket?"

"Sea salt. Our vendor left it out of our order. We don't have enough to get through the evening."

McCabe smiled. "And it didn't occur to Chelsea to just announce to any diner who complained that salt's bad for you."

"She thought of that, but I vetoed the idea. Can't expect the diners who are only occasional vegetarians to be purists."

"That's why I love you, Stan. You acknowledge the need for salt, chocolate, and fat, along with fruits and veggies."

Stan wiped his hands on a cloth and poured wine from the

bottle on the counter into a glass. "And good wine from the grape," he said.

He brought the glass over to her.

"Thank you," McCabe said. "This is exactly what I need."

"Long day?" he said, picking up his knife again.

McCabe watched him attack the mountain of kale in front of him.

"And not much to show for it," she said.

"Case getting you down? Want to talk about it?"

"Not really," McCabe said, and leaned back against the wall.

"How's it going with your brother?"

"He and Pop are watching soccer together these days. He and I are awkward."

"Thought of sitting down with him and getting it all out in the open?"

"We did that once. It didn't work."

"But you're both older now."

"And he's still in a wheelchair. A super-duper wheelchair, but a wheelchair. And I'm still walking and running." McCabe took a sip of her wine. "So it's the same old, same old."

"Maybe you'll be able to get to know each other again now that he's back in Albany."

"Maybe," McCabe said.

Stan went on with his work, a big man with a weight lifter's build, who was sensitive enough to know when to let a conversation lag.

McCabe settled into the noise around her, letting her body relax.

Chelsea burst into the kitchen. A five-four dynamo carrying a tote bag filled with cartons of salt. She dropped the tote bag on the counter.

"There was a woman standing right there in the middle of the supermarket offering samples of grilled bioengineered beef strips."

"Well, at least, they were grilled," her husband said.

"Do you know how they—"

"Hannah's here," Stan said.

Chelsea whirled toward McCabe's corner. "Hi, girl. You made it." She came over and gave McCabe a hug. "Love that top."

"You should," Hank said. "You gave it to me two Christmases ago."

"I know. I just wanted to remind you that I have excellent taste. How's it going with—"

A crash, a tray of dishes hitting the tile floor, sent Chelsea dashing. "Back in a moment and we'll talk."

McCabe shook her head at Stan and slid off her stool. "I'm going to get out of the way and go listen to the music for a while."

"Okay, I'll tell Chelsea to catch up with you out front."

McCabe kissed him on the cheek. "Thanks for letting me hang out in your kitchen."

"Always glad to have your company, slugger. Come over to the house for breakfast on Sunday. Real waffles. I promise."

"In that case, I'll be there. Unless I have to work. Right now, I'm going to go claim my table. I have a reservation tonight. I'm going to go sit at one of your tables like a real customer. And I want my check, Stan."

He held up his hand in pledge. "We will send it to you, ma'am. Can't have a cop always eating here for free."

"Nope, neither a cop nor a friend."

At shortly before midnight, when the last set was over and most of the supper crowd had departed, Chelsea plopped down in the other chair at McCabe's table.

"Now we might actually have a chance to talk."

"I came for dinner and the music, Chelsea Ann. I told you the third time you popped by that I was fine tucked here in my corner. Your new appetizer and dessert menus are excellent, by the way."

Chelsea shook her head, "And healthy, in the event one of our customers decides to have appetizers and desserts instead of a balanced meal. Stan says you're coming to breakfast on Sunday. Bring your dad, too."

"You know that's not going to happen. Retired or not, Sunday is Pop's day of rest. Breakfast in bed with his newspaper."

"The man does know how to take it easy."

"Except now he needs to get more exercise."

"Is he beginning to perk up?"

"I think he may be turning the corner."

Chelsea said, "That reminds me, did I tell you that our lawyer has a new associate in his office?"

"No, you didn't mention that," McCabe said.

"Six-three, gorgeous, funny—"

"No, Chelsea."

"But he's—"

"No, Chelsea."

"You just spent a Friday evening sitting alone at a table—"

"It was exactly how I wanted to spend my Friday evening. What happened at the doctor's?"

Chelsea made a face. "I really hate getting up on that table with my legs in the air. You would think they'd have figured out a more dignified—"

"Chelsea Anne, tell me—"

"She said I've healed from the miscarriage. It's okay to have another try at a baby."

"This time, it will be all right."

"It better be. This time, Mother Nature better not even think of keeping me from being a mother."

"That's exactly the expression you had on your face the day you punched Joey Morgan in the stomach."

Chelsea smiled. "I couldn't believe I'd really done that. Not until everyone started applauding."

"What Joey didn't know was that he could only push—sorry." McCabe reached for her purse and her buzzing ORB.

"Maybe it's your father, making sure you're having a good time," Chelsea said.

McCabe looked and shook her head. "Work."

She said her name and listened. "I'm on my way."

"Sorry, I've got to go," she told Chelsea.

"Your serial killer case?"

"The droogie boys' case. My witness, Mrs. Givens . . . they broke into her house and beat her up."

"Oh God," Chelsea said. "That poor old woman."

McCabe heard the weeping before she got to the waiting room in the ER.

Inside, a group of people were huddled together, clutching one another.

McCabe walked over to the two evening-shift detectives who had caught the call. "She didn't make it?"

"Just died," Grace Eubanks said with a glance at the family. "The perps beat her around the head. If she'd lived, she probably would have had brain damage."

Dwight Parker looked up from his ORB. "But we got a break. The old girl put up a fight. FIU found some drops of blood on the way out the door. One of the little pricks was bleeding when they ran out."

"Good," McCabe said. She tucked her hands into her jacket. ERs were like morgues—always cold. "I guess I should go over and speak to the family."

"I hate that," Eubanks said. "That's the worst part."

"She wasn't going to testify," McCabe said. "She had taken some lullaby, and she couldn't remember the details of what happened. She came by to tell me that she couldn't testify."

Parker said, "We saw your notation about that."

"Are you going back there tonight? To look for witnesses?"

"As soon as we finish up here," Eubanks said.

"Mind if I ride along?"

Parker touched her arm. "Just go home and get some sleep," he said. "We wouldn't have called you out, but we thought you'd like to know."

McCabe nodded. "Yeah, thanks."

McCabe took the long way home. Fog swirled around the streetlights. Outside, on the steps of brownstones, Friday night was still playing itself out. Laughter, curses, bottles passed back and forth. Couples courting or breaking up. Tired, cranky toddlers outside with their adults because of the scare since a rat had bitten a baby in her crib.

No pest-free, climate-controlled conditions for poor folks who lived in old houses. You could only afford that if you moved in and gentrified. Then you could even go green and have solar panels. On a muggy October night, you could entertain your friends in the comfort of your own air-cooled apartment instead of meeting them on the stoop and hoping for a stray breeze.

In the street where Mrs. Givens had lived, police cruisers were lined up in front of her house, lights strobbing, cops moving back and forth.

McCabe parked in the next block. Looking in her rearview mirror, she watched a FIU detective come out of the building carrying a container.

Up the street in front of her, a white boy in a hybrid had pulled up to the corner. A black kid, who couldn't have been more than twelve, strolled over. A moment's conversation and an exchange of cash for product. Bold as brass. Maybe they assumed the cops were too busy dealing with a murder to worry about a drug deal.

McCabe reached for her ORB.

When the white boy pulled away from the curb, she put her siren on.

Lucky for him, he decided to stop. Equally fortunate for him, he was scared shitless and did what she told him when she ordered him out of his car.

By the time her backup arrived, she had him cuffed and ready to go. She gave the uniforms a description of the juvenile dealer. They knew him. Knew his street name.

Assuming the surveillance cameras on that corner were working, they would have the drug deal on video. Not that that meant anything. Everyone involved would probably still walk. A waste of her time and effort.

It was almost one o'clock when she got home. McCabe pulled into the driveway and sat there staring at the closed garage doors.

She left her car in the driveway, got out, and went in through the back door. In the kitchen, she poured herself a glass of mango juice.

The house was quiet except for the snoring from Pop's room when she passed.

McCabe undressed and got into bed, then lay there thinking about Mrs. Givens, who hadn't wanted to have any more bad dreams and who had ended up dead anyway.

She needed to get up in the morning. She turned off the lamp and shut off her mind. No more tonight. Let it go.

15

Vivian Jessup's condo overlooked Central Park. Remembering the statue of Alice in Wonderland near the boat pond in the park, McCabe thought that was appropriate. When she was a child, McCabe had always begged her father to take her to see the Cheshire Cat, the Mad Hatter, the White Rabbit, and the Dormouse. Alice hadn't been of as much interest to her. But maybe Vivian Jessup had gotten pleasure from the statue featuring a character she had played as a child.

And what about the *Alice*-themed tearoom around the corner? Had they recognized Jessup whenever she went in and given her a seat of honor? Served her a little cake saying *Eat Me,* accompanied by tea in a bottle labeled *Drink Me.*

Baxter joined her at the windows. "See something?" he asked.

"Just thinking Jessup must have enjoyed her view."

McCabe turned as she heard their NYPD escort finish her call.

"Sorry about that," Detective Maggie Soames said in her Brooklyn accent. "My ex wants the kids this weekend. I had to explain to him why he is not taking my kids along on a road trip with his new girlfriend." The crow's-feet around her eyes deepened as her mouth curled in amusement. "That's one of the good things about being a cop, right, McCabe? When a woman with a gun speaks, men listen."

McCabe said, "How many children do you have?"

"Two boys, ten and twelve, and a daughter who's four. I love 'em to death, but they're a handful. Especially when my ex spoils them rotten whenever he has them." Soames glanced around the room. "It's a shame to end up dead when you've got digs like these."

"Amen to that," Baxter said.

"So shall we get started?" McCabe said.

"Want to split up and each do a room?" Soames asked, pulling out the gloves she had brought along.

"Sounds good to me," McCabe said. "I'll do this room and try to check what's in the glass cases against the *Alice* collection inventory the insurance company sent over."

Soames said, "All yours. I definitely don't know what to look for there."

"Me, either," McCabe said. "Only thing I have going for me is that I've read both books and seen the movies."

Soames laughed. "My kids saw the last movie they made. A serious mistake to let my four-year-old see it. She had nightmares for two nights running. Want me to get the bedroom?"

"Thanks," McCabe said. "Here's the inventory of the jewelry that's supposed to be here in the apartment. Apparently, she kept most of her good stuff in a safe-deposit box. But everything is security-coded."

"Makes our lives easier," Soames said.

"I'll get the kitchen," Baxter said.

"And whoever finishes first gets the bathroom," McCabe said.

She put on her gloves and started going through the drawers of the antique credenza that held a place of honor along one wall. Photo albums labeled with the names of the plays in which Jessup had appeared, with photos of Jessup herself, scenes from the play, cast members.

In the next drawer, some of the items that appeared on the inventory—*Alice* collectibles—playing cards, coloring books, of value because of their age and uniqueness, the insurance company rep had said.

The bottom drawer contained magic lantern slides, bookplates, and hand puppets.

McCabe checked the items in a glass cabinet, then worked her way around the rest of the living room.

She stopped to examine the framed photos on display: ones of various family members; one of Jessup in her late teens with mother, father, and sister, standing behind the chair of a distinguished-looking older man. The grandfather, McCabe thought, who, according to Vivian's official bio, had gone to England after World War II and founded the family's theater dynasty. There was a photo of Vivian, now a grandmother, beaming down at a young woman in a bed who was holding a baby in her arms. Other photos had apparently been taken at last year's Tony awards.

"Mike," McCabe called out.

"What?" he said, coming to the door of the kitchen.

"Look who," she said, pointing.

He came closer, peering at the photo of Vivian Jessup and her escort at what seemed to be a post-award party.

"Teddy in his tux," he said. "With his arm around our victim."

"Well, he did say they were old friends," McCabe said. "But no celebrity gossip came up on the Web to suggest they had ever been a twosome."

"Maybe they managed to keep their private lives private," Baxter said.

"A real feat if they could pull that off. If they were involved, I wonder if Thornton's fiancée knew."

"If she did, she might not have been thrilled when Vivian turned up wanting Teddy to back her play."

McCabe shook her head. "But Jessup was the third victim in a series of murders. Unless we assume that the person who killed the first two women was only marking time until he or she got to Jessup—"

"Or maybe we've got ourselves a copycat killer."

McCabe said, "We didn't release the information about the phenol. But Clarence Redfield did know there was something linking the two murders."

"And clammed up when he was questioned at the station on Thursday," Baxter said.

"And so far he hasn't written any more about his serial killer theory in his thread. So we don't know what he knows, how much he knows. But, as far as we know, Redfield had no reason to kill Jessup, even if he knew how the first two murders were done."

"And the fiancée, who might have had a reason, had no way of knowing about the phenol," Baxter said.

McCabe frowned. "Unless somehow Ted Thornton found out about it."

"How?" Baxter said. "He and the mayor are pals. But unless one of the brass told her, she doesn't know the details of the murders. So unless Teddy has eyes and ears in the department who are feeding him information . . . But even if he did, would he have passed on the information to his fiancée?"

"And if he did, would she have wanted to eliminate her rival enough to risk having him wonder when his good friend Vivian became the third victim?" McCabe picked up a chess piece in the shape of a dormouse from the set on the side table. "But there's something off about all this, Mike. Remember what Agent Francisco said about serial killers having patterns, choosing their victims based on certain characteristics?"

"I thought you weren't buying what Francisco was selling?"

"I was simply questioning her theory about our perp being someone with a medical background. From what I've read, she's right about serial killers having preferred types. And that's the part that we all agree doesn't fit here. He kills two twentysomething hometown girls. And then he kills a forty-seven-year old Broadway actress who's visiting."

Baxter glanced at Jessup's photographs. "She was superhot for forty-seven, but there was no way he could have mistaken her for early twenties. Not even in low light."

"So what are we missing?"

"Don't know what you're missing, guys," Maggie Soames said from the doorway of the hall leading back to Jessup's bedroom. "But I've found some interesting reading."

16

Albany, New York
Empire State Plaza
10:47 A.M.

Bruce Ashby took one of the elevators up from the parking garage. The doors opened on the concourse floor. He peered out, then stepped back out of sight.

"This is the floor you requested," the automated voice informed him. "Do you want another floor instead?"

He slipped out of the elevator, taking cover behind a column.

Lisa had stopped at the mouth of the North Corridor, which led out onto the concourse. She looked to her right toward the wing housing the legislative offices, glanced up at the signs overhead, then turned to the left.

God, don't tell me she's going to the damn museum, Ashby thought.

He moved up to the entrance of the North Corridor. He needed to give her a head start.

She was wearing a red silk blouse and was easy enough to follow. Especially on a Saturday, when only a few state workers were around and no busloads of schoolchildren were milling through the miles of corridor.

But the lack of people also meant that he had less cover and had to stay farther behind her. He stepped out into the concourse.

She moved with a slender, long-legged stride past the closed bank, card shop, and flower stand, past the empty dining hall housing the food court, past the display of artwork, where she stopped to look at a painting, forcing him to turn and study the announcements on a bulletin board.

She moved on. He followed.

At the end of the corridor, she went through the glass doors. She took a few steps in the direction of the stairs leading up to the exit. Then she glanced to the left and toward the auditorium and the elevators and escalators leading up to the museum. She decided to go that way rather than outside and across the street.

But she was going to the museum. All this, and she was going to look at Indian wigwams and Adirondack wildlife. Maybe she wanted to ride on the damn carousel.

He waited a few minutes and then followed her up the escalator to the museum floor. He stepped back when he realized she had stopped at the information desk.

She spoke for a few minutes to the woman sitting there, and then she headed toward one of the exhibit rooms.

Ashby went in the other direction, circling around.

When he spotted her again, she was studying the artifacts from the archaeological digs in Albany—the distillery and the broken pottery and other items excavated years ago, before a parking garage had gone up.

Ashby watched her take out a palm-size camera. He sagged back against the wall and almost laughed out loud. Now the trip to the graveyard was beginning to make sense. Ted, giving one of his history lessons, had been talking last night about the British lord who was buried in the vestibule of one of the churches on State Street. The only British lord buried on American soil. Undoubtedly, she intended to amuse Ted with a photo montage of what he had described as "underground Albany," all the bones and artifacts dug up or still buried in various places around the city.

He watched as she finished taking her photographs and slid the camera back into her bag. She turned back toward the lobby.

In the lobby, she paused, glanced toward the escalators back down to the concourse, then decided to go into the gift store.

Through the glass walls, Ashby watched her browse. Finally, she chose something too small to make out from where he was standing. She paid at the counter and slid her purchase into her bag. Then she came out and stepped onto the escalator.

Ashby waited until he was sure she was at the bottom of the second set of escalators. Then he followed. When he peered into the corridor, she was halfway to the glass doors leading back onto the concourse. When she had passed through them, he strode up the corridor. He waited at the glass doors until she was almost out of sight, then stepped into the concourse.

At the flower stand, she turned. She looked back along the length of the concourse, staring straight at him. She blew him a kiss.

Ashby choked, cold panic and colder rage spreading through him. He watched her walk away, disappearing in the distance. What the devil was he going to tell Ted? But she might decide it would be wiser to keep her mouth shut. . . .

17

New York City

They had set the ORB that Maggie Soames had found in Jessup's bedside table on the credenza. They projected the pages on the opposite wall.

"Is this what women call 'erotica'?" Baxter said.

"Looks like she was writing it, not reading it," Soames commented.

Baxter said, "Guess this was her leisure-time activity when she got bored writing that play about Lincoln, Booth, and the actress."

McCabe said, "This is the kind of thing that makes you hope you'll have time to clean out all your closets and drawers before you die."

Baxter slanted her a glance. "You about to confess to having a few secrets, partner?"

McCabe shrugged. "We all have secrets. Even if it's only a boxful of keepsakes that nobody else has ever seen. And we die, and someone comes in and starts pawing through them."

Soames said, "Well, better that we found this before her family did."

"Yes, definitely. And I'm really glad you found it, Maggie, because it might be useful. But—"

"You're just saying?" Soames said.

McCabe nodded. "I'm just saying."

Baxter was reading. "This is about an actress. A young actress having an affair with an older married man."

Soames said, "If you go back to the beginning, it's supposed to be set in 1995, when the young actress arrives in the City."

"About the time Jessup would have arrived," Baxter said.

McCabe said, "She calls the actress Kate Sheridan. And the older man, the lover, is Richard March."

"And by chapter two, they're going at it hot and heavy, in all kinds of creative positions," Baxter said.

"Didn't you say something about a book that Jessup was trying to buy from someone?" Soames asked.

McCabe said, "From a collector. Is there—"

"Go to chapter five," Soames said. "I don't know if it has anything to do with your collector, but she mentions a book."

McCabe scanned the chapter. "The wealthy tycoon gives the struggling young actress the first edition of a book by her favorite author. 'Not a practical gift, but a gift that she treasured.'"

Baxter read, "'An author Kate had adored since she was a child.' As in Lewis Carroll?"

"That would matchup with what Professor Noel told us about the 'friend' who gave Jessup a Dalí edition of *Alice* when she was still a poor unknown," McCabe said.

"So you think this little tale might really be based on Jessup's life?" Soames asked.

"Seems like it could be," McCabe said. "That makes me curious about the identity of the lover."

"If he kept up that pace with young actresses," Baxter said, "he's probably dead by now."

McCabe scanned through the documents. "There's nothing else on this ORB. Just those six chapters of her book."

Soames said, "And, of course, this couldn't be the ORB that she took with her to Albany."

McCabe shook her head. "No, this one is a bonus. The ORB she had in Albany is still out there somewhere. I wonder if Jessup's publicist knew she was writing a novel, too."

"We could interrupt that meeting she had with that other client and ask," Baxter said.

"Let's do that."

McCabe took out her ORB.

In spite of her distress about her client's untimely death, Vivian Jessup's publicist had not been able to find time that morning to meet with them. As she'd explained, she had been Jessup's publicist for only a few months, since the publicist Jessup had been with for seventeen years had died. And the truth was, Vivian, whom she'd absolutely worshiped, so talented, had been a bit difficult to work with. . . . They just hadn't been simpatico. And she had another client, who had a major emergency, was having an absolute meltdown, and needed her immediate attention.

During that first call, Ms. Kirkpatrick had informed McCabe that she had deleted the tag from the *Alice* collector that she had sent to Vivian Jessup. No need to keep it. Yes, she understood forensics might be able to recover the tag. Reluctantly, she had granted access to her Jessup file.

Before she could disconnect, McCabe had asked where she, Ms. Kirkpatrick, had been on Wednesday evening. Ms. Kirkpatrick was somewhat annoyed, since she had clearly been trying to reach her client, Vivian Jessup. However, she supplied the name and location of the reception she had attended, and the nonprofit fund-raiser she had gone to later that evening with another client.

Ms. Kirkpatrick was not pleased to hear from McCabe again. When McCabe said she was calling to ask about the book Jessup had been writing, Kirkpatrick said. "I don't know anything about it. She didn't mention it to me." A pause and a change of tone: "How near is this book to being done? It might be something that her family could pursue, even though poor Vivian . . ."

McCabe said, "She had written only the first few chapters. I don't think they'd want to bother."

"But I should follow up with them about the play. Call and offer my condolences and let them know I'm available to help . . . if they want to pay tribute to dear Vivian by going forward—"

"I'll let you get back to your other client and his emergency," McCabe said.

"Yes, I do have to run. But they are going to dim the lights on Broadway for dear Vivian tonight. At eight, if you're still here. And please do keep me posted."

"We'll absolutely do that, Ms. Kirkpatrick. Bye now."

"Nothing?" Soames said.

"Other than Ms. Kirkpatrick beginning to think about how she might make some money off her deceased client?"

"She was way slow on the uptake with that one," Baxter said. "Guess the murder thing slowed her down."

They were leaving Jessup's condo when her neighbor's door opened. An elderly woman wearing a caftan and a turban peered out at them. "Are you the cops?"

McCabe nodded. "Yes, ma'am. I'm Detective McCabe and—"

"I have Vivian's cats."

"Her cats?"

"Kitty and Snowdrop. She asked me to feed them while she was out of town. Tell her daughter they're here with me when she wants them."

"We will. Ma'am, could we speak to you about—"

"I don't know anything. I can't help you."

"We'd just like to ask if you've seen—"

"I haven't seen anything." She started to close the door, then opened it a crack to say, "I watch the cop shows. I know the kind of thing you're looking for. If I knew anything that could help you find the son of a bitch who killed her, I'd tell you."

The door closed.

"That was to the point," Soames said. "Anyplace else I can take you guys before you catch the train?"

McCabe glanced at Baxter. "Have you ever been to the Alice statue in the park?"

"When I was a kid. Why?"

"Just thought we might swing by and have a look. I've always liked it. And, who knows, maybe we'll get inspired."

"You never know what might turn on a lightbulb," Soames said. "No problem. It's right across the street. My kids have all had their pictures taken with that statue."

When they got to the park, they walked down the hill, past the New Yorkers and the tourists who were enjoying Saturday outside. At the boat pond, a few of them were having brunch at the café. Small model boats sailed across the water.

McCabe, Soames, and Baxter walked into the area of paths and benches that surrounded the eleven-foot metallic statue of Alice and her friends. A group of Japanese students was posing in front of the statue. Four middle-aged white women with southern accents were waiting their turn.

When they were done, McCabe moved closer. She ignored Baxter's grin as he watched her move around the circle, reading the quotes from the book.

"Inspiration strike yet?"

"Not yet. Could be I'm just picking up on Jessup's obsession."

"Could be," he agreed.

Soames said, "Me personally, I've got this thing about obsessions. When a vic has one, I always wonder if it had something to do with getting him or her dead."

McCabe glanced up. "Me, too. But, in this case, we've got two other victims who have nothing to do with *Alice in Wonderland* or the theater. . . ."

Baxter had his mouth open when she turned to him. "Damn," he said.

"What?" Soames said.

"We didn't look for that," McCabe said. "With the first two victims, we didn't look for whether they had performed in a middle school pageant or the senior play. We were looking at the present, here and now, with the first one. Who had reason to want her dead. And then when we had the second, when we knew they both had died the same way, we were looking at what connected them, what they had in common."

Soames nodded. "The same friends. Or going to the same clubs, or working out at the same gym, or being in the same dance class."

McCabe had her ORB out, waiting for the connection.

Baxter said, "We checked for whether they had gone to the same schools or attended the same church. Volunteered for the same cause. Dated the same guy."

"But you didn't ask if either of them had been in a school play when she was a kid," Soames said.

"Because there was no reason to ask that then," McCabe said. "But now we have Vivian Jessup, the third victim—Lou, it's McCabe. . . . We want to check something out. . . ."

McCabe and Baxter were on the train back to Albany when Lieutenant Dole got back to them. "I've got Yin checking with the victims' families about the school play thing," he said.

"Thanks, Lou. It's just an idea, but we didn't want to miss anything."

"Meantime, McCabe, you'd better check out Clarence Redfield's thread."

She reached for her ORB. "Is he threading about Vivian Jessup?"

"The Givens case. Check back with me when you get into the station. Jessup's daughter's in town. The mayor's already been over at Thornton's house, paying her condolences. We need to set up an interview with the daughter."

"Yes, sir, we'll let you know when we arrive."

"What's up?" Baxter said as she disconnected.

"The mayor's been paying her condolences to Jessup's daughter, and Redfield's been threading again."

McCabe brought up Redfield's node on her ORB.

"Wonder if the mayor considered that Redfield might thread about how she didn't pay her condolences to the families of the first two victims," Baxter said.

"Right now, he's focusing on the Givens case." She read Redfield's thread, then passed the ORB to Baxter. "Here's what Mr. Redfield has to say:

". . . I am forced to comment on the ineptness of the APD, particularly Detective Hannah McCabe, who was assigned to all three serial murder cases and to the case of Mrs. Margaret Givens. Not only have three women—including the Broadway star Vivian Jessup, a visitor to our city—died at the hands of this serial killer but last night Mrs. Givens, a poor black woman who had been terrorized by juvenile sociopaths and witnessed one of their violent crimes when they savagely killed the young man who came to her aid . . . last night, Mrs. Givens, forced to live in chronic fear in her crime-ridden neighborhood, became another Albany PD statistic when young hoodlums, who call themselves "droogies" after the violent, sadistic gang members in A Clockwork Orange, broke into her house and beat her . . . beat her so badly that she died in a hospital emergency room without regaining consciousness. We understand Detective McCabe was taking the evening off to have dinner at a club and listen to a little cool jazz. That's what she was doing while Mrs. Givens was being murdered. Do your job, Detective McCabe, or give your badge to someone who can and will. You and the rest of the APD are failing to protect the citizens of this city."

Baxter passed the ORB back to her. "Want me to put a hit out on him for you?"

"Actually," McCabe said, "I have a friend who would probably be willing to punch him in the stomach for me."

"Would this be a man friend?" Baxter asked.

McCabe looked up from the screen and caught his grin. "I keep my personal life personal, Mike."

"Does that mean you don't have much of a personal life?"

She closed her ORB. "After this, I may not have a job."

"Was that what the lou said when he told you to check it out?"

"No. But the commander and the chief aren't going to be thrilled about—"

"Who cares if they're not thrilled? You're a good cop, and Redfield's an asshole."

"And this is bad press. If any of the mainstream media pick it up . . ." McCabe shook her head. "If they start poking into my background—"

"You mean what happened when you were a kid?'

"So you *have* heard about that?"

"I thought I'd let you mention it first," Baxter said. "What's the media going to make out of that? Way I hear it, you were a little nine-year-old hero."

"That," McCabe said, "was the spin they put on it."

Baxter said, "You killed the man who had broken into your family's home and who had just shot your brother."

"He shot my brother when I came in with my father's gun in my hands. If I hadn't done that, he might have just left."

"Or, the more popular theory, he would have shot your brother and then shot you because he'd been caught in the act and he'd come to the burglary with a gun in his pocket."

McCabe shook her head. "If the media should rehash the story, my brother, Adam, won't be thrilled with me, either."

"Tough, because I bet that's the way Jacoby's going to go with this. He'll tell your story to counter Redfield's—"

"Oh shit," McCabe said. She leaned her head back against the seat.

"It never came up before? Since you've been a cop?"

"Once . . . when I graduated from the Academy. But since then . . . none of my cases . . . I've never been the lead investigator in a case that attracted so much media attention. And, of course, Redfield wasn't around before."

"As I said, partner, Redfield can be made to disappear."

McCabe laughed. "Thanks. But if he pulls anything else I'll just send my friend after him. She's got a killer right hook."

"This friend of yours . . . you're not by any chance hinting that you're gay?"

McCabe looked sideways at him. "What's with this needing to know who I sleep with?"

"Well, I'm not . . . gay, I mean." He settled back in his seat, feet up on the metal footrest. "So if you'd ever like to have a fling with a much younger man . . ."

McCabe threw her crumpled iced coffee cup at him.

"That's better," he said, settling deeper in his seat. "Cops don't cry."

McCabe sighed. "This one does. Last night for Mrs. Givens."

"Good. Holding in your emotions can shorten your life."

"Thank you, Dr. Baxter." McCabe looked down at the scratch on the back of her hand from the fence two days ago. "How do you think Redfield knew what I did last night?"

"Who did you tell what you did last night?"

"No one."

"What about the cops who gave you the call about Givens?"

"No. I just said I was on my way."

"Maybe they heard the music or the sounds in the background."

"They might have heard people talking and guessed I was in a restaurant. But no music was playing. The last set was over. And even if they had guessed where I was, why would they tell Redfield? So how did he know that I'd been out listening to jazz?"

"'Cool jazz,' as he put it. And he said 'club,' not 'restaurant.'"

"Of course he did. 'Club' sounds worse."

"How much do we know about Clarence Redfield? Other than what you told me about the chemical engineering degree. And the mother he came back to Albany to take care of and the wife and baby who died."

"That's about it. I think I should see what else I can find. If he wants to play games, I should be ready to play, too."

"Deal me in on that," Baxter said. "Hey, where do you park your car at night?"

"Park my car? At home."

"No, I mean, do you have a garage?"

"Yes, but I don't usually bother to put my car . . . Are you suggesting—"

"That someone could have gotten to your car there or somewhere else and—"

"A tracker?"

"The guys in vice used them now and then," Baxter said. "No way to know if you've got one without doing a sweep of your car."

"But if I do have a tracker on my car, that would explain how Clarence Redfield knew how I spent my evening."

18

Albany, New York

McCabe and Baxter drove across the bridge from the Albany-Rensselaer train station. The Egg looked like a granite spaceship tilted on its platform, and the towers of the Empire State Plaza stood out against the sky. They went through the underpass, by the parking entrances to the plaza. By the time, they reached the intersection for State Street, McCabe had finished her conversation with Lieutenant Dole.

She put her ORB down and turned to Baxter. "Jacoby has a press conference scheduled later this afternoon. He's going to provide updates on the case and respond, assuming it comes up, to any questions about Clarence Redfield's thread. Since they don't intend to bar Redfield from the press conference, they are pretty sure it's going to come up."

"How are they going to handle it?"

"By stating the facts. By explaining that the first two murders happened a few weeks apart and I happened to catch each case because Jay O'Connell and I were available when the calls came in. By explaining that Thursday same thing happened to me regarding a case that came in three weeks after the second murder. That last night, I had completed my shift and was on my own time. And that Ms. Givens had told us on Thursday morning that she did not intend to testify."

"Jacoby going to mention what happened when you were a kid? I heard you ask them not to, but—"

"Lieutenant Dole says that if it comes up, Jacoby intends to give them the facts about what happened. But he's not going to push it."

"Guess I was wrong."

"For which I'm grateful. Turn left on Lark."

"Why? Where are we going?"

"A funeral home. The CO got a call from Ted Thornton. Jessup's daughter is there making arrangement for her mother's body. Thornton thought we might want to interview her there and save ourselves a trip out to his place. He and his fiancée, Lisa, are there, too."

Baxter made the turn. "This really sucks. I wanted to see Roz again."

Greer Jessup St. John did not look like her mother. She was a plus-size woman who seemed comfortable in her skin. If her mother had preferred classic styles, Greer St. John went for the gusto. With complete disregard for any expectation that mourners should wear black, she was clad in a calf-length red-and-white-stripped halter dress and high-heeled red sandals. Her red earrings were retro hoops. Red-and-white-striped bangle bracelets clanked on her arms when she turned to meet them. Her lipstick and nail polish were matching shades of red. Her sable brown hair was caught up in a ponytail that dangled down her back. And somehow she managed to carry it all off.

Eyes red and damp, she leaned into the sheltering arm of her tall, attractive husband, "Ron." Dr. Ronald St. John, pediatric surgeon, whose mother-in-law had reportedly adored him.

The meeting was taking place in one of the family "meditation" rooms. Ted Thornton had assured them that he and Lisa, who was in the ladies' room, would be happy to wait outside until they had finished their talk.

After expressing their sympathy, McCabe asked her first question.

Greer St. John sighed. "I make puppets," she said. "I'm a professional puppeteer."

McCabe wasn't sure how to respond to that. The question she had asked was about the last time Greer had communicated with her mother.

"That must be interesting," she said.

"What I meant was that my mother and I were working on a puppet show for a fund-raiser. We do the show together every year in D.C. at Thanksgiving for the children of soldiers."

"Oh, I see," McCabe said. "So you and your mother spoke about the puppet show that you—"

"On Wednesday afternoon, when she called."

"Was this going to be an *Alice in Wonderland* puppet show?" Baxter asked.

Greer shook her head. "We always do something Alice, but this year we had planned to do scenes from *Through the Looking Glass* instead of *Wonderland*. I've been working on flower puppets and insects. Mom . . . my mother called to see how they were coming along."

She twisted her hands in her lap and looked as if she was about to burst into tears.

McCabe said. "If you don't mind my asking . . . Greer is a lovely name. It makes me think of Greer Garson. But I would have thought that you mother would have named you—"

"Alice?" Greer St. John smiled through her tears. "That would have been overkill, even for Mom. But Greer is an *Alice* reference. Greer Garson starred in *Mrs. Miniver,* and if you've ever seen the movie—"

"I have," McCabe said. "But it's been so long ago that I don't remember—"

"There's a scene when Mrs. Miniver and her husband, Clem, are in the bomb shelter with their children. She—"

"Oh, of course, I had forgotten that. She reads *Alice in Wonderland* to the children to get them to sleep."

"And by naming me Greer when everyone would have expected her to name me Alice, my mother provided herself with endless opportunities to point out the influence of Lewis Carroll on popular culture. Luckily, I do happen to like the name."

"So do I," McCabe said. "When you spoke to your mother on Wednesday, did anything seem to be bothering her?"

"No, she was really upbeat . . . upbeat in a creative person's way. She said she was ripping her hair out by the roots over one of Henrietta's monologues in the play. But she was excited about how it was all coming together."

"Did your mother mention any plans that she had for the rest of the day?"

Greer shook her head. "I had a minor crisis on my end. We have a new German shepherd puppy and he'd gotten one of the baby's shoes. And I told my mother that I needed to go . . . to get . . ."

"The shoe from the puppy?"

Greer nodded. "I told her I would call back later, but then there was one thing after another. And . . . I was going to call her back the next day when I had more time to talk. I . . . oh God . . ."

Her husband held her. "Detectives, I think that's about all my wife—"

"Yes," McCabe said. "Just one more question, Mrs. St. John."

Greer raised her head and swiped at her eyes. "Yes, I'm sorry. Please, what do you need to know?"

"Did your mother mention an Albany collector who offered her a Dalí edition of *Alice in Wonderland*?"

"Yes, she did mention that. You don't think that man—"

"We don't know who he is at this point. Your mother's ORB is missing, and her publicist deleted the tag that she forwarded to your mother. Forensics will try to recover the tag, but did your mother happen to tell you the man's name? Or anything else that might help us to locate him?"

Greer shook her head. "No, she just told me about being contacted and that she was trying to arrange to see the Dalí volume and the stamp case."

"That was what she told you on Wednesday afternoon?"

"We didn't talk about that on Wednesday. We really didn't cover anything other than the puppet show and her update on her play . . . and then I said good-bye and went to chase the puppy."

McCabe said, "I'm sure she understood that. Normally, it would have been nothing that either of you would have thought twice about."

Greer St. John straightened and nodded. "Thank you for saying that."

"It's true," McCabe said. "Things happen and you do what seems the right thing to do at that moment." She stood up. "If you should think of anything else, please give us a call. Here's my card."

She and Baxter said their good-byes and stepped into the hallway.

A woman as elegantly fine-boned as Greer St. John was voluptuous, her pale blond hair in a chignon, rose from a bench and put the funeral home brochure she had been reading back in the rack.

"Amazing how many different options there are for coffins," she said. "Hello, I'm Lisa. Ted had to step out for a moment."

"Thank you for waiting, Ms. Nichols," McCabe said. "We won't take up much of your time. Let's go in here."

They went into one of the other two meditation rooms.

The interview looked as if it was going to be both short and routine. Lisa Nichols confirmed everything her fiancé had said about their travel between Albany and New York City. She had, she said, known Vivian only a short time. They had first met about six months ago in New York when she and Ted encountered Vivian at a gallery opening. Ted had introduced the two of them.

"Thank you, Ms. Nichols," McCabe said. "We just have to make sure we've touched base with anyone who might be able to provide us with information."

"I'm sorry I can't be of more help. I really liked Vivian."

From the corner of her eye, McCabe saw Baxter shift in his chair. He probably wanted to ask Nichols the same question she did: "So you didn't mind that your fiancé and Jessup might once have been lovers?"

Instead, McCabe said, "You and Ms. Jessup did have a lot in common."

Lisa Nichols blinked. A flutter of long lashes over hazel eyes. "A lot in common?" she said.

"What should I call it? Being creative people . . . understanding the creative process. Ms. Jessup was an actor. You're a photographer. I wanted to tell you how incredible I thought your photographs were."

"You've seen some of my photographs?"

"In Mr. Thornton's gallery. The wall display. The action shots of people engaged in dangerous sports."

Nichols smiled. "That was how Ted and I met. I was a last-minute replacement for the photographer who was supposed to go along on one of his mountain-climbing expeditions."

McCabe said, "So you climb mountains, too?"

Nichols laughed. "No. Not for a major exhibit or any amount of money."

"Afraid of heights?" Baxter said.

"Terrified. But with telephoto lens, I was able to get the shots Ted wanted. He had to do without the shots from the helicopter that the other photographer had planned to do."

"But you go up in his airship," McCabe said.

"I was heavily medicated the first time. Three glasses of champagne. And I'm actually okay in large planes when I only have to see the ground going up and coming down. The airship is like that when you're not up in the cockpit. Is there anything else I can—"

With perfect timing, the door opened and Ted Thornton stuck his head in. "All done?'

"Yes, we are," McCabe said. "Thank you, Mr. Thornton, for arranging this. And thank you for your time, Ms. Nichols."

"Even though I haven't been that much help," Lisa Nichols said.

Baxter said, "But now we can cross you off our list of people to interview."

"We'll be in touch if anything should come up," McCabe said.

She and Baxter were out in the hall when something else occurred to her. The question they had forgotten to ask. Feeling like
Peter Falk in an old *Columbo* episode, she retraced her steps.

"Excuse me, Mr. Thornton . . . one more thing . . . the other two
victims . . . and this is a question for you, too, Ms. Nichols. Did either of you come into contact with the other two victims?"

Ted Thornton raised an eyebrow, "To the best of my knowledge,
Detective McCabe, I've never met either of the young women."

Lisa Nichols shook her head. "I saw their photos on the Web
yesterday, along with Vivian's. I don't recall ever having seen them
before."

"And the names weren't familiar, either?"

"No," she said.

"No," Thornton said, "and no need to ask . . . to ask Greer and
Ron. We were all looking at the photographs together."

"Thank you," McCabe said. "Just thought I'd check."

"Now, Detective McCabe," Thornton said, "did you really think
we wouldn't mention something like that?"

"Not really, Mr. Thornton. But sometimes if you ask a question,
it sets off another related train of thought."

"What did you think?" Baxter said when they got back to the car.

"About what?" McCabe said. "Or should I say who?"

"Lisa Nichols," he said.

"I'm not sure," McCabe said. "Interesting that she was the one
who wore a black dress to the funeral home. Maybe she just has a
well-developed sense of the traditional."

Baxter said, "Or maybe she knows blondes look hot in black."

McCabe took out her ORB and began to make her interview entries. "I wonder what Vivian thought of Lisa."

"The daughter didn't mention anything."

"No. And I guess if her mother had been seriously bad-mouthing
Ted Thornton's fiancée, Greer and her husband would have stayed at
a hotel, no matter how many reporters were hanging around."

Baxter glanced over at her ORB. "Do we have anything yet on whether the first two vics were in any plays?"

McCabe shook her head. "No notations in the master file."

"Guess no one's been able to catch up with anyone who knows yet."

They got back to the station in time to see the last news van pull away.

"Jacoby's press conference must be over," Baxter said.

"Glad we missed it," McCabe said.

They met Lieutenant Dole in the hallway. He gestured for them to go into his office.

When he followed them in and closed the door, McCabe said, "Is something wrong, sir?"

"Your partner was right, McCabe. Your car was transmitting."

"So someone wanted to know my whereabouts." McCabe swallowed. "Could they tell anything about who might have installed it?"

"They sent it to the lab. Could be a few days before anything comes back."

"And in the meantime? What—"

Knuckles rapped and the door opened just wide enough for the commander to stick his head into the room.

His gaze, not at all turtlelike, fastened on McCabe. "You want off the serial killer case, Detective?"

"No, sir, I don't," she said.

"Then stay alert out there. And get me some results."

"Yes, sir."

He drew back his head and closed the door.

"You heard the man," Lieutenant Dole said. He sat down at his desk and looked up at McCabe and Baxter. "We're going to have another task force meeting on Monday morning. Keep working on whatever you have until then."

Back out in the bull pen, Baxter said, "Want to go over what we have again now or come in tomorrow morning and give it another shot?"

McCabe dropped down in the chair at her desk. "May as well give it another run-through now. We might find something we should follow up tomorrow."

"Who said Sunday was supposed to be a day of rest?"

"What I'm hoping," McCabe said. "Is that our killer thinks three is the perfect number. No more victims before we can figure out what the connection is between the first three."

"Hey, Hannah," Yin said as he came in. "I got that information you wanted from the families. I just entered it in the MF."

"Thanks, Walt," McCabe said, and swung toward her monitor.

Yin snagged his thermo jacket from his desk chair. "Call me if you need me to explain my notes. Got to run. Tonight's our anniversary. Casey made dinner reservations at that fancy French restaurant down on Pearl Street."

"Happy anniversary," McCabe said.

"Have fun," Baxter called after him.

"This is interesting," McCabe said.

"What do we have?"

"Nothing on playing Alice or anything with an obvious connection to Jessup. But Sharon Giovanni was an angel in a Sunday-school pageant. Bethany Clark's sister says Bethany was in the chorus in a high school production of *Oklahoma*."

"Which means they were both on a stage at some point."

"Yeah, but there's something else that's more interesting. Something that Sharon's mother remembered. Yin talked to her first. When he called Bethany's sister to ask her about plays, he followed up with another question. She remembered something, too."

"What?" Baxter said.

"That Bethany had taken part in the student presentations at the end of a summer science program. Both girls did. They were both in a two-week summer science camp for twelve- to fourteen-year-year old girls."

"But we checked their school records. There was nothing—"

"The program wasn't sponsored by their schools. To get in, the participants submitted essays about why they wanted to attend the camp. It was sponsored by a women's group that wanted to encourage girls to go into science-related fields."

"That's it?" Baxter looked over her shoulder at Yin's notes. "That's the link between the two of them? Why didn't one of the families remember this before?"

"They didn't go to the same schools. They weren't friends. I guess neither family thought about a science camp." McCabe frowned. "Look at this. Yin says he thinks there was something else that Sharon's mother remembered about the camp. Something she was holding back."

"Why would she have brought it up in the first place if she was going to hold something back?" Baxter said.

"Don't know," McCabe said. "Maybe it was something she hadn't thought of in years and when she began to remember, she decided it wouldn't reflect well on her daughter."

"Yin looked up the year of the camp. Sharon would have been what . . . twelve years old that summer? What could a twelve-year-old girl—"

"Hate to break it to you, Mike, but twelve-year-old girls are not—"

"Forget I asked that. I grew up with two kid sisters."

"Are you up for a couple of more interviews before we call it a day?"

"Let's do it. And maybe we should find out where Yin and his wife are having dinner and order the guy a bottle of wine."

"For a lead like this, amen," McCabe said. "Wanna bet that fancy French restaurant he mentioned is Chez André?"

19

Sharon Giovanni's mother said, "She wanted to be a doctor . . . with NASA, if you can believe that. When she was a kid, she was always watching reruns of that *Enterprise* show . . . you know, the one with the lady doctor . . . Presser?"

"Crusher," McCabe said. "Dr. Crusher."

"That's it. The show with that Luke guy with the bald head playing the captain. Anyway, that's the kind of doctor she wanted to be." Mrs. Giovanni looked up from the box she was going through. "I kept telling her that we weren't going to get up in space like that anytime soon, but she said she could be a NASA doctor anyway. God, that girl was jumping up and down when that UFO thing happened. I was scared to death, and here she was, going, 'Mom, if a ship came here, that means we might decide to go out there.' "

McCabe looked at the assortment of items Mrs. Giovanni was taking from the box and placing neatly on her daughter's bed. She said, "Sharon's adviser at Hudson Valley told us that Sharon would have had an excellent chance of getting a scholarship when she transferred to a four-year school."

"She had applied to UAlbany and a bunch of other schools. She was worried that she wouldn't get into medical school if she couldn't get into a really good university to finish up."

Baxter said, "If you want to just dump all of that out, it would be faster."

Mrs. Giovanni shook her head, "Sharon was so careful of her things. We didn't have much. That's why she had to go to community college first and take a job. But that girl was particular about what she did have. Everything in its place . . . I know if she saved it, it'd be here in one of these boxes from her closet."

McCabe said, "I don't remember seeing it when we were here before. We did go through both boxes—"

"But you weren't looking for it then," Mrs. Giovanni said. "If you aren't looking for something, you can look right over it."

"That's true. While you're looking for the program for the presentations, could we talk a little about the camp?"

"Like I told that other detective who called, it lasted two weeks. They went every day for classes taught by these science teachers the group had hired. And they would go on field trips to different places. Like the Museum or that Art Institute . . . you know, the one on Washington Avenue. They went there to see the mummies. And they . . . I know it's here somewhere. . . . Sharon always saved things like that. . . . She was always meaning to put all her odds and ends into scrapbooks when she had time."

McCabe looked over the woman's head at Baxter.

She said, "Detective Yin thought you might have recalled something else, Mrs. Giovanni? Maybe something Sharon told you about the camp?"

Mrs. Giovanni put the New Year's Eve 2017 napkin she was holding down on the pile. "I don't think the program's here. Maybe she didn't save it after all."

"That's okay. We'll see if we can find a copy from the group that sponsored the camp," McCabe said. "Mrs. Giovanni, do you—"

"She told me about how this girl was making fun of this other girl. And then the girl who was being teased, she ran away when the teaching assistant stepped out of the room. And they couldn't find her. Sharon was really upset when she told me about it."

McCabe said, "But you hesitated to tell Detective Yin. Why?"

"I remembered the program that they did at the end of camp . . . and then it came back to me about. . . . I had forgotten what happened that week. But it wasn't Sharon's fault. It was the other girl, the one who was teasing the girl who ran away."

"Did someone say it was Sharon's fault?"

"The girl who was teasing the other girl was sitting beside Sharon and she passed Sharon this picture that she had drawn."

"A picture of the girl she was teasing?" McCabe asked.

Mrs. Giovanni nodded. "The teaching assistant made Sharon give her the picture. When she saw what it was, she took Sharon and the girl who drew the picture out into the hall and scolded them both. Sharon tried to tell her she wasn't doing anything, but the teaching assistant said they were being disruptive and she was going to tell the teacher when she came back. The teacher had left the teaching assistant in charge while she went to set up this experiment the girls were going to do later."

"I see," McCabe said. "And at some point, the girl who was being teased ran away?"

Mrs. Giovanni nodded. "The teaching assistant let Sharon and the other girl go back into the classroom, and she started telling them about the movie she was supposed to show them while the teacher was gone. But then she had a text on her cell phone, and she said she needed to return the call. She stepped out into the hall and closed the door. And that was when the girl who was making all the trouble started calling the girl she was teasing names and telling her she was going to kill her if she got her into any more trouble. And the girl she was bothering started crying and got up and ran out the door on the other side of the room."

"What did the teaching assistant do when she came back?" Baxter asked.

"Sharon said she had turned down the lights for the movie. She didn't even notice the girl was gone. Then finally one of the other girls told her. Sharon said then the teaching assistant ran out, and the teacher came back looking upset. And they started asking them questions about why the girl ran out. And the other girls told on the one who had been teasing. And the teacher told the teaching assistant to stay there and finish showing them the movie. And she left again. I guess she went to tell the other teachers that the girl was gone, and they must have started looking for her."

Baxter said, "Did they find her?"

Mrs. Giovanni nodded. "But she . . . this boy had picked her up in his car."

"Was she molested?" McCabe asked.

"That was all Sharon heard. Two of the teachers were whispering about it in the hall. But then the next day, the mother came, and she was upset and yelling, and they got her into the office. Sharon said they called the teaching assistant in there, too, and then she came out crying . . . and she left and didn't come back. But I looked and there was never anything about it on the news or in the paper. So maybe it wasn't that big a thing."

"But Sharon was upset about it?" McCabe said.

Mrs. Giovanni nodded. "Sharon was really tenderhearted and she felt bad about the girl who was teased. The girl didn't come back to camp after that day when she ran away."

"Did Sharon tell you the girl's name?"

"No. But the girl who was teasing her was . . ." She glanced at Baxter. "She was teasing her about her . . . about having big breasts. The other girl was teasing her about how she shouldn't be there in a science camp because all her brains were in her . . . her breasts. She was calling her names about that. And she drew this picture and passed it to Sharon. Sharon said she wrote something on it."

"What?" Baxter asked.

Blushing, Mrs. Giovanni said, "Tits Galore."

McCabe said, "And you're sure that Sharon never mentioned the girl's real name? Or the name of the girl who teased her?"

"No. She didn't even want to talk about it, but I could tell something was wrong."

"But she went back to camp the next day?" Baxter asked.

"She wanted to have a chance to do the presentation that she had been working on. And there were only another three days left in the camp session."

"Sharon must have been really excited about her presentation," McCabe said. "What was it about?"

"About? It was about what might happen to astronauts . . . to their bodies on long trips in space . . . like to Mars." Mrs. Giovanni smiled. "She did her research and then she watched all these movies to see if the way it was in the movies was how it really might be."

"If she had put in so much time on her presentation, it's understandable that she would have wanted to stay for the rest of camp," McCabe said.

"And what happened was that other girl's fault . . . she and the teaching assistant. The teaching assistant should have been watching the girls instead of being out in the hall talking on her phone."

McCabe said, "Is there anything else you can tell us about the camp, Mrs. Giovanni? We know this all happened years ago, but the camp is the first link we've found between Sharon and Bethany Clark."

"Bethany Clark? The other girl who was killed? She was at the camp, too?"

"Yes, she was."

"Do you think she could have been one of the girls Sharon told me about?"

"We won't know that until we talk to Bethany's sister," McCabe said. "Mrs. Giovanni, Bethany was killed first. Thinking back, do you remember Sharon acting at all oddly after—"

"No, she was just like usual. Sharon was always working so hard at her job at the warehouse or on her schoolwork. I don't think she had even heard about what happened . . . about Bethany Clark." Mrs. Giovanni went still. "Do you think if she had heard . . . if she had heard Bethany Clark's name, she would have known who might have killed her?"

McCabe said. "There's no reason to think that. Sharon and Bethany were at the same science camp when they were children. For two weeks. After that, as far as we can tell, they never saw each other again."

"But Albany isn't that big a city," Mrs. Giovanni said. "Maybe they did see each other. Maybe they saw each other again and somehow that's why they were both killed. Oh God, if it had something to do with what happened all those years ago . . . If my Sharon's dead because—"

"We don't know why Sharon was killed yet, Mrs. Giovanni." McCabe touched her shoulder. "We've upset you. You should have some company tonight. Do you have someone who can come and stay with you?"

"Yes. My sister."

"Then why don't we call her? Ask her if she'll come over. Okay?"

"Okay. But do you think this is really about—"

"We don't know what it's about yet. All we have now is a link between Sharon and Bethany."

"Which still leaves Vivian Jessup," Baxter said.

"That means it couldn't be about the science camp," Mrs. Giovanni said, taking heart from Baxter's observation. "Even if the girls met there . . . he killed that famous actress, and she had never even met Sharon and Bethany."

That, McCabe thought, was another question they had to answer. Whether somehow Vivian Jessup had been linked to two girls who had attended a science camp. Or a third girl who had run away because she was being teased.

"Let's call your sister," McCabe said to Mrs. Giovanni.

Bethany Clark's sister, Francine, invited them into her kitchen, where she was making dinner for her husband. Through the screened back door, they could see her husband and a couple of his buddies sitting out in the yard with bottles of beer.

"We cooked outside all this week when it was so hot. Tonight, I told Eddie that I was going to make some real food. The kids are doing a sleepover at their friends' house, and I was sick to death of hamburgers and hot dogs." She looked up from the sauce that she was stirring. "You're here because of that detective who called? The one who wanted to know if Bethany had ever been in a play?"

Seated at the kitchen table, McCabe said, "Mrs. Petrie, what we'd like to talk to you about is the science camp that Bethany attended. It turns out that Sharon Giovanni also attended that camp."

Francine Petrie put the cover back on her sauce. Then she came over and pulled out a chair at the table and sat down. "Tell me," she said. "If you know something, tell me."

"We need your help to try to put the pieces that we have so far together," McCabe said. "Detective Yin told us that you remembered the science camp that Bethany attended and the presentations that she took part in at the end of camp."

"We all went. My folks . . . all of us . . . we always made a big fuss over Bethany because she was the baby of the family. I remember Bethany had done this project where she'd made a volcano. She had all these diagrams on the computer to show, too. And she explained about how volcanoes form and then she made her model spew out the lava and run down this mountain. Everybody applauded."

"Sounds like she learned a lot at the camp," McCabe said.

"She really had fun there," Francine Petrie said. "But are you telling me that the camp is connected to Bethany being killed?"

"We're telling you that we know now that both Bethany and Sharon attended the camp. Did Bethany or your parents mention an incident that happened during the time she was at the camp? A few days before it ended?"

"What kind of incident?"

"Involving a girl who ran out of the classroom, left the building. The teachers were looking for her."

Francine Petrie shook her head. "I don't . . . I wasn't living at home at that point. My cousin Jackie and me had gotten an apartment . . ."

"Think carefully, Mrs. Petrie. Anything that might have been mentioned in passing."

"I . . . Wait a minute . . . there was something . . ." Mrs. Petrie leaned her forehead on her hand. "What was it?"

Baxter said, "Something about—"

"Wait . . . just let me think for a minute."

Baxter glanced at McCabe. Then they sat there, looking around Mrs. Petrie's well-lived-in kitchen with the children's drawings taped to the refrigerator and the stuffed toys piled in a basket in a corner by the breakfast nook. The kitchen smelled of garlic and simmering tomatoes. It was warm from the cooking, but a breeze came now and then through the open door.

"All right, I've got it," Mrs. Petrie said. "It was after the presentations were over, and we were walking around the room, having a closer look at the exhibits. We were looking at an exhibit that one of the girls had built . . . a miniature greenhouse . . . and the girl was talking to some other people about it and she said, 'Deirdre helped me figure out the irrigation system.' And then she looked over at Bethany. And Bethany grabbed my mother's arm and said, 'Come on.'"

"That was all?" McCabe asked.

"No . . . as we were walking away, I heard my mother whisper to my aunt, 'Deirdre's that teaching assistant who caused the problem . . . got the girls all upset.'"

Baxter said, "Was that it? Did your mother say what the problem was?"

"No, she . . . Bethany brought over her favorite teacher from the camp. The teacher was telling my mother how well Bethany had done. I didn't even think about it again."

Both of Bethany Clark's parents were dead. Bethany had been living in the family home alone since her youngest brother had married and moved to Vermont.

McCabe said, "Your aunt—"

Francine Petrie shook her head. "She died last year. All of that generation are gone."

"Do you think your mother would have told your brothers what—"

"Mom never told the boys or my father about things like that. She said men just made things worse by charging in like bulls in a china shop. And I don't think whatever it was really involved Bethany. She seemed fine . . . except for that moment when the other girl mentioned Deirdre and they looked at each other."

"I'm curious," McCabe said. "How do you remember the name Deirdre after all these years?"

"Because my cousin Karen had named her baby Deirdre, and she was complaining to everyone who would listen because her mother-in-law was calling the baby 'Dee Dee.'"

"I see. You said the girl who had mentioned Deirdre and your sister looked at each other. What kind of look exactly?"

"A kid's look. The other girl . . . she mentioned Deirdre . . . and then she saw Bethany standing there . . . and it was like she'd said something and she wished she hadn't."

"Like maybe she was scared or frightened?" Baxter asked.

"Frightened? No . . . why would she be frightened because Bethany heard her? It was like when you say something and it's awkward because it reminds people of what nobody's talking about."

McCabe said, "And you think the girl had reminded herself and Bethany of whatever happened with Deirdre, the teaching assistant?"

Mrs. Petrie nodded. "That's what it felt like. It was just that moment and my mother whispering to my aunt and then it was over. And we all went out to a diner and had a family dinner. It was a good evening."

"Did Bethany ever talk to you about the science camp? Did she ever mention the girls she met there?"

"No. Like I said, I had moved into my own place by then. I wasn't seeing her as much. During that last week of her science camp, my cousin Jackie and I were up in the mountains, staying at the camp that Jackie's boyfriend's family had up there. We had come back in time for Bethany's program that Sunday afternoon."

"So," Baxter said, "You're sure Bethany never mentioned Sharon Giovanni back then. What about later? Recently? Maybe saying she had run into someone from science camp?"

Mrs. Petrie shook her head. "I never heard Bethany mention that camp again after that. She . . . later she sort of lost interest in books and school. . . ."

"Why do you think that happened?" McCabe said. "It sounds like she was really smart."

Francine Petrie smiled—a brief, weary smile. "The ugly duckling becoming a swan. At least that was what our mother said. Bethany was awkward and skinny when she was a kid. But then when she was about fifteen, she started to blossom. And suddenly she was a really beautiful girl, and the boys were flocking around her." Mrs. Petrie shrugged. "It's hard for some girls to be popular and stick to their books at the same time. I kept telling Bethany . . ." Tears filled her eyes. "She should have been in college, getting her degree, not working at some waitress job and then out partying with those wild friends of hers. And they let her walk to her car alone . . . half-drunk . . . in the dark . . . and she ends up dead."

She stood up and went back over to the stove. "I can't think of anything else to tell you," she said. "I need to finish dinner."

"Then we'll go now," McCabe said. "Thank you for talking to us."

Francine Petrie turned and looked at her. "One of Eddie's friends showed us that thread that Redfield man wrote about you. I know the police are doing all that they can on this, and that you've been working hard on this since day one. Don't let them get you down."

"I . . ." McCabe stammered in her surprise. "I appreciate your saying that."

Francine Petrie put the spoon she had been using to stir the sauce down on a saucer. "It's the twenty-first century and some men still can't stand it when a woman's in charge. Got to claim she doesn't know what she's doing. I told Eddie and my brothers that. I get it sometimes on my own job."

"What do you do?" Baxter asked.

"I'm a truck inspector. I know how to handle myself, but every now and then a driver tries to give me grief. Or date me. Same difference."

. . .

In the car on their way back to the station, Baxter said, "How do you like our girl Bethany as the bully?"

"Because she made a volcano for her science camp project?"

"And because seeing Bethany after she'd mentioned Deirdre, the teaching assistant, got the other kid all shook up."

"It would make sense that a girl who was awkward and skinny would resent another girl who was . . . further along in the process. Of course, we don't know if Sharon was telling her mother everything that happened."

"Yeah, but Sharon was the hardworking college student who wanted to be a doctor in the space program. And our girl Bethany was waiting tables by day and partying by night."

"What would be really helpful," McCabe said, looking up from her ORB, "would be if we could find someone who was involved with Girls in Science, the women's group that sponsored the science camp."

"Still nothing?"

"According to Research, nothing's coming up on the group after that summer. They rented the building for one month. The woman who was the president was a research biologist. She signed all the paperwork. Unfortunately, she's dead."

"Dead?" Baxter said. "When?"

"Five years ago. Complications following elective surgery."

"Elective surgery? What kind?"

"Liposuction. She developed an infection."

"What about the other officers?"

"The vice president was the wife of an engineer. Her husband's out of the country. A project in Brazil. She went with him. They're trying to reach her. The treasurer was from L.A. She moved back there and started her own graphic arts company. The company went under, and she ended up broke. Declared bankruptcy. No address after that. But they're trying to trace her."

"I wonder where the money came from to rent the building and run the camp," Baxter said. "Did they do it on their own dime?"

"I wouldn't think so. It doesn't sound like any of them was

wealthy. Maybe they were able to get a grant. But I'll remind Research to see what they can find about the source of the money."

"So are we going to call it a day now?"

"It's almost eight o'clock. Sounds like a good idea to me."

"I hope Yin and his wife are enjoying the wine."

"Me, too," McCabe said as they pulled up to the police garage.

"Want me to follow you home?"

McCabe looked at him. "I think I can manage to get there alone."

"I thought with the tracker they found on your car—"

"Someone—in all likelihood, Clarence Redfield—wanted to know where I was going. Now he won't unless he's willing to take the chance of trying to get another one in place. And he knows we're onto him."

"What if it wasn't Redfield?" Baxter said.

"Who else would it be?"

"Just remember what the CO said and watch your back."

McCabe opened the door of the sedan and picked up her field bag. "I always do that. And in this case, forewarned is forearmed."

On the way home, she passed a group of women gathered on a street corner. They were holding up huge glow-in-the-dark signs that were obviously a response to Clarence Redfield and KZAC. One of the signs read WE'RE NOT AFRAID OF THE DARK. The other said THE NIGHT IS OURS TOO.

They were on a corner that seemed safe. McCabe hoped so anyway. All they needed were victims who had become victims while refusing to be made afraid.

20

McCabe woke up at the first hint of dawn. She hadn't closed the blinds completely, and light filtered into the room. She squinted, thought of going back to sleep, and decided instead to go for a run. If she moved quickly, she might be able to get out and back before the humidity began to build.

Outside, she took a cautious breath of air and tasted a hint of the smoke drifting from the north. Best to start with a brisk walk to loosen her muscles, then build to a run.

She had some time. She and Baxter had agreed to go in at eleven. She had nothing to do until breakfast at Stan and Chelsea's house.

Odd, the order of that in her mind. Not Chelsea and Stan's house. Chelsea ran the restaurant. Stan ran the house. Ask her where she'd rather eat, and Stan's place won out every time. Real waffles with real maple syrup and Canadian bacon.

She'd deserve that bacon after putting up with this smoke.

She had picked a route toward New Scotland Avenue rather than Western Avenue. Handy to be on the same street as two hospitals if she should pass out.

But there was no point in being reckless. McCabe took out her mask and slid it on, glanced at her vitals monitor, then slipped into a loping run.

Baxter's friend with lung cancer and his question about cloning . . . was that something that Adam had thought about? But Adam didn't need a clone. What he needed was an android body. One that looked like his own. Another body into which he could transfer what was Adam.

Soldiers who had lost their arms and legs in battle were given new limbs, computerized body parts that their brains coordinated. Adam could not tell his own immobile legs to move. But he wanted to walk again on his own two legs.

He had rejected the option of replacing his empty eye socket with a prosthesis.

If and when he could chose, would he even be willing to take the other option. To leave his wheelchair to become Adam in an android body?

If it were me, would I choose that? McCabe wondered.

But even the possibility could be a long time away. Long before android hosts were available, Adam or someone else might have a breakthrough that would make it possible for him to walk without computerized braces on his legs or an exoskeleton.

McCabe glanced at her monitor again and picked up her pace.

At the stoplight across from Washington Park, McCabe jogged in place, debating a run through the park versus heading toward downtown. Sunday-morning quiet hung over Madison Avenue, and she was tempted to turn toward the streets that would lead her to the Empire State Plaza.

The shrill sound of a siren turning onto Madison Avenue sent her into the park.

By the time she'd done the circuit around the lake, she would have logged over three miles. She would still have the return run home. More than enough when she hadn't been out all week.

Her mother would never have believed this would happen. That the day would ever come when Hannah, her "wild child," would have learned how to pace herself.

Now, if she could only manage to put the pieces of the serial killer case together before the commander reassigned her to finding stolen Zip cars. A task force, yes. But she and Baxter were still the primaries on the Jessup case.

And she had been working on the other two cases since the beginning. They now needed a task force because she and Jay O'Connell and the other detectives who had been lending a hand hadn't been able to figure out what was going on before another woman was killed. Clarence Redfield was right about that much at least.

McCabe touched the button on her vest. Maybe music would help unfreeze her brain.

First up, "Harlem Nocturne." All she needed was a trench coat and a rainy night in the city.

And the Wizard of Oz to give her a brain.

What movie had the teaching assistant been showing that day?

McCabe stopped, hands on knees, catching her breath.

Silly question. But they hadn't asked. Not that Sharon's mother would probably have known.

She touched the button to silence the music.

"Ask Sharon's mother if she knows what the movie was," she said into the recorder on her vest.

She walked for a few minutes, then started to run again.

She stumbled to a stop when a fat gray opossum wobbled across the path in front of her. When he was out of sight, she ran on.

Back to her playlist. By the time she'd reached the lake, Mike Hammer's theme song had given way to Aaron Copland's *Appalachian Spring*.

It was only after the music changed that she thought of Lisa Nichols, the blonde who might be a femme fatale. No reason to think that except for the fact Nichols was beautiful and wore black. And she was the fiancée of a very wealthy man. And Vivian Jessup, the woman who might have been that man's former lover, had been murdered.

But even if she'd had a motive for killing Jessup, why would Lisa Nichols target two young women from Albany?

That was the problem. Two of the murders might go together. Two of the victims had shared a common experience. But that left Jessup, who didn't fit.

But it had to fit, unless this wasn't what it looked like. Unless there were two related murders . . . and then the third committed by someone else, copying the method of the first two.

They had talked about that during the task force meeting. The KZAC radio host had suggested it when he was interviewing Clarence Redfield. Mike had brought it up, too.

But the thing was, a copycat killer would have had to know how the first two victims had died. Clarence Redfield had hinted that he knew. But when they'd finally had a chance to question him about what he knew and the source of his information, Redfield had lawyered up.

McCabe glanced upward as the starlings that had been sitting in an oak tree took off in a flutter of iridescent wings and squawks.

Either Redfield knew enough about how the vics had died to know it was by the same method or he knew that and also knew what the method had been. Either he had an informant in the department or he had some other way of knowing.

And the only other ways he could have of knowing was if he were the killer himself or in contact with the killer. Maybe that was going to be his next big thread. About how the serial killer had talked to him about the murders and the incompetence of the APD. It wouldn't be the first time a killer had communicated directly with a member of the press . . . if you could call Clarence Redfield that.

Redfield had even mentioned Jack the Ripper during his radio interview on KZAC. Someone claiming to be the Ripper had sent letters to the London press of his day.

McCabe slowed to a walk to take a long sip from the water tube attached to her mask. One serial killer who had killed all three women. Or someone who had been able to duplicate the method of death of the first two and had hoped the police would attribute

Vivian Jessup's death to the same person who had killed Bethany Clark and Sharon Giovanni.

And if the first two murders were for revenge or some other such motive, the victims had not been chosen at random. The killer had gone after them one at a time.

And then after Vivian Jessup?

Science camp. Broadway actress. *Alice*, the Red Queen, and the yellow brick road.

And *Lolita* thrown in for good measure. Ted Thornton had mentioned Vladimir Nabokov when he was discussing the mayor's "It Happened Here" initiative. He had said Nabokov had come to Albany to capture butterflies in the Pine Bush.

McCabe made another note to her recorder, "Check on Nabokov and Albany visit. Check link *Lolita* and *Alice* books and authors."

Had Lewis Carroll ever come to Albany? Probably not. If he had, then his number-one fan, Jessup, would have made the trip up from the City to see what he had seen. She had not come to Albany until she had learned about the John Wilkes Booth connection.

McCabe broke into a run again. Feet pounding, she ran across the wooden bridge that arched over the lake.

When the weather was pleasant, anglers came out to try their hand at the fish the city stocked in the Washington Park Lake. Most caught and released their catch. When the water in the lake was as stagnant as it must be now, that was a sensible precaution.

She ran along the paved upper path, heading back toward the lake house and the amphitheater and bleachers. Summer theater in the park.

Thornton had said that he'd appeared as Richard III in college. Did his aide-de-camp, Bruce Ashby, have any theater connections?

This afternoon, she and Baxter were going to have to sit down and spread out all the pieces. Check and cross-check until they came up with another lead to follow.

Maybe one more lap around the lake before she headed home.

·   ·   ·

McCabe was stepping out of the shower when her ORB buzzed.

"Just calling to make sure you're all right," Chelsea said when she picked up.

"All right? Am I late? I thought Stan said nine-thirty."

"You haven't seen the story in the *Chronicle*?"

"No. What story?"

"Hold on, and I'll send it to you."

Towel wrapped around her, McCabe stood there in the middle of her bedroom, reading the article.

"Hannah?" Chelsea said.

"Rain check on breakfast? I have something I need to do."

"What?"

"Go see Adam before he reads this."

"He's probably seen it already."

"In that case, I'm sure he'll have a few things he'd like to say to me."

"That might be a good reason to stay out of his way for a couple of days."

"That's not how it works. Talk to you later."

Adam opened the door of his apartment in his bathrobe and pajama bottoms. His long-toed feet were bare on the footrests of his wheel-chair.

"Sorry, did I get you out of bed? Pop was still asleep, too, when I—"

The sound of a cabinet door closing drew her eyes toward the kitchen. A woman with black hair to her waist, wearing white shorts and a blue T-shirt with Asian characters, smiled and waved. "Hi, I'm Mai. One of Adam's colleagues at UAlbany."

"I'm Hannah. Adam's sister."

"Nice to meet you, Hannah. Are you staying for breakfast?"

"Thanks, but I just came by for a quick conversation with Adam."

Adam turned in his wheelchair. "Let's go out on the balcony. Excuse us, Mai."

He closed the French doors behind them and brought his chair to a stop beside the balcony railing. "What's up?"

"This." McCabe passed her ORB with the article on display over to him.

She looked out across the green space that the four apartment buildings in the complex shared. If Adam stayed in Albany, he would probably buy a place of his own. He'd had a condo in Chicago.

"Did you talk to this reporter?" he asked.

"No," she said. "I didn't know about the article until Chelsea called me this morning. But I was afraid this might happen. When they're covering high-profile cases, reporters like to include human-interest stories about the people involved in the investigation." McCabe cleared her throat. "I was hoping now that we have the task force, they wouldn't notice me."

"According to the article, you're the lead investigator."

"I'm the investigator who caught the case. I was there when the call came in and the lieutenant needed to send someone to the scene. Mike Baxter responded, too."

"Nothing much about Baxter in the article. In fact, he doesn't seem to be mentioned at all."

"No. The article's about you and me."

" 'Lead Cop on Serial Killer Case a Child Hero.' Catchy."

"Adam, I am so sorry. I hope this . . ." McCabe glanced toward the closed French doors. "I hope this won't be awkward for you with Mai and your other colleagues."

"Why should it be? They already know how I got in this chair."

McCabe's breath caught in her throat. Before she could speak, Adam smiled.

"Don't sweat it, sis. You were the hero of our little saga. And it is just a newspaper article. After the hatchet job that guy Redfield did on you on his thread, you could probably use some good press."

"Right," McCabe said. "I'd better go and let you and Mai have your breakfast."

He followed her to the door. "Drop by anytime."

"I'll call first next time." McCabe waved to the woman in the kitchen. "Nice meeting you, Mai."

"You, too, Hannah. See you again soon."

If Mai thought that, she must not know how many women had passed through Adam's life. Of course, he might be more careful when it came to colleagues. And, of course, they might only be friends.

But being in a wheelchair had not changed the attraction women of all ages seemed to feel for Adam. That at least was something that had been salvaged. But McCabe had never been sure if he considered that a blessing or a curse. Maybe it only made it worse when he thought of some day meeting a woman with whom he would want to spend more than a few months . . . and wondered if she would want him for a lifetime.

Her father was in the kitchen when she got back. Like Adam, he was in his pajamas and robe, but he had slippers on his feet and was moving between stove and counter.

He was loading a tray with his breakfast, whole-wheat toast, scrambled egg whites, turkey bacon, blueberries, and green tea. Good. He was sticking to his diet plan.

"You back from Chelsea's already?" he asked.

"I didn't go. I had to go see Adam."

"See him about what?"

She went over to the wall and brought up the *Chronicle* node. "This," she said. "An article about me and Adam."

Angus put down his tray and came over to read the display. "What did your brother have to say about having the story rehashed?"

"He said not to worry about it . . . that I could use some good press after Clarence Redfield's thread. Did you see that thread?"

"I saw it. Your brother's right. If some reporter were going to do this story, it couldn't have come at a better time. After Redfield's thread, you needed some humanizing."

"Learning that I shot a burglar when I was nine should certainly humanize me for the readers of the *Chronicle*."

"What else would they expect you to do in that situation? Your brother was struggling with a man with a gun. The man shot him."

McCabe closed out the *Chronicle* node. "As Mama pointed out to me when we were waiting to see if Adam would live or die, he was shot because he was trying to keep me from being shot."

"I loved your mother. And she was distraught at the time, so you have to cut her some slack. But sometimes she could be full of crap. I've told you that."

"I know you have."

"Then why are you even thinking about it?"

"Because it's hard not to think about it. Aside from the *Chronicle* article, now that Adam's back—"

"Well, do you want him to go away again?"

"No, I want us to be brother and sister again. The way we were that day when we walked into the house together laughing."

"You can't go back in time."

"I know. If I could, I would turn as I'm walking out the door and remember to reset the security system."

"If your mother hadn't thought a nine-year-old ought to wear deodorant—"

"If I'd remembered to put it on when I was getting dressed—"

"If Adam hadn't told you to hurry up and get ready if you wanted to go with him to the park to watch him play soccer. Or if I hadn't bought that gun. Or if your mother and I had stayed home that Saturday instead of driving to Boston. We can 'if' ourselves to death. And it'll still come back to the fact that nobody was responsible for what happened except the guy who broke into our house."

"I know that. And I'd like to be able to make peace with it once and for all. But I look at Adam in that wheelchair—"

"All right, then tell him to get the hell out of that wheelchair so you can get on with your life."

"Pop—"

He glared at her. "It ain't going to happen. Until your brother or someone else comes up with a medical or technological miracle, he is not going to have legs that function on their own. So you can either learn to live with the fact he's in that wheelchair or you can make yourself crazy and drive your brother away once and for all."

"Drive him away? It isn't just me. Adam—"

"Adam what?"

"Can't you see that he . . . sometimes he . . . I think he resents the fact that I—"

"You don't think he ought to be pissed now and then that you're whole and he ain't? And did he ever tell you that he resents you?"

"No."

"Then how do you know he does?"

"You make it sound like I'm being childish—"

"You are. He might be now and then, too. And, God knows, sometimes he can be his mother's son. One of his little looks or the way he says something. But he loves you. You're still his sister. Just the way you were your mother's daughter."

McCabe said, "Right. Of course, we can both acknowledge that Mama loved Adam best."

"Sure she did. He was her favorite, the way you're mine."

"And you don't think there's anything wrong with those family dynamics?"

"It might be wrong, but that's the way humans are. We love the way we love, and you take it or leave it. And my breakfast's gotten cold while we've been standing here talking about it."

McCabe sighed. Whatever else Pop was, he was a realist, prone to pragmatism, she thought. He never quite got that it wasn't always that easy for the rest of them.

Not that it was always that easy for him, either. If it were, he wouldn't have drunk himself half to death when Mama died.

"Hearts don't break," he had informed her in one of his drunken hazes. But for a while, she had thought his would.

"I'll heat your breakfast up for you." She took his plate from his tray. "Pop, changing the subject—"

"Good. About time."

"The case I'm working on. We're trying to find some information that doesn't seem to be there."

Angus sat down at the table. "What kind of information?"

"If I tell you this . . . and I'm only telling you because I really need to know—"

"Stop filibustering and get on with it."

"You have to promise me first that you will keep this to yourself."

"Who am I going to tell? If you're talking about me telling your brother—"

"I'm talking about you telling anyone. I know when you get hold of a good story, you find it hard—"

"As you keep reminding me, Ms. Detective, I'm retired now. Where am I going to write about it?"

"Maybe in that book you might get around to writing." She filled a mug with hot water and added another tea bag. "Or, who knows? You might decide to start your own thread." She turned back to him and smiled. "I wouldn't put that past you."

"Wouldn't you? What is it that I know that you don't? Must be important for you to be willing to take a chance on me keeping it to myself."

"The serial murder case. We've finally found a link between the first two victims." She set his breakfast plate and the fresh mug of tea on the table in front of him. "When they were kids, both attended a two-week summer science camp for twelve- to fourteen-year-old girls sponsored by a women's group. We're trying to reach the officers of the group, but what we know so far is that something happened during the time the girls were at the camp."

"What?"

McCabe sat down across from him. "A bullying incident. A girl was being teased by another girl. The girl who was being teased ran away when the teaching assistant was out of the classroom. She was picked up in a car by a boy. We don't know what, if anything, happened. She was found. But she didn't go back to the science camp. Instead, her very angry mother went in the next day. The teaching assistant was called to the office. She left crying. She didn't go back to the camp, either."

"Sounds like a real dustup."

"It may have been. But so far, what we have is based on what we were told by the mother of one of our murder victims. No one seems to have called the police that day when the girl ran away from camp."

"Got any names for these people?"

"No, other than Bethany Clark and Sharon Giovanni, our two murder victims, who both attended the camp. Sharon told her mother what happened. According to her mother, Sharon was involved because the girl who was bullying the other girl drew a picture and showed it to Sharon. Both the bully and Sharon got into trouble when the teaching assistant saw the drawing and called them out of the classroom to scold them."

"But, according to her mother, Sharon was as innocent as the driven snow in all this?"

"Claims her mother. Actually, Bethany, our other murder victim, seems more likely to have been the instigator. Her sister remembers an odd little incident involving Bethany." McCabe looked at him across the table. "Does any of this ring a bell?"

"Who was running the camp?"

"A group called Girls in Science, which as far as we can tell, was organized specifically to sponsor the camp."

"Where'd the money come from?"

"Good question. We don't know yet. None of the group's officers seems to have been wealthy. We're thinking they might have had some type of grant. By tomorrow, we should have access to any paperwork that they filed."

Angus scooped some egg whites onto the toast he had smeared with strawberry jam. "This would have been when? 2009?"

"2010."

"Hand me my ORB over there on the counter."

McCabe got up and brought it to him. "You remember something?"

"Not off the bat. But all of the crime stories the paper covered that year are on here. Indexed. What month?"

"First two weeks of July."

She waited while he scanned the files.

"Robbery . . . hit-and-run . . . arson . . . missing baby found with father." He shook his head. "Nothing coming up on a runaway girl."

"She probably wasn't missing more than a few hours." McCabe said. "So you don't recall anything?"

"I didn't say that. I just said we didn't report on anything like that."

"So you do remember something?"

"I didn't say that, either."

"Pop, you're making me crazy here."

"Make yourself some breakfast and let me finish mine." He took another bite of toast. "I've got my notes for that week here in another index."

McCabe shook her head. "I don't understand why you can't write a book about your life and times as a reporter and editor when you have your notes organized right down to the week."

"I wrote the notes as journal entries. That doesn't mean I can make any sense of them years later. I've got some entries after your mother died, when I must have been on weeklong benders. Don't know how in the hell I ever got anything written fit to print."

"Because you're an extraordinary writer, even under those circumstances."

"Quit trying to butter me up and eat. I'll tell you if I find anything."

McCabe went over to the fridge and found herself a cup of yogurt. She tossed in a handful of walnuts and took a banana from the fruit bowl, then sat back down at the table.

"Umm," Angus said.

"Umm, what?"

"Probably nothing useful. Got a note here about sending a reporter to interview Ted Thornton. Thornton knew Jessup, didn't he?"

"They were old friends. When was this interview?"

"Monday, July twelfth, 2010."

"What was the interview about?"

"Thornton's plans to expand his business interests in the Capital Region. The reporter asked a question that Thornton didn't like, and Thornton said, 'Interview over,' and got up and walked out. I wrote a note to myself about arrogance and power. I was thinking of writing an editorial."

"Did you?"

"Looks like I was working on it a few days later, but then they started to get a handle on the oil spill in the Gulf. My editorial turned into a piece about modern disasters and their aftermath. I couldn't work Ted Thornton in."

"But Thornton was here in Albany in July 2010."

"Hadn't built his mansion yet. He was renting a house on Willett Street, across from Washington Park. Rumor was that he was going to try to buy up all of the houses along there. That was the question that made him get up and walk out on the interview."

"You mean when your reporter asked about the rumor?"

"Didn't like being questioned. Whatever he was considering, he seemed to change his mind before he moved on it. Nothing to do with what you're interested in."

McCabe broke off a piece of banana and stirred it into her yogurt. "I asked Ted Thornton if he knew anything about our first two victims. He said he had never heard of them."

"Since they would have been young girls back in 2010, unless you're implying that Thornton—"

"I don't have any reason to think that. But it does occur to me that with his interest in various modes of transportation, he probably also has an interest in science."

"So you're thinking he might have had something to do with the summer science camp?"

"He donates lots of money to charities and good causes through his foundation. Maybe back in 2010, he made a donation to a science camp." McCabe scooped up another spoonful of yogurt. "Whatever these murders are about, if it somehow started with the science camp, then there's a motive that we might be able to get a handle on. Not some whacked-out psycho who likes shooting women up with phenol."

"Sometimes serial killers have motives that make pretty good sense. Greed, for example. The payoff from the insurance policies they have on their victims."

"I think we can assume that isn't the case here."

"Didn't say it was. Just agreeing with you that your killer may not be foaming at the mouth."

"It would be a whole lot easier if he were. Easier to spot him."

"You got reason to be certain the killer's a man?"

McCabe pushed back her chair and stood up. "Forensics has been able to put together a profile from the trace evidence on the victim's bodies. They aren't prepared to swear in blood, but the indicators are male, European ancestry. Of course, we could have a killer who is leaving fibers and hairs for us to find."

"So it could be a woman."

"With the method of death, there's no reason why it couldn't be. But as Agent Francisco would remind us, most serial killers who kill women are men." McCabe dropped her yogurt container into the recycle bin, the banana peel into a compost can. "Thanks for the info, Pop. I've got to get to the station. Baxter and I are going to spend some time going over what we have."

"Don't work too hard," Angus said.

He had been saying that for years. Her reply was a part of the same ritual: "I won't."

21

Baxter came in a few minutes after she had settled down at her desk. He was carrying a Cambrini Bakery box. "Brain food," he said.

"Bless you," McCabe said.

"Since we're probably going to be here long enough to order pizza, we may as well make it a complete pig-out."

"And repent and start over once the case is solved."

Baxter leaned back in his chair. "You see any solution in sight? I checked the master file, and we still don't have anything useful on that women's group that sponsored the camp. They organized as a nonprofit. No record of any other activity by the group after they rented the building, hired the instructors, and put on a two-week science camp."

"I swore my Dad to secrecy and asked him if he remembered his newspaper covering anything about a girl running away from summer science camp."

"Did he?"

"No, and he was able to check the index of the articles for that month. Nothing." McCabe took a sip of the 'coffee' that one of the detectives on the morning shift had made. She wrinkled her nose and put her mug down. "But he did come across something else in his notes from that month. Ted Thornton was here in Albany. One of my father's reporters went to interview him."

"But Ted Thornton said he had never heard of either vic."

"Maybe not. But I'm wondering if he might have made a donation to the women's group that sponsored the camp."

"And if he did?"

"No idea. But at least we'll have found something linking all three victims."

"And that would be our good friend Theodore. How do you want to handle finding out?"

"We should have some more information about the group from Research by tomorrow morning. But, in the meantime, we could run this by the lieutenant and see if there's any problem with contacting Ted Thornton and asking him directly."

"Thornton will probably refer us to Ashby."

McCabe picked up her ORB. "I hate to interrupt the lou's time off. He and his wife go bowling on Sunday morning."

"Bowling?"

"They love the game. Whenever they both have a Sunday morning off, they go bowl a few games."

"What does the lou's wife do?"

"ER nurse."

When Dole answered, she could hear the clash of bowling balls in the background. When she had explained their theory about Thornton as a possible donor to Girls in Science, he said, "Go ahead and ask him about it and see what he says. If it was a legitimate nonprofit, he shouldn't have anything to hide. If he stonewalls you, we'll pull the CO in on it. But the general agreement on this is that as much as possible we treat Thornton the same way we would anybody else."

"That's what we were thinking, sir."

"Let me know if you get anything useful."

"Good luck with your game."

"I'm going to need it. The woman just got another strike."

"What'd he say?" Baxter asked.

"Go ahead and check with Thornton. Try to handle him the same way we would anyone else."

"Until he makes it clear that he's not?"

"You got it. But Thornton did tell us he wanted to be helpful."

"This means I get to see Roz again," Baxter said, grinning.

McCabe shook her head, "You and that robot."

"The woman of my dreams. Low-maintenance."

When McCabe reached Bruce Ashby, he gave the okay for them to visit. Ted, he said, would be happy to answer any other questions they might have.

"I wonder if Clarence Redfield would be as happy to see us," McCabe said after she had passed that on to Baxter. "I was thinking about Redfield when I was out running this morning."

"What about him? Other than whether you're going to get your friend to beat him up."

"I was thinking some more about what we talked about. That we still don't know how Redfield knew that we had a serial killer. During the press conference, Jacoby shut him down before he could say what it was that he knew about how the two victims had died. We still don't know how much he knows. Or how he knows."

"You thinking Redfield should be on our list of suspects?"

"Only wondering about him," McCabe said. "If you were the killer, wouldn't it be a great way of staying off the suspect list to be out there accusing the police of being incompetent and engaging in a cover-up."

"Yeah, it would be. On the other hand, we could have someone in the department who's feeding Redfield information."

"That's more likely. Either that or Redfield's been in contact with the killer. But I think at the task force meeting tomorrow, we should put Redfield on the table. See how people are feeling about how he might fit into this."

"Want to swing by and pay him a visit after we see Thornton?"

"Maybe we'd better wait until we have something that we can use as a conversation opener. If we just drop by, he'll probably call his lawyer and claim I'm harassing him because of his thread."

"Okay. However you want to play it."

"That's what I like," McCabe said. "An agreeable partner."

Baxter pushed back his chair and stretched. "Does being agreeable buy me about five minutes to make a call?"

"Sure, go ahead. I'll meet you at the door."

McCabe glanced up from her ORB as he walked away. Probably the same woman he was calling on Thursday after the autopsy. Probably telling her he was going to be tied up most of the day and making a date for later.

She glanced back down at the screen in front of her. She had no reason not to trust Baxter . . . unless being easy to get along with made him suspect.

After all, he didn't have to mention the call. He could have said he needed to make a pit stop in the john. Could be that was where he was going to make his call.

Bruce Ashby opened the door at Ted Thornton's house.

"Where's Roz?" Baxter asked.

"Who?" Ashby said.

"Rosalind. The maid."

"Oh, she . . . I happened to be passing, so I signaled her that I would let you in."

"Thanks for letting us drop by," McCabe said. "We'll try not to take up too much of Mr. Thornton's time."

"I should have told you when you called that this will have to be short. Ted and Lisa are taking Greer and her husband down to the City on the airship later this afternoon. The memorial service for Vivian is tomorrow."

"A public service?" McCabe asked.

"Private. For Vivian's close friends and associates. Cremation rather than burial."

Horatio, the cat, did not appear, either, as they followed Ashby back through the house. This time, their destination was a room filled with cushioned wicker furniture, green plants, and sunlight from the windows that made up one wall. Lisa Nichols and Ted Thornton were sitting in adjacent chairs, with a table between them. They were sharing the Sunday paper over coffee and croissants.

There was no sign of Greer St. John and her husband, Ron.

Thornton stood to greet them, waving them to the sofa across from where he and his fiancée were seated.

"Need me, Ted?" Ashby asked.

Thornton passed the cup of coffee he was pouring to McCabe. "Please help yourself to sugar and cream. Are you . . . uh, going to have any questions that Bruce might be helpful in answering, Detective McCabe?"

"Thank you," McCabe said. "And, yes, actually we do have a question that might require Mr. Ashby to check his records."

"Then, Bruce, why don't you join us?"

Thornton poured coffee for Baxter and gestured for Ashby to serve himself. When everyone was seated with the cups in hand, he said, "Now, how can we help you?"

Lisa Nichols, chic in white slacks, black tunic top, and strappy black high-heeled sandals, crossed her legs. She had been silent, but she seemed interested in what had brought them back for another interview.

McCabe, both of her feet on the floor, took another sip of her coffee, which was excellent, and set the cup on the table at her elbow.

"We need to ask about a donation that you might have made to a nonprofit organization back in 2010," she said. "The organization was called Girls in Science. It was a women's group that sponsored a two-week summer science camp for girls twelve to fourteen."

Thornton raised an eyebrow. "I take it . . . take it . . . this organization has some relevance to your murder investigation."

"We've learned that Sharon Giovanni and Bethany Clark both attended this science camp."

"But I'm . . . uh, pretty sure Vivian wouldn't have," Thornton said.

"No," McCabe said. "But it did occur to us that your foundation might have made a donation to the group. It would have been a worthy cause and one that you might have supported because of your interest in innovations in transportation."

Thornton nodded. "'Innovations in transportation.' I like that phrase. Not your usual cop phrase."

"Cops aren't generally illiterate, Mr. Thornton."

"No, of course not . . . of course, not. I meant no offense, Detective McCabe. What I was getting at in my clumsy way is that most cops . . . in my admittedly limited experience . . . prefer plain, blunt language rather than multisyllable phrases."

"Depends on who we're talking to," Baxter said.

"Yes," Thornton said, smiling back at him. "And, of course, given Detective McCabe's wordsmith parents—"

"Who are not the subject of this conversation, Mr. Thornton," McCabe said. "Do you recall making a donation to Girls in Science? Or being contacted by anyone from the group?"

Thornton turned to Ashby, who already had his ORB in his hand. "Anything?"

"Searching," Ashby said.

"While Bruce is doing that, what would it mean if I had donated to this group? With regard to your investigation, that is?"

McCabe shook her head. "No idea, Mr. Thornton. To be honest, we're fishing right now. We're trying to reach the only officer of the organization who is still available, but she's out of the country with her husband. In the meantime, we're trying to find out whatever we can about the group and the camp. One of the questions we need to answer is who paid for the camp."

"I think I've got it," Ashby said. "A check for twenty-five thousand dollars. March seventeenth, 2010."

McCabe tried to keep her excitement from showing. They were finally getting a break or two. "Do you have anything else?" she asked Ashby.

"No . . . at least nothing . . ." He sent a glance in Thornton's direction.

Thornton said, "Go ahead with whatever it is. We have no secrets from our friends here."

"Ted, the donation wasn't through the foundation. You wrote a personal check."

Thornton frowned. "I did? Doesn't ring a bell. Do you remember anything about it?"

Ashby shook his head. "I was a little distracted during that time." He glanced at McCabe and Baxter. "My father'd had a stroke. I was going back and forth to Wichita to help my mother. He died later that spring."

Thornton cleared his throat. "Sorry, Bruce, old man. I should have remembered." He frowned. "Did I make the check out to this group?"

"No, to someone named Rachel Kincaid. But the memo says "For science camp.""

Thornton was still looking puzzled. "Is that it?"

"You have a notation. Apparently, a memory jogger. Shall I read it?"

"Go ahead."

"'The Naked Jungle.'"

"Ah, now it comes back to me." Thornton's smile widened. "Charming woman. We met at an event, and I asked her what she did. She said she was a biologist and studied army ants. And that reminded me of a movie I'd loved when I was a kid."

"Charlton Heston has a plantation in South America," McCabe said. "Army ants are on the march toward the plantation—"

"Consuming everything in their path," Thornton said. "Plants, animals, men. But our hero, Charlton Heston, stands . . . stands his ground with Eleanor Parker, his lovely bride by proxy. Dr. Kincaid and I had a . . . a fascinating chat about the accuracy of the movie and her own research on ants."

"And then you wrote her a check for twenty-five thousand dollars?" McCabe said.

Thornton flashed his lopsided smile—his "Oh shucks" smile. "She mentioned that the funding had fallen through for the camp that she and some like-minded women had planned to launch that summer. There was no time for her to go through the usual process of applying to my foundation." He shrugged. "Actually, I stay out of that anyway. There's a committee that makes those decisions. But this camp sounded like a good cause." He glanced at Ashby. "Bruce, we must have the paperwork on it somewhere. She said she'd send it along."

Ashby made a note. "I'll look for it tomorrow. You probably gave it to the accountants."

"Who undoubtedly made sure that I received the appropriate tax deduction. So we should be able to . . . to track that down for you, Detective McCabe."

"Thank you, we'd appreciate that."

"Is Dr. Kincaid the person you're trying to reach?"

"No," McCabe said, watching his expression. "She's dead."

But it was Lisa Nichols who reacted to the news. "Dead? Dead how?"

McCabe gave that two beats. "Of natural causes," she said. "Or, at least, while under a doctor's care. Did you ever meet Dr. Kincaid, Ms. Nichols?"

"No, I don't know anything about her." She stretched her upper body, like a cat rippling its back. "It was just when you mentioned she was dead . . . for a moment I was afraid you were going to say she had been murdered, too."

Thornton said, "How long ago did she die, if we may ask?"

McCabe said. "Five years ago. Did you see her again after that evening?"

"No, that was the only time we ever encountered each other."

"So you had no involvement in the summer science camp that you paid for?" Baxter said.

"None at all. I wrote the check and then forgot about it," Thornton said. "My forgetting . . . may have been helped along a bit by the excellent champagne that I seem to recall was being poured that evening."

McCabe said, "This event . . . what kind of event?"

"A fund-raiser for African famine relief. There was a speaker. A missionary who had worked in the Congo and other countries. I was there because I was one of the honorary chairs. And Dr. Kincaid was there because she had spent time in the village where the missionary had her headquarters."

"So the missionary was a friend of hers?"

Thornton smiled. "As much of a friend as a woman inclined toward sainthood and a woman inclined toward sin . . ." He shot a glance in Lisa Nichols's direction.

"Don't mind me," she said.

"It was only a flirtatious exchange over our champagne glasses, my love. I had a plane to catch."

"But you wrote her the check before you said good-bye," Lisa said, a smile curling her own lips.

"It sounded like a worthy cause." He turned his attention back to McCabe and Baxter. "But I will admit . . . being unattached at the time . . . that I did have a vague notion of seeing the lady again when I returned from wherever it was I was going."

"But that didn't happen?" Baxter asked.

"No. By the time I got back, she had slipped my mind. I hadn't thought of her again until today."

Bruce Ashby, who had been quietly sipping his coffee, glanced at his watch. "Ted, if we're going to make that stop on the way to the airport . . ."

"Is there anything else I can help you with, Detective McCabe? As Bruce may have told you, we're going down to the City this afternoon."

"Yes, he did mention that." McCabe glanced toward the door. "How is Mrs. St. John doing?"

"As well as can be expected. She slept in this morning, and she and Ron are having breakfast up in their suite."

"Then we won't disturb them." McCabe stood up. "Please give her our best."

Thornton stood, as well. "I'll do that. And please do keep us posted."

"I'll show you out," Ashby said.

McCabe nodded at Lisa Nichols. "Sorry to interrupt your morning."

Nichols shook her head. "No apology needed, Detective. I just hope you're able to catch the man who killed Vivian and those two young women."

She sounded sincere.

Back in the car, McCabe checked her ORB. "Hey, they've found her."

"Who?" Baxter said.

"Jean Lockhart, the vice president of Girls in Science. She sent us a tag from Brazil with her contact info. She's standing by for our call."

"Great. Maybe she can tell us who the girls were who were involved in the teasing incident."

"It was almost ten years ago. I hope she still remembers. If we're lucky, it's in a file somewhere."

They called Jean Lockhart when they got back to the station.

"No," she said. She was sitting at a table, with a swimming pool in the background. A glass containing a beverage that looked like iced tea was in front of her. "No file. The last thing we wanted was a paper trail."

"Why was that? If there had been an incident—"

"The girl's crazy mother was threatening to sue us. We were scared to death she would find out that Ted Thornton was funding us and go after him. All we wanted to do was get through the next few days and then fold our tent and slip away."

"When the girl left the camp . . . we heard that she was picked up by a boy—"

"Who may have had some ideas. But when he found out she was only thirteen, he dropped her off on a street corner. She called her older sister, and the older sister and her boyfriend went to pick her up."

"So the mother's concern was about what might have happened," McCabe said.

"And we agreed with her that what happened shouldn't have happened. We fired the teaching assistant who let it happen. But the woman was still ranting and raving."

"She was probably still scared," Baxter said. "What happened with the guy in the car could have turned out really bad."

"We knew that. And it scared us, too. But none of us could afford to be sued. We had been trying to do a good thing with the camp."

"A science camp for girls was a good idea," McCabe said. "Let's talk for a moment about the two girls the teaching assistant reprimanded that day before the girl who was being teased ran away. We know that one of the girls called into the hall by the teaching assistant was named Sharon Giovanni. The other girl we are interested in was named Bethany Clark."

"Bethany? What did you say the last name was?"

"Clark. Bethany Clark."

"That sounds right. She was the one who was accused by the other one . . . Sharon, did you say?"

"Sharon Giovanni. What was it that Sharon said?"

"Sharon accused Bethany of teasing—*harassing* would have been a better word—the girl who ran away. She said Bethany had drawn a picture."

"That's what we had heard," McCabe said. "What did Bethany say about that?"

"She said she was only playing. That she hadn't meant to upset the girl . . . whatever her name was."

"Did Bethany's parents come in?"

"Her mother came in. And, of course, she took Bethany's side."

"What about Sharon's mother?"

"We didn't call her in. Bethany seemed to be the problem. That is, she seemed to be until the next day, when the other girl's crazy mother came in."

"Why do you keep calling the mother 'crazy'?" Baxter asked.

"Because there was something wrong with the woman. She was either half-drunk or half-high on something. And the way she came in ranting . . . it was over the top, even given what had happened."

"Ms. Lockhart," McCabe said, "would you try one more time to remember the woman's name or her daughter's name?"

"The daughter had one of those made-up names."

"A made-up name?"

"You know how some parents want to use both the father's and the mother's name, and they put the two together. A name like that."

"Okay. What about the mother's name?"

"No idea. The last name must not have been distinctive, or I'd at least remember that much."

"That helps. So we're looking for a common surname and an unusual first name for the girl," McCabe said. "Would you happen to remember what school she attended?"

"I'm sure I never knew that. I got called in with the rest of our board after the mess broke out. We had set the camp up, but then we left it to what we thought were the experts. The director had excellent references. She was the one who took charge of hiring the teachers and other staff."

"So it was a very hands-off board?" McCabe said.

"We wanted to do something that we thought was important. But it wasn't as if we didn't all have day jobs."

"What about the teaching assistant? Anything you can tell us about her?"

"The director called her in while we were there. She was really distressed and apologetic about what had happened. She said she'd thought the telephone call she stepped out of the room to make was urgent."

"Did she tell the board who she called?"

"Her boyfriend. He send her a text message saying he had an emergency. She went out into the hall to call him back. His emergency turned out to be his lucky pen."

"His lucky pen?" Baxter said.

"He had a job interview that afternoon and he was calling her because he couldn't find his pen and he thought she had it." Lockhart shook her head. "I remember that because when I heard it, I thought of what I would have done to him if he had been my boyfriend and caused me all that trouble over a stupid pen."

"I guess he didn't know she was going to get into trouble," Baxter said.

"He should have had better sense than to send her a message saying it was an emergency when she was working."

McCabe said, "The TA's name. We believe her first name was Deirdre. Would you happen to remember her last name?"

"Not a clue."

"Nothing unusual or—"

"I don't think I really heard it."

"Does the first name sound right?"

"Probably . . . all I really remember about her was that she was a college kid and she looked miserable. I felt bad for her. But she had gotten us into the mess we were in."

McCabe said, "Would you have any idea how we might go about finding the camp director?"

"I don't really remember how we found her in the first place. I think someone recommended her to Rachel."

"That would be Rachel Kincaid, the president of your board of directors?"

"Yes." Lockhart grimaced. "If you want the truth, it was a bad experience, and I tried to forget about it. We ended up arguing among ourselves over what we should have done differently. We had been good friends before our little venture into the world of nonprofits."

"Have you stayed in touch with any of the other board members?"

Lockhart shook her head. "There were only seven of us. Four of the seven were advisory. Three of us, the officers, were the working board. We thought that was about all we'd need for a summer camp. We had plans to expand if we pulled that off."

"And when you didn't, the group disbanded?"

"As quickly as we could."

"Was Ted Thornton aware of what had happened?"

Lockhart hesitated. "We decided not to tell him. We thought if we could deal with the girl's crazy mother . . . . Aside from everything else, it was embarrassing. Here we were, competent professional women, and we couldn't even run a two-week science camp."

"Do you think Thornton might have found out in some other way?" McCabe asked.

"If he did, he never contacted us . . . unless he and Rachel talked."

"We understand that it was Dr. Kincaid who persuaded Mr. Thornton to fund the science camp."

"Yes. They met at a fund-raiser and she had a chance to make our pitch for funding in person." Lockhart reached for the glass. She took a long sip. "Sorry, I should have done this inside. It's getting hot out here."

Baxter said, "We won't keep you much longer; then you can have a dip in the pool."

McCabe said, "Only a few more questions, Ms. Lockhart. Do you think Dr. Kincaid might have told Ted Thornton about the incident?"

"She was really worried that the mother might push the lawsuit. But the rest of us wanted to wait and see what happened before we talked to Thornton. After all, he wasn't a member of our board."

"Did the rest of the board tell Dr. Kincaid not to involve Mr. Thornton?"

"I don't know if we told her that specifically. We talked about it and agreed that we should wait. She never told us that she had told him."

"And I gather the girl's mother calmed down and decided not to sue."

"Actually, that was kind of strange."

"Strange how?" Baxter asked.

"We were there for our emergency board meeting when the mother came in and pitched her fit. She said she had already spoken to a lawyer. We were bracing ourselves to be served with papers in a lawsuit the next day."

"But you weren't?" McCabe said.

"No, not the next day or the day after. We couldn't decide if we should contact her. We were afraid if we did, we'd get her all stirred up again. We even wondered if she might turn up at the closing event for the camp."

"The presentations that the girls were doing?"

"Yes. We thought she might turn up there and make a scene in front of the other parents. But nothing. Finally, we decided we had no choice but to try to contact her before we closed down operations, to see what she intended to do. But we couldn't reach her. The telephone number we had was no longer working. No one responded to the e-mails we sent. Finally, Rachel and the camp director went to the address we had on file. The landlord said crazy mama and her two children had left the day after she'd stormed into our board meeting. She took off without leaving a forwarding address."

"And she didn't contact the group again?"

"No. That was the last we ever heard of her."

"You mentioned her two children," McCabe said. "Do you know anything about the other daughter? The older sister?"

"No, only that she and her boyfriend went to pick up the younger sister when she called." Lockhart took another sip of her tea. "Rachel said something about the landlord telling her that the older sister took care of the younger one when the mother was gone."

"Gone where?" Baxter asked.

"I suppose he meant gone out. To work, or wherever she went."

McCabe said, "You've been really helpful, Ms. Lockhart. Is there anything else you can tell us? Something we haven't asked?"

Lockhart shook her head. "I just hope this murder case you're working on didn't start with what happened at our science camp. How could it have?"

McCabe said, "We don't know that it did. All we know right now is that the camp is where our two victims came in contact. But that may have nothing to do with the reason they were killed."

"I hope not." Lockhart sighed. "But I had a bad feeling when we closed down that somehow that wasn't going to be the end of it."

.   .   .

"Okay," Baxter said after they had ended the transmission. "We've got a mother who rants and raves, possibly while under the influence. Threatens a lawsuit but by the next day has taken off with her two daughters in tow."

"It would really help if we had the woman's name." McCabe leaned back in her chair and twirled around. "What about the schools? Maybe we can get them to cooperate and go through their files. We know the daughter had an unusual first name that could have been a combination of her parents' names. Maybe when the mother packed them up and moved, they left town. In that case, we're also looking for a student who didn't go back to school that fall."

"Sunday afternoon," Baxter said. "We aren't going to be able to do anything about the schools until tomorrow."

"And in the meantime," McCabe said, "about all we can do is add what Lockhart gave us to the file and walk it through one more time."

"Okay, let's start from the top."

They were staring at the images and notes displayed on the wall when McCabe remembered the to-do list she had made when she was out running. She picked up her ORB and hit the playback.

"Ask Sharon's mother if she knows what the movie was," her voice said. "Check on Nabokov and Albany visit."

"What movie?" Baxter said. "And who in Albany?"

"Nabokov, the author of *Lolita*. Remember Ted Thornton mentioned that Nabokov stopped here to hunt for butterflies?"

"So what?"

"So I don't know what. We've got two young women who were students in a science camp. We've got Vivian Jessup, who played Alice when she was a child. Then there's Lewis Carroll, whose reputation has occasionally been besmeared because of those photographs he used to take of young girls. And Ted Thornton, who mentioned the author of a book about a man obsessed with a child."

"So are you suggesting—"

"No, I'm just saying we should make sure we've eliminated something that might be staring us in the face."

"There's nothing about how the women were killed to suggest a sexual motive."

"No. And Ted Thornton probably mentioned Nabokov when he was talking about the mayor's initiative because it's really arctic that a famous author came to Albany to go butterfly hunting. . . ." McCabe frowned. "What did Greer St. John say about making insects and flowers for the show that she and her mother were planning?"

"She said this year they were doing *Through the Looking Glass* instead of *Alice in Wonderland*." Baxter grinned. "I went over to my folks' house yesterday to see if they still had my kid sister's copy of the books."

"You did?" McCabe said.

"The way you've been going on about Alice, I wanted to be able to hold up my side of the conversation."

"Then I should have gone back for a look at *Through the Looking Glass*, too, because I only vaguely remember the whole thing with the insects and the flowers."

Baxter grinned. "Got you covered. I found the chapters in question on the Web."

He brought up the node that they wanted.

McCabe stood up and moved closer, staring at the illustrations. "Okay, we've got flowers that talk. Tiger-lily, who tells Alice that flowers can talk 'when there is anybody worth talking to' . . ."

"Great line," Baxter said.

"And Rose and Tiger-lily discuss Alice's color and the fact that her petals don't curl properly."

"And a Daisy has a line about the bark of a tree going 'bough-wough,'" Baxter said.

"Clever nonsense designed to delight a child," McCabe said. "And we're probably wasting valuable time."

"I don't know," Baxter said. "I enjoyed reading about the looking-glass insects again. Had to go make myself a snack when I got to the Bread-and-Butterfly."

"Who lives on 'weak tea with cream in it,'" McCabe read, quoting the Gnat.

"There is one thing," Baxter said. "The flowers that the killer left at the first two crime scenes."

McCabe turned and looked at him. "A red poppy at the first, a tiger lily at the second. There are no poppies in *Alice*. But there is a poppy field in *The Wizard of Oz*. Dorothy falls asleep there."

"Hold on a minute. *The Wizard of Oz*?"

"Sorry. You missed that conversation. And I was too busy arguing my point about the phenol to bring it up during the task force meeting."

"To bring what up?"

"The conversation Pete Sullivan and I had when Lieutenant. Dole and I were in the Comm Center having a first look at the Jessup crime scene on the cam. Pete and I were discussing where the crime scene was in relation to the police kennel and horse stables and the community garden. And he mentioned the 'yellow brick road' out there—"

"Oh, yeah, I remember something about that. The bricks in the old bridge road."

"I wondered out loud to Pete if there might be some link to the case. *Alice in Wonderland*. *The Wizard of Oz*. But, as Pete pointed out, Vivian Jessup's body was not left on our yellow brick road."

"But," Baxter said, "since we're having our literary hour, we might as well have a look at Dorothy's poppy field."

"And get it out of the way," McCabe said. She did a quick search: "Dorothy. Poppy field."

The chapter came up on the wall.

McCabe said, "I had forgotten that. The title of the chapter."

"I never read the book. Just saw the movie when I was a kid."

"If you think about it," McCabe said, "it's kind of a scary story for kids." She read the title of the chapter out loud. " 'The Deadly Poppy Field.' "

Baxter got up and they stood there reading the chapter together.

He said, "So the Lion passes out from the poppy fumes and the Scarecrow and the Tin Woodsman have to leave him there in the field because he's too heavy to carry. And they're sorry that they have to leave him to die because he was a 'good comrade' even if he was 'cowardly.'"

"But they have been able to rescue Dorothy," McCabe said. "And they carry her to safety."

Baxter said, "Read that last line. 'They carried the sleeping girl to a pretty spot beside the river, far enough from the poppy field to prevent her breathing any more of the poison of the flowers, and here they laid her gently on the soft grass and waited for the fresh breeze to waken her.'" He grinned. "Think L. Frank Baum's trying to tell us something, partner?"

McCabe told herself not to get too excited. But a tingle went down her spine. "Okay. Vivian Jessup was left to sleep by a river . . . a stream . . . the Normanskill. And she had been put to sleep by a poison." She stared at Baxter, giving him a chance to stop them both from getting carried away. "But she didn't breathe the poison. She was injected with it. And Vivian Jessup played Alice, not Dorothy."

Baxter shrugged. "Alice. Dorothy. What's the dif? Both little girls are wandering around in wacky worlds. Maybe our killer likes both books."

"Or is as wacky as a fruitcake himself."

"I think that's drunk as a fruitcake," Baxter said.

"That would be rum cake, Michael." McCabe smiled at him. "Think we're punch-drunk."

"Or on a sugar-substitute high. But I also think we just might be onto something."

"Maybe," McCabe said. "The water might explain why Jessup's body was dumped where it was. But he didn't move the first two bodies."

"Because it was too late to save them," Baxter said.

"Except he's the one who killed them. And there's nothing to indicate he tried to revive Jessup."

Baxter shook his head. "I give up. You're determined to shoot down my brilliant theory. Ready to order a pizza and get some protein?"

"Yeah," McCabe said. "I think we need it." She went back over to her desk and sat down in her chair. "When we try running this particular theory by the task force tomorrow morning, Agent Francisco . . ."

"Guess we'd better work on it some more."

"The movie that the TA showed the girls that day at the science camp. I had a note to myself that we should ask Mrs. Giovanni if she knew what it was."

"We can be pretty sure it wasn't *Lolita*," Baxter said. He was on his ORB, ordering the pizza. "Are you an anchovies, woman?"

"No," McCabe said. "But I don't mind if you have them on your half. Pepperoni for me."

"You going to call Sharon's mom?"

"Might as well. Even though the odds that she'll know the answer to the question aren't that good. But, since it was a science camp, I think we can rule out movies about little girls in fantasy worlds."

"Not necessarily. They might have been studying special effects."

"The name of the movie?" Mrs. Giovanni said, sounding puzzled and looking confused. "I don't know. Is it important?"

"Probably not," McCabe said. "Don't worry about it. We'll be in touch if—"

"Oh, no, wait!" Mrs. Giovanni waved her hand to make sure McCabe wouldn't cut her off. "Wait. They might be able to tell you at the library."

"The library?" McCabe said.

"I remember Sharon said the teaching assistant told them she was late that morning because she'd had to wait until the library opened to pick up the movie. It was an old black-and-white movie and the teacher couldn't find a copy to buy."

"Any idea which library?" Baxter asked.

"Which library?" Mrs. Giovanni looked confused again. "The . . . I assumed she meant the one on Washington Avenue. That's the one Sharon used to go to. But I don't . . . She could have meant one of the branches."

"We'll find the right one," McCabe said. "The movie itself—did Sharon say anything about what the movie was about?"

A pause, then a nod. "Ants. The movie was about ants."

"Ants?" Baxter said.

"Sharon said that girl who was teasing the other girl . . . when the teaching assistant went out into the hall to talk on the phone . . . the mean girl asked the poor girl she was teasing if she'd like some big old ants like that in her pants. And then she whispered something in her ear. That was when the other girl ran out of the room."

"Thank you, Mrs. Giovanni," McCabe said. "You've been a great help."

"I'm glad. I don't know what I've told you, but I'm glad if I've helped."

McCabe said good-bye and turned to Baxter. "To quote you, Mike, 'bingo.' "

"A movie about ants?" he said. Where does that get us? Back to Ted Thornton's memo on his check about the Charlton Heston movie?"

"Maybe. But, even more important, it might also get us the teaching assistant's name. If she checked out a movie—"

"She would have had to use her library card," Baxter said, grinning. "I'm slow sometimes, but eventually I get there."

"A black-and-white movie about ants shouldn't be too hard to identify."

"I bet it was one of those 1950s sci-fi movies. You know, the kind with the giant insects."

"That would make sense," McCabe said. "As I recall, *The Naked Jungle,* the Charlton Heston movie, is in color. A black-and-white sci fi movie would be perfect for a summer science camp. Unless they went serious and showed them an old documentary."

"I'm betting on the sci-fi movie."

"Okay, you're on. Winner springs for lunch tomorrow." McCabe glanced at the clock on the wall. It was almost three o'clock. "This is October, right?"

"Last time I checked."

"Just making sure. As I said, I'm getting punchy. In fall, the public libraries go back to their regular Sunday-afternoon schedule. They're closed on Sunday during the summer."

"I'll take your word for it. I haven't been in a library in a while."

"I do occasional book runs for my dad," McCabe said. She picked up her ORB and touched the icon for Research. "We'd better check the university libraries, too, just to be safe. They have film collections."

"Problem, though. Even if we can identify the movie, there is the little difficulty of getting a library to tell us who checked it out."

"All we can do is go to the ADA on that one. I'm not holding my breath that the library will give us the information, but— Kelsey? Hi, it's Hannah McCabe. We need some help finding a movie title. . . ."

They might not be able to get the library to give them the name of the patron who had checked out the movie, but, McCabe thought, this felt like real progress.

"Not going to happen," Mark Paxton said. He was the ADA on duty. McCabe had called him after speaking to the lieutenant and getting clearance.

"Mark, can't you even—"

"Is this related to a terrorist threat or a matter of national security?"

"I've told you—"

"That you're fishing for a name of someone who might be somehow involved in your murder investigation. Not going to happen. Libraries do not open their patron records unless it's a matter of national security."

"Then there's no way we can get the name?"

"Unless you find another patron who was at that library on the day in question and happens to recall seeing who checked out the movie."

"Okay, I get the picture." She sighed. "No pun intended."

"Look, I'm sorry, Hannah. But no point in wasting your time or mine. Call me if there's anything I really can help with."

"Thanks."

"No go?" Baxter said.

"Only if we can find an observant patron who happened to see the transaction in question and can provide the name."

Baxter tilted back his head and stared up at the ceiling. "We could try to get any surveillance video the library has for the parking lot that morning. Of course, we're talking nine years ago."

"And if they haven't long since recorded over or tossed it, if they knew why we wanted it, we'd still need the FBI with a national security subpoena in hand."

Baxter sighed. "See this is the kind of stuff Howard Miller complains about. Eleven years of lefty liberals in the White House, stacking the Supreme Court, and law enforcement has to jump through hoops to get anything done."

"Lucky for him, or he and some of his buddies would be under indictment," McCabe said. "Any other bright ideas?"

"Traffic-cam videos," Baxter said. "But they aren't stored."

"And if we're talking about the main library on Washington Avenue, that parking lot is in back. It faces houses. Unless our teaching assistant went out of the lot and back up the hill onto Washington, the only cameras would probably have been the ones in the library lot."

Baxter twirled in his chair. "Okay, let's say she did go out of the parking lot and head back up onto Washington Avenue. We've got businesses on both sides of the street. A bank across the street."

"And we're still talking about surveillance video from nine years ago." McCabe shoved her hands through her hair and pulled it away from her scalp. "We're so close. It feels like we're so damn—"

"A television camera crew," Baxter said.

"You know what a long shot this is," McCabe said, but she reached for her ORB again.

"The library's in downtown Albany. If we're lucky, some newsworthy event was happening that morning."

McCabe said, "Lieutenant Dole, sorry, it's me again. The ADA says no chance on the library patron information, but Mike had another idea. We're thinking television camera crews. If one happened to be in the area that morning . . . Yes, sir, I know if we ask for the information . . . I know . . . Yes, sir, that sounds like a good idea."

"Well?" Baxter said.

"He's going to call Jacoby. He thinks Jacoby might be able to get the local stations to cooperate without having to promise them too much."

"Assuming they won't do it out of civic-mindedness."

"Assuming that." McCabe shook her head. "This is such a long shot."

Baxter grinned. "We've been good. Done our chores and brushed our teeth. We're due for another break right about now."

They got their break. It came later that evening. Lieutenant Dole tagged McCabe at home to tell her that the commander and Jacoby had talked and Jacoby had reached out to the local television stations. One of them had been so eager to get a jump on the competition that it had initiated an immediate search of its archives for any relevant footage. And the archivist found video of a camera crew covering the setup for a championship wrestling match at the City Armory. The crew had been doing interviews with fans and passersby while also filming the arena setup.

When she finished reading the message, McCabe reminded herself that they would have the car they were looking for only if their teaching assistant had driven past the library or had parked in the lot in back of the library and then gone up the hill and onto Washington Ave en route to the summer science camp on Madison. But at least they had video from which they could try to pull license numbers and hope for a match with a female driver who would have been in her late teens or early twenties.

Unless she had been driving someone else's car or had taken the bus or gotten a ride with her boyfriend.

But they had at least a shot at finding what they were looking for.

The television station had already sent over the video. McCabe debated getting dressed again and going back to the station.

But she was exhausted, and she knew Baxter must be, too.

She sent him a tag, letting him know his idea had paid off. Then she went out into the kitchen and made herself a turkey sandwich and a cup of cocoa.

The house was quiet because Pop was out. He'd gone down to the City for a reunion with an old buddy from his days as a foreign correspondent. "An overnighter," he had said in the note she had found on the bulletin board. "So don't wait up."

Truth be told, she was glad to have the house to herself. Pop wasn't hard to live with, rarely played the heavy father. She did what she wanted and he did what he wanted, and they were company for each other. But now and then, it was nice to have the place to herself and enjoy the solitude.

Pop probably felt the same way when she spent the occasional night out, so she felt no guilt about thinking it.

McCabe settled down on the sofa in the living room in her cotton nightgown and robe. Stocking feet on the coffee table, she brought up the movie menu.

According to Research, the movie that the teaching assistant had picked up had probably been *Them!* It had been, and still was, in the Albany Public Library catalog.

She owed Baxter lunch. He had bet it was a sci-fi movie, not a documentary.

According to the description from Research, the movie was about giant ants, mutants produced by nuclear radiation.

McCabe scanned through "classic sci-fi."

There it was.

She read the notes and settled in to see how the New Mexico State Police and the FBI would handle the infestation.

"Okay, that's why the teacher chose this movie," McCabe said out loud when the father-daughter team of entomologists arrived to provide their expertise. "A female scientist. Dr. Kincaid's 1950s counterpart."

Of course, the downside of a movie about giant ants was that it might give sensitive children nightmares. But presumably girls of between twelve and fourteen had been way too sophisticated to be frightened by a black-and-white movie made in 1954.

Still, the giant ants were pretty good. According to the notes, the special effects had been nominated for an Oscar.

McCabe took another bite of her turkey sandwich and settled back for some mindless entertainment that had nothing to do with the case, other than one girl's taunt to another: "Want those big old ants in your pants?"

Had Bethany Clark, middle-school bully, improved with age? What they knew was that she had worked as a waitress and, during her off-hours, she had liked to party with what her sister had described as her "wild friends."

But there was nothing to indicate Bethany's friends had been any wilder than other young people their age.

At age twenty-two, Bethany Clark had been a beautiful young woman. But had she been kinder than she was when she was thirteen, skinny, and awkward?

When the movie was over, McCabe decided, she'd read through the entries on Bethany's social network node again. At first glance, there hadn't been much there. But maybe, with the additional information they had, some throwaway remark would stand out this time around.

McCabe wiggled her toes and took a sip of her cocoa. Not the appropriate drink for a warm evening in October, but the house was on cooldown. And with luck, even if other people were doing the same thing, the Northeast would make it through the night and right through December without a repeat of the three-day blackout they'd had in the spring.

22

"Mike, look at this," McCabe said when Baxter walked into the bull pen the next morning.

"What? The video from the TV station?"

"No, I was waiting on you to get started with that. But I found a really interesting entry on Bethany's Web node."

"I thought you said you and O'Connell had gone through all those already."

"We did. But I thought I'd look again now that we know about the science camp." McCabe highlighted the entry on the wall. "Read this."

Baxter read out loud: "THE DIET GODS WILL PUNISH SIN- NERS. Really wanted hot fudge sundae today. Swore I'd do another thirty crunches at gym. Broke down and stopped at place out on Wolf Road. Cute guy working counter. Decided to sit at table outside even if it was hot. Then realized had forgotten to get water. Went back inside. Came back and ANTS crawling ALL OVER my sundae. TOTALLY GROSSED OUT. Little brats at next table laughing like hilarious. Diet gods laughing, too.'"

Baxter finished reading. "When did she write this?"

"August eighth, 2019," McCabe said. "A few weeks before she was killed. I wonder how the ants got on her sundae."

"The kids were giggling. Maybe they did it. Or maybe the ants were on the table and rushed for the sundae as soon as she walked away."

"Maybe," McCabe said. "Or maybe someone else scooped up the ants from the ground and sprinkled them on Bethany's sundae. Maybe nobody was paying attention but the kids, and they thought it was a good joke. And anyway, you hop in your car and you're out of there."

"But what's the point?" Baxter said, sitting down in his desk chair. "If she thinks the ants got on the sundae on their own, then what's the point?"

"If it's a message and she didn't get it the first time, maybe you send it again."

"Okay. Does she mention ants again?"

"No. I did a search, and ants only come up in this one entry."

"Does she mention anything else that seems odd now that we know about the science camp?"

"Nothing that jumps out at me so far. But it's going to take me another couple of hours to finish rereading."

Baxter took a sip of the iced coffee he had brought in. "You really think the ant thing means something?"

McCabe shrugged. "I have ants on the brain. I watched that movie last night. *Them!*"

"Great movie, right? I saw it years ago, when I was a kid."

"And you probably recalled that movie had a female scientist."

Baxter grinned. "That's why I was betting they'd watched a movie instead of a dull old documentary about ants. So let's see if we've got anything on the TV station video."

"We're going to need help from the lab to see what we have."

"Task force meeting this morning. After we take a first look, maybe we can get some help from the State Police."

. . .

By that afternoon, they were at the State Police lab with Whitman, the investigator assigned to the task force. He had helped them to expedite the forensic examination of the video from the television station.

Cahill, the lab tech, was manipulating the images on the screen. The license plates of the cars on Washington Avenue between 8:30 and 9:30 that morning nine years ago were being scanned into the database.

Within seconds, the driver's license photos of the registered drivers who fit the criteria appeared on the screen.

"Six possibles," Baxter said.

Two of the possibles were black, the other four white.

"No one's mentioned the teaching assistant's race," McCabe said. "I should have thought to ask Jean Lockhart. Mrs. Giovanni and Bethany Clark's sister didn't meet her, but if the teaching assistant wasn't white, someone would probably have mentioned that to them."

"How do you figure that?" Baxter said.

"Because nine years ago, white was the default setting for race. If a person wasn't white, a white person would be inclined to mention his or her race, especially in a situation like this one. If this doesn't work, we should check with the people we've interviewed just to make sure they weren't all being politically correct by not mentioning that the bungling teaching assistant was black."

"Politically correct because you're black?" Whitman said.

"That sometimes happens," McCabe said, not getting into the biracial discussion. "Anyway, let's look at the four white possibles first."

It took less than half an hour to locate all six of the young female drivers in the database. Within the next hour, they had reached four of the six. All denied having worked as a teaching assistant in a science camp back in 2010. The husband of the fifth, reached at Albany

Med, said that his wife was in labor. Between contractions, she informed them she didn't know what they were talking about and didn't care. The sixth possible was in London, where she had been living and working for the past three years. McCabe left a tag asking the woman to contact her or Baxter. But when they reached her mother, she said her daughter had never been a teaching assistant.

"One of them could be lying," Baxter said.

Whitman said, "None of them sounded like it. But we can dig some more."

"Maybe we've struck out," McCabe said.

"Or maybe not," Cahill, the lab tech, said. "I know you guys are interested in cars, but I've been playing around with the video, and I might have something. The camera angle's bad, but I've managed to enhance the image. This is an image in the side mirror of the TV mobile van."

They gathered around her, peering at the blurred image of a woman walking away from the main entrance of the library. Her hair was caught up in a ponytail under a baseball cap, which threw her face into shadow. She was slender, wearing a short denim skirt, T-shirt, and sandals. She had something in her hand that she was putting into the tote bag she was carrying.

Cahill zoomed in.

Baxter said, "Damn, woman, you're good."

Cahill pushed back her lank brown hair and smiled. "See what's in her hand. That looks like a VCR container to me."

"Me, too," McCabe said."And that's what we're looking for. The library had retained some of the old movies in that format. For which we should be grateful. A DVD would have been harder to spot."

"Hey, what's that writing on the bag she's carrying?" Whitman asked.

"Let's have a look," Cahill said.

She manipulated the image until the Gothic white lettering on the black cloth tote bag was visible.

"*The Next Man*," McCabe said. "Wasn't there a play with that title?"

"Don't ask me," Whitman said. "I don't do theater."

"Easy enough to find out," Cahill said. She pulled up her search engine. "Here we go. *The Next Man* opened on Broadway in November 2009."

"Okay," Whitman said. "We've got a dead Broadway actress. And now we have a teaching assistant walking around with a tote bag from a play."

"If she is our TA," McCabe said.

"I'd bet good money on it," Baxter said. "Next question: Was Vivian Jessup in that play?"

"Yes, she was," said Cahill. "Here she is in the cast list."

"I think we just hit pay dirt," Whitman said.

Baxter grinned at McCabe. "Do I get to choose the restaurant?"

"Yes," McCabe said. "Now, would you like to have a go at telling us what this is all about?"

"You got me there, partner."

"Whatever it's about," Whitman said, "it looks like you might be right that our serial killer hasn't been choosing his victims at random."

McCabe glanced at the screen. "Or, maybe, her victims." McCabe smiled at Cahill. "That really was incredible work. Would you give us a copy of the image and the info that you found on the play?"

"Coming right up."

"What next?" Whitman asked as they were walking down the hall. "We still need to identify the teaching assistant."

"If you were the director of a summer science camp, how would you go about finding a TA?" McCabe said.

"Check with the local colleges," Whitman said.

Baxter said, "College science programs."

"We have at least eight or nine colleges in the immediate area. All of them have science programs." Whitman said. "The director of the science camp might have come from one of those programs, too."

"Definitely," McCabe said. "And I think that it would also be a good idea to follow up with Meredith Noel, the theater professor at

UAlbany. She might have some thoughts about Vivian Jessup and *The Next Man*."

"Okay," Whitman said. "While you two are doing that, I'll work on the college science programs angle."

This time, they met with Meredith Noel in her office in the Department of Theatre Productions. She looked a little uncertain about finding herself talking to police detectives again.

McCabe said, "We're sorry to bother you again, Professor Noel. But we're hoping you can help us. We looking for information about a play that Ms. Jessup appeared in."

"Oh, I see," Noel said. "Which play?"

"*The Next Man*."

Noel shrugged. "A mediocre play, But Vivian was wonderful in it."

"According to what we've been able to find, the backer of the play was a business mogul named Richard Osmond."

Noel hesitated, then said, "When we talked before, I didn't want to gossip, but now that this has come up . . ."

"Now that what has come up, Professor Noel?" McCabe said.

"When I mentioned the Dalí edition of *Alice in Wonderland* that Vivian had when she first moved to New York . . . the one that was stolen in the burglary . . ."

"What about it?" Baxter said.

"I think that Richard Osmond may have been the friend who gave it to her. We had dinner together last week . . . that would have been on Tuesday. My husband was out of town, so we kicked off our shoes and let our hair down." She smiled slightly. "Although I was more than a little astonished when I stopped to think about it, that I was sharing a girlfriends' night with Vivian Jessup."

"And while you were having this girlfriends' night, she said something about the Dalí edition?" Baxter said.

"She was telling me about her career, and she mentioned a 'wonderful but very married man named Richard' who had helped her when she first arrived in the City and who had been there for her over the years."

"And you think Richard Osmond might have been the friend she was referring to?" McCabe said.

"Vivian said this man had died a few years ago and she still missed him." Noel looked from McCabe to Baxter. "Osmond died a few years ago of a heart attack."

"Do you know what happened to his wife?" Baxter asked.

Noel said, "I looked it up. She remarried less than a year later. Her new husband is an old family friend."

"According to the bio we saw," McCabe said, "Osmond and his wife had no children."

"I think that's right," Noel said. She ran her fingers through her spiky hair. "You do know that he was Ted Thornton's mentor? The reason Ted Thornton came up here to Albany."

Baxter said. "We did see Thornton listed as one of Osmond's business associates. But Detective McCabe and I don't keep up enough with the wheeling and dealing of the financial world to be up on the details."

"Neither do I," Noel said. "I was just curious enough to look Osmond up. And that was when I saw his connection to Ted Thornton."

"And you were already aware of Thornton's friendship with Vivian Jessup," McCabe said.

"Yes," Noel said. "But I don't think . . . I think any romantic relationship she had with Osmond was over long before she met Ted Thornton. And I'm not even sure that she and Ted Thornton were ever involved in that way. So I didn't want to gossip."

"We understand," McCabe said. "There is something else we'd like to ask about. Would you be able to tell us if one of your theater students had worked as a TA in a summer science camp back in 2010?"

"Good grief, that's almost ten years ago. I've only been here seven years. And it's not the kind of information that would be recorded anywhere unless a student put it on his or her vita or in a funding application. You might be able to get Ian's secretary to try to look it up. But why would you think one of our students would be working at a science camp?"

"We have a theater connection that we're trying to follow up," McCabe said. "We have a young woman on a video from 2010 who we think was the TA at the summer camp that our first two victims attended as kids. In the video, she's carrying a tote bag with the title of the play we asked about."

"You mean *The Next Man?*"

"That's the play," Baxter said.

"But anyone who attended the play . . . or didn't . . . might have picked up a tote bag. It was probably available as a promotion. And with a title like that, it's the kind of accessory a young woman might enjoy carrying around."

"To get her flirt on?" Baxter said.

"You could put it that way," Noel said.

"All good points," McCabe said. "But we were hoping we'd get lucky and someone here would know the young woman we're looking for."

"Sorry I can't help. But if you really think she might have been one of our students, you might ask Ian to have his secretary look through the files."

McCabe slid out of her comfortable armchair. "Thanks. We'll do that on our way out."

When they stopped in his office to ask, Ian Carmichael shook his head. "Before my time, too. But Maude might know."

He went to the door and called his secretary in from her desk in the outer office.

When he had repeated their question to Maude, she said, "I can go through the files. But it might take a while."

"Thank you," McCabe said. "We hate to put you to the trouble, but this is rather important."

Maude frowned. "Did you say I'm looking for one of our students who worked as a TA at a science camp? You did say science?"

"Yes," McCabe said. "Did you think of something—"

"There was this student . . . it must have been at least that long ago . . . she had this boyfriend who was a TA for a biology course. I remember because he came into the office once with a lab specimen in a glass jar. It was really disgusting-looking."

"Was the student . . . your theater student, was she dark-haired?"

"She was always changing her hair. Streaks of color, wigs, feathers . . . whatever she felt like when she got up that morning . . . and clothes to match. That child was born for the stage, but I can't imagine why anyone would have hired her to be a teaching assistant at a science camp."

"But would you check her file to see if someone did?" McCabe said.

"It would help if I could remember her name," Maude said. "I ought to recognize it when I see it on the list of students from that year."

"If she's the person we're looking for," McCabe said. "Her first name would have been Deirdre."

"Unless she was in the habit of changing her name, too," Baxter said.

"They've been know to do that," Maude said. "Theater students like trying on stage names."

Ian Carmichael said, "I've got a meeting, but I'm leaving you in good hands with Maude."

He picked up his briefcase and went out the door.

At her desk, Maude flicked through files, making an occasional mumbled comment.

"Here we go," Maude said. "Deirdre Chase. That was the child's name."

"Bingo," Baxter said to McCabe.

The young woman in the photo was smiling, wearing a white blouse with ruffles under a plaid vest. A tam set at a jaunty angle atop her dark shoulder-length hair.

"Nothing about a science camp in her file," Maude said. "But that doesn't mean anything."

"Do you happen to have her present address?" McCabe asked.

"The last time she updated her contact information was in 2017. She was moving around quite a bit before that, so this address may not be current. She hasn't responded recently to our alumni contacts."

"When did she graduate?" McCabe said.

"Spring semester, 2011."

"Could we have the address from 2017?" Baxter said. "That'll give us somewhere to start."

They went back to the station and tried the contact information that they had for Deirdre Chase.

"No go," McCabe said. "Let's get Research to see what they can do."

While they were waiting, Whitman from the State Police called. He had struck out so far on finding a science program at UAlbany or at a local college where someone remembered a student who had worked as a TA at a science camp.

McCabe told him about Deirdre Chase. He sounded almost as pleased as they were. "We're getting there," he said. "I'm still waiting for several people to get back to me. Maybe we'll be able to locate the summer camp director, too."

"Or, if we have the wrong Deirdre on this end," McCabe said, "maybe one of your leads will pan out."

Whitman said he was on his way home and would check in with them tomorrow.

"Maybe we should go home, too," Baxter said, stretching.

McCabe nodded. "No point in putting in overtime when there's nothing else we can do."

She was straightening up her desk when her ORB buzzed. "McCabe," she said.

She listened and then signaled to Baxter, who had stopped to see who it was. "Thank you. That's terrific."

"Got it," she said to Baxter. "Research found Deirdre Chase in Seattle. She's with a repertory theater company."

"Three hours earlier there, so that makes it about three-fifteen. Want to try her?"

McCabe nodded. "Let's see if we have anything."

When they reached the theater, Chase was in rehearsal. The stagehand McCabe spoke to promised to give her the message.

McCabe and Baxter settled down to wait.

Chase called them back about forty-five minutes later. "The science summer camp. God, I hadn't thought about that in years."

"Then you were a TA at the camp?" McCabe said to the woman, whose streaky blond hair was in beaded braids.

Chase nodded. "I was the only TA. Kevin, my boyfriend at the time, was a biology major, and he had seen the flyer posted on the bulletin board. They were looking for a science major, but the flyer emphasized they wanted someone who was mature and competent and good with children. Kevin promised to help me bone up on any science stuff I needed to know. But he said I would be a teacher's assistant and the girls were only twelve- to fourteen-year-olds, so there wouldn't be a lot that I'd have to do that I wouldn't be able to figure out."

"So you applied?" Baxter said.

Chase grinned. "And charmed the director's support hose off. I told her all about how my grandfather had been a doctor and I had loved spending time with him when I was a child. That much was true."

"And she thought you'd be good with the girls?" McCabe asked.

"Kevin was right. They had several teachers. All they wanted the TA to do was to be in the classroom when a teacher had to step out and to help set up experiments and go along on field trips." Chase tilted her head. "But what is this about? If you went to all this trouble to find me, it must be something important."

McCabe nodded. "We'd like to ask you about something that happened during the science camp. We understand you left after an incident involving a student who ran away."

Chase grimaced. "Among the first of my many jobs that turned into minor or major disasters. The only place I'm competent is in a theater." She shook her head, setting her beaded braids swaying. "When the other girls told me that she'd left, I went running out after her and couldn't find her. That was seriously scary. I deserved to be fired over that one."

"Can you tell us about what happened?"

Chase said, "Yes. But first, why don't you tell me what this is about? I've got two police detectives in Albany interested in the fact that I was a TA at a science camp nine years ago. Before I say anything else, tell me what's going on."

McCabe caught Baxter's glance in her direction. "We're investigating three murders, Ms. Chase. They seem to be the work of a serial killer and—"

"Wait. Does this have something to do with Vivian Jessup?"

"Then you've heard about her murder?" Baxter said.

"Even out here in Seattle. But I missed the early news reports. I was at a workshop over the weekend," Chase said. 'When I got back, I heard that Vivian Jessup had died . . . been murdered. And that it had happened in Albany and they thought a serial killer . . ." She turned pale. "My God, what does this have to do with the science camp? Why are you—"

"Ms. Chase," McCabe said. "Just take a deep breath, and I'll try to explain. Okay?"

Chase nodded. "Yes. Okay."

"The first two victims, Bethany Clark and Sharon Giovanni, were students at the summer science camp—"

"Oh my God. Oh God." Chase was on her feet. "I . . . They were the two girls who—"

A man's voice said, "Dee? What's all the commotion?"

"Vivian Jessup," Chase said to him. "The serial killer who . . . I knew the first two victims when they were kids."

"Jeez." The man came into view and clasped Chase in his arms.

"Ms. Chase," McCabe said. "Ms. Chase, please, we do need to ask you some questions."

Chase turned back toward them. "I want David to stay. This is David, another actor here and a good friend."

"All right," McCabe said, realizing Chase would tell him about the conversation anyway. "But Mr.—"

"Jahn," he said.

"Mr. Jahn, please treat this conversation as confidential."

He nodded. "I understand. My father's a lawyer. But, of course, I'm only here as Dee's friend. I don't have a law degree."

"And we are not questioning Ms. Chase as a suspect at this time. We are only interested in learning more about what happened at the summer science camp where she was a TA."

Deirdre Chase finished blotting her eyes with tissues from the box that Jahn had handed her and sniffed. "I'm sorry to go to pieces like that. But this is . . . it's really awful."

McCabe said, "We understand. But we hope that with your help we can figure out what's going on."

"You said Bethany and Sharon were the first two victims."

"Yes. And we haven't been able to find anyone who can tell us in detail about the teasing incident."

"You think what happened . . . their being murdered was because of that?"

"We don't know why they were murdered. All we know is that they both attended the science camp and that the TA, who we have now confirmed was you, reprimanded Sharon and another girl, who we believe was Bethany Clark, for teasing a third."

Chase nodded. "Yes, it was Bethany. I felt bad about Sharon because Bethany admitted she was the one who had been teasing Johnnie Mae and—"

McCabe said, "Was that Johnny with a *y*?"

"No, with an *i* and an *e*. Johnnie Mae Dupree," Chase said. "Bethany teased her about that name, too. Johnnie Mae's mother was from the South. Louisiana or somewhere."

"The board member we spoke to thought that the name—which she couldn't remember—might have been the combination of the two parents' names."

Chase said, "No, Johnnie Mae said her mother had named her after a singer that her mother used to like. I made the mistake of commenting on her name when I was getting to know them. Bethany jumped right on that."

Baxter was on his ORB. He said, "Would the singer have been Johnnie Mae Matthews, a soul singer from Detroit?"

Chase said, "I don't remember the singer's last name. But I know Bethany looked it up and then she teased Johnnie Mae some more because the singer was a black woman."

"So all three girls were white?" McCabe said.

"I think Johnnie Mae was biracial. I know her mother was white. Or at least she seemed to be when she came to camp that day looking for my head. But her father, who I gathered had left or died or something, he might have been black or biracial. Johnnie Mae was olive-skinned, with wavy black hair and dark brown eyes and a cute little figure. Which explains why skinny Bethany hated her."

McCabe said. "But it seems Bethany turned out to be a late bloomer."

"Did she?" Chase said, and then shook her head. "Not that it helped her. I can't believe she and Sharon, too . . . Sharon seemed like a sweet girl. Bethany got her into trouble by showing her the drawing that she'd done of Johnnie Mae. I didn't know poor Sharon was an innocent bystander until I had them both out in the hall."

"Tell us about later, when you left the classroom and Johnnie Mae ran away," Baxter said.

Chase said, "I wish I could claim it was all my ex-boyfriend's fault." She balled up the tissue in her hand. "He texted me that he had an emergency. I went out into the hall to call him back. He was trying to reach me because he couldn't find his lucky pen and he had a job interview that afternoon. He wanted to know if I had seen his pen or had it."

McCabe nodded. The same story that the board member had told them.

"So you finished the call and then went back into the classroom?" she said.

"And I started the movie that I was supposed to show them. But there was a weird vibe, and I asked what was going on. And someone pointed to Johnnie Mae's seat and I realized she was gone. And Sharon said Bethany had been teasing her and had whispered something in her ear and Johnnie Mae had jumped up and run out of the other door."

"What happened then?" Baxter asked.

"I told them all to stay in their seats, not to move a muscle. And I ran out to look for Johnnie Mae. When I couldn't find her, I went to tell the teacher for that session. Everyone panicked, and they decided the only thing to do was to call the police, because it would be worse if something happened to her and they hadn't called."

McCabe said, "So a report was made to the police?"

"The camp director was going to call, but then she decided she should call Dr. Kincaid, the chairperson of the board, first. I'm not sure what happened after that. If they called the police or not. The teacher who was running that session and I went out in her car to see if we could find Johnnie Mae."

"When did you find out Johnnie Mae had been located?" Baxter asked.

"Not until we got back. We had driven all over town and gone out to Crossgates Mall and Colonie Center and everywhere we could think of a kid might hop on a bus and go. When we got back to the camp, the other girls had gone home for the day. The director told us that she had finally been able to reach Johnnie Mae's sister. The sister said that Johnnie Mae had called her and she was all right. The sister and her boyfriend were on their way to pick her up."

That, too, matches what we heard from the board member, McCabe thought.

"What happened after that?" she asked.

"The director, Mrs. Nash, gave me this look and told me we would talk about this tomorrow. And I got the hell out of there as fast as I could."

"The director's first name?" McCabe asked.

"Oh . . . I don't remember," Chase said. "I only remember her last name because it was the same as the last name of my best friend in preschool."

"What about the teacher of the session you were monitoring?"

"Campbell, like the soup. I think her first name might have been Karen or Carol. Something like that."

"Do you know where either of them worked during the rest of the year?" Baxter said.

"I think Mrs. Nash used to be a high school biology teacher and then she was an administrator of some kind. But she had retired. And Mrs. Campbell had been teaching somewhere else, but her husband got transferred to Albany, and she was working those two weeks at the camp while she looked for a full-time teaching job for fall."

"Do you know what her husband did?" McCabe asked.

"No. Worked for some company."

"Okay," McCabe said. "Would you take us through what happened the next day?"

"I had been awake most of the night. Had a big argument with my boyfriend and then ate and cried and ate some more. So I was feeling really lousy when I got to camp. Mrs. Nash called me to her office, and three members of the board were there. They wanted me to tell them in my own words what had happened in the classroom."

"Was the teacher there, too?" Baxter asked.

"She had already spoken to them. They wanted to see me alone."

"Go on," McCabe said.

"I had just gotten to the part about returning to the classroom and finding Johnnie Mae gone when her mother arrived. She was yelling and cursing outside the conference room. Mrs. Nash's assistant came in and told her who it was. Then Dr. Kincaid, the chairperson of the board, told Mrs. Nash to let Mrs. Dupree come in."

"What happened then?"

"The board members tried to make nice and tell Mrs. Dupree how sorry they were for what had happened. I said I was sorry, too. But Mrs. Dupree was yelling and cursing and threatening to sue."

"Did she seem to be intoxicated?" McCabe asked.

"Or maybe on some kind of drug. Not completely out of it. But really hyper. She yelled and screamed and said they—the board members—would be hearing from her lawyer."

"What happened then?"

"She stormed out. And it was really quiet for what seemed like forever. And then Mrs. Nash said she'd like to speak to me outside. That was when she told me that I was fired." Chase smiled without humor. "I knew it was coming, but it still hurt. I started crying, and she said she was sorry but that she and the board had no other choice."

Her friend David, who had been silent until then, said, "Sounds like they had planned to fire you all along. They didn't confer after the girl's mother showed up."

Exactly what McCabe had been thinking. "Did you finish out the day?" she said.

"No. I went and got my stuff and left right then. I was too humiliated even to ask for my paycheck."

"Did they remember to send it?"

"The next day, I received a special-delivery letter from Dr. Kincaid saying the situation had been regrettable but that they appreciated my hard work prior to the incident. She asked me to please be discreet and not discuss what had happened." Chase paused. "And there was a check enclosed for three times the salary that they had promised me for those two weeks."

"Sounds like they were willing to pay for your discretion," her friend David said.

"They didn't have to bother. It was too humiliating for me to go around talking about it."

"And no one other than the board members ever asked you about what had happened?" McCabe said.

"That was the last time I talked about it until now. I didn't even tell my friends and family what happened."

"What about your boyfriend, Kevin?" Baxter said.

Chase made a face. "Kevin and I were over. We'd had that big fight about the fact that he had sent me that 'urgent' message about his stupid pen. Especially when it turned out to have been in his jacket pocket the whole time."

"Ms. Chase, thank you for talking to us," McCabe said.

"You'll let me know what happens, right?" Chase said. "I mean if I need to hire a bodyguard or something in case this serial killer turns up out here."

"Yes, we'll let you know if we have any reason to believe you might be in danger," McCabe said. "In fact, we'll contact the police there, just to give them a heads-up."

"And I'll be around, too," Chase's friend David said, putting his arm around her again.

"Good," she said, giving him a watery smile.

Before they could forget they were still on-screen, McCabe said, "Ms. Chase, there is one more thing. *The Next Man* tote bag that you were carrying that morning when you picked up the video at the library. Where did you get it?"

"I'd talked Kevin into going down to the City to see the play a few weeks earlier."

"And Vivian Jessup was in the play on the day that you saw it?"

"Yes. She was one of the leads."

"I don't suppose you happened to get a chance to speak to her."

Chase shook her head. "I wanted to wait at the stage door, but we'd gone to the matinee and Kevin was starving. He wanted to get some dinner before we caught the train back to Albany. So I bought the tote bag and we left."

"So you never met Vivian Jessup?"

"I wish. I loved her. She was so great."

McCabe said, "I don't suppose Bethany, Sharon, or Johnnie Mae ever mentioned the play or Vivian Jessup."

"No . . . except Bethany asked about my tote bag. About what *The Next Man* meant. And I told her it was a play."

"Did you mention Vivian Jessup?"

"I don't . . . I think I mentioned the play was a musical and Vivian Jessup was playing a secretary in love with her boss. And Bethany said something like 'Who's Vivian Jessup?' "

"And what did you tell her?"

"That Vivian Jessup had played *Alice* in a musical when she was a kid and that now she was known as 'the Red Queen' and was a Broadway star."

"Did any of the three say anything when you told them that?" McCabe asked.

Chase smiled. "They looked completely unimpressed. Bethany even made a show of yawning."

"Thank you," McCabe said. "We'll let you—Wait, one more thing. Did the movie *The Wizard of Oz* or the 'yellow brick road' here in Albany ever come up?"

"No," Chase said. "I know we didn't talk about that movie, and I didn't even know there was a yellow brick road in Albany. There is?"

"Check the Web. You'll see the node," McCabe said. "We will let you go now, but we'll be back in touch if there's anything else."

"Okay," Chase said. "I think I'm going to go find myself a drink."

"Not a bad idea," Baxter said once McCabe had disconnected. "How about debriefing the case over a couple of beers?"

"Thanks, but I'm about cased out right now. I'm going to send all the names that Chase gave us to Research and then head home."

23

McCabe stopped at the barricade across the Western Avenue entrance to Washington Park. A uniform she recognized was standing there. She waved to him.

He walked over to her car. "Hey, McCabe, how you doing?"

"Hi, Joe. Why's this entrance blocked?"

"They're filming a scene for another movie. Got Hollywood here every few months now, huh?"

"Yeah, we do. What's this one about?"

"Don't know. But the scene's supposed to be a family birthday celebration in the park. Kid runs and falls and knocks out a tooth. Mommy and Daddy get into a big argument about who should have been watching him. Mommy slaps Daddy for one of his comments. He punches her. Relatives of Mommy chase Daddy and beat him senseless. That's why they got the emergency vehicles." He grinned. "I hear it's supposed to be a comedy."

McCabe shook her head. "Sounds like it. Take it easy, Joe."

She waved and backed up, making a U-turn. Whenever she did that, she flashed to one of Pop's *Andy Griffith* reruns, with Gomer Pyle yelling, "Citizen's arrest!" when Deputy Barney Fife made a U-turn after giving Gomer a ticket.

Mayberry RFD. Safe, dull, and no daddy punching out mommy on a movie set in the park. No real-life droogie boys killing an old woman. No serial killer with who knew what motive on the prowl.

Of course, she would probably have died of boredom as a cop in Mayberry. Taking in the wash from the clothesline for a citizen wasn't quite her idea of "protecting and serving." She liked solving crimes.

But the downside was that every crime had its victim. And if you were a cop, you didn't just play Sherlock Holmes. You had to deal with victims who had been hurt by offenders who were sometimes victims themselves.

Take Gary Motley. Gary Motley, the armed burglar she had shot after he'd shot her brother. He'd had his own story. A single, hardworking mother who'd loved him and done the best she could. And his favorite teacher, who had sexually abused a smart, handsome little boy and left him angry and bitter. A life that had gone from bad to worse because nothing he had tried to do right had worked out as it should have.

And then he had broken into a house with a gun and shot someone and been shot and killed himself. By a nine-year-old girl. About the age he was the first time he'd been abused by his teacher.

Justice, McCabe thought, is a difficult commodity to come by. About as elusive as a star in another solar system.

McCabe heard the groan before she saw her father. He was stretched out on the sofa with an ice pack on his head.

"Pop? Are you okay?"

"Not so loud," Angus said. "Speak softly or not at all."

"Pop, you don't have a hangover. Tell me that you don't—"

"I won't tell you anything. Just be quiet."

McCabe opened her mouth and closed it again. She had learned as a child, watching her mother nag, that it was pointless to keep talking when her father wasn't prepared to listen. She would wait until he was back on his feet from what had obviously been a high old time in the City with his buddy. And then she would remind him about what his doctor had said about drinking after his bypass surgery. She would remind him, and he would do whatever he wanted to do anyway.

"I'm going to make myself some dinner," McCabe said. "I don't suppose you want any."

"No, I don't. And stay in the kitchen, so I don't have to smell it."

To distract herself from being aggravated, McCabe decided to make something more satisfying than a peanut butter and jelly sandwich.

She touched the countertop, pulling up the virtual drawer that contained her recipes. She wanted the one for pasta fagioli that she had gotten from Mrs. Castelleno, their next door neighbor.

Another minute to run a check of the required ingredients against what she had in the pantry and refrigerator.

All right. She was good to go.

Ten minutes prep time, forty minutes to cook the old-fashioned way. And soup on the table, with a crisp salad and garlic bread.

While she was eating, McCabe used the kitchen table as a wall for her ORB. She figured she might as well finish going through Bethany's node journal again.

If Bethany had been smart when she was thirteen, she was determined to downplay her intelligence as a twentysomething. She raved about the new job she'd gotten a few months earlier, still a server in a restaurant, but a more fun place to work. New job or not, her life seemed to be work, shopping, clubbing, and more of the same. Men were mentioned frequently, but none of them by proper names. And there was nothing that seemed to hint at a dangerous, potentially homicidal encounter.

But any man who had been interested in Bethany Clark would have had no trouble keeping track of her comings and goings. She had believed in keeping her public informed.

Another one of Pop's topics for rants. That the concept of privacy had vanished.

No expectation of privacy in public places with surveillance cameras everywhere. And no sense of what should be private among young people who believed everything should be shared, from holograms of the clothes they were trying on in a store to an instant critique of the sexual performance of the person they had just bedded.

"All right, Bethany," McCabe said, "do we have a real wacko serial killer? Or someone you pissed off long ago when you were a kid, who finally got revenge?"

"Stop talking to yourself," Angus said from the doorway, "and make me a cup of coffee, would you?"

"Busy, Pop. Make your own."

He grunted and started across the floor. "Showing your disapproval, are you?"

"Yes," McCabe said, "I am."

He made his coffee and came over and sat down in his chair at the table.

"Anything new on your case?"

"A lot more of the pieces, but no answers."

"Want to talk it through?"

"I've been doing that all day with Baxter. Right now, I just want to sit here and stare at Bethany Clark's journal and hope something will spring out at me."

"If she had known somebody was out to get her, she sounds like the kind of girl who would have made sure other people knew it."

"Unless the reason someone was out to get her was something she didn't want other people to know about."

"What have you got on her? And what happened with Ted Thornton? You were real curious about him the last time we talked."

"Pop, I can't—"

"Don't give me that 'I can't talk about it.' You were willing to talk when you wanted to pick my brain."

McCabe met his scowl. "I could use some more information. So let's horse-trade. I'll trade you an update for the answer to another question."

"Deal."

"You're still sworn to secrecy."

"Understood."

McCabe waved her hand, closing the display of Bethany's journal. This is what we know so far," she said.

When she was done, Angus looked as if his hangover was much improved. In fact, he was leaning forward, listening intensely.

He needs, McCabe thought, something to do with his time. Write the book or get out of the house and take up a hobby. Do something that occupies his mind.

"This is a doozy," he said. "We got a little bully who ends up being killed nine years later."

"But we don't know that was the reason she was killed. And Sharon was killed, too. She seems to have been an innocent bystander. And then there's Vivian Jessup."

Angus nodded and scrubbed at his day's beard with the back of his hand. "It all requires some thought."

"Exactly what Baxter and I have been doing," McCabe said. "So has the task force. With the aid of forensics and an FBI profiler. And we still haven't figured it out."

"Then you haven't been thinking about it right. Haven't been turning it on its head and looking at it upside down."

"I've been standing on my head and looking at it every way from Sunday. We all have."

"So, what do you want to ask me, Ms. Detective?"

"About what was going on in Albany back in 2010. What was happening in the city?"

"You were here."

"I know I was here. And I was on the job by then. But I wasn't really paying attention to things like Ted Thornton's move into the city. What else was going on that I might not have noticed?"

"If you'd been reading my newspaper, you'd know."

McCabe tilted her head at him. "You mean to tell me everything that you knew about what was going on actually ended up in the paper? Okay, I'll just pull up the archives and read it for myself."

Angus scowled at her. "Let me get my notes and see what I said about that year."

"Thanks, Pop."

24

New York City

In his penthouse apartment in Manhattan, Bruce Ashby was stretched out on his sofa, staring up at the ceiling. The skylight gave him a view of the night sky. The stars were out, sparkling after the thunderstorm that had passed through.

He thought of rousing Rufus, his sleeping bulldog, to go out for a walk. But he was too comfortable to move.

The downside of working for Ted was that on any given night, he could never be sure whether he would be at home in his own apartment or in Albany because Ted had decided he needed him there.

Ted's damn cat despised Rufus. The dog spent those nights when Ashby was in Albany with the woman who lived one floor down and was willing to walk Rufus with her own fox terrier, Fifi. "Boyfriend and girlfriend" she called the two dogs when she was being coy.

Ashby closed his eyes and considered his problem. Not Rufus and Fifi and her feather-brained mistress.

Lisa. Beautiful Lisa, who was, at least for the moment, Ted's fiancée.

Ted had always tended toward attractions. But Lisa was turning out to be more difficult to get rid of than the others.

Ted thought he was in love with her and was willing to overlook the discrepancies that Bruce had uncovered and dutifully reported to him.

Suddenly the great romantic, Ted said Lisa would tell him about her past when she was ready.

And she might. If she were around that long.

Ashby intended to make sure she wasn't around that long.

He smiled to himself, stretched his arms over his head, and went back to his contemplation of the view through his skylight.

If only he could send Lisa straight to the moon.

25

Angus looked up from his ORB and said, "I don't have to remind you that 2010 was the year that Faulkner retired as police chief and the mayor and the Common Council hired that hotshot from Connecticut to replace him."

McCabe grimaced. "No, you don't have to remind me of that. Community relations in Arbor Hill and the South End were already shaky when Faulkner left. And in less than a year, our hotshot new chief had even managed to alienate the middle-class folks in neighborhoods like Pine Hills and the campus district."

"And it still took another year to get rid of him."

"By then, the cops were ready to join the marches on City Hall. It wasn't any safer for us than for anyone else." She shook her head. "But he sure did look good on paper. And he sounded good at first."

"Fascists can be as charming as hell when they want to be," her father said. "Make all kinds of sense unless you're listening close."

McCabe smiled. "You said that in your editorials when you were demanding he be fired."

Angus scowled at her. "Didn't mean to make life hard for you with those editorials, daughter. Guess I never told you that."

"It was all right. By then, he had other things to worry about. Going after me wouldn't have helped his cause."

Angus nodded. "I knew you could handle yourself." He turned his attention back to his ORB. "Aside from the ruckus the police chief caused that year, let's see what else we've got."

"Not just crime, Pop. Anything that looks interesting."

"Understood."

"What was the mayor doing in 2010?"

"Living out in the suburbs. I don't have it here, but she and her husband didn't move into Albany until around late 2011 or early '12, when they bought that house and started renovating it. Then she decided to run for the Common Council."

McCabe said, "She rose up through city government pretty fast, didn't she?"

"Had the right connections. Having a husband who's a banker don't hurt."

"A banker. I hadn't thought about that. I wonder how that plays out with Ted Thornton."

"Money men always play together." Angus eyed her. "The mayor and her husband on your list of suspects now?"

"No, of course not. Or at least I don't think so. But Ted Thornton keeps turning up all over this. And he and the mayor do seem to be cozy."

"Maybe that's something for her husband to worry about, not you."

McCabe smiled. "She and Thornton did go on that canoe ride together. You think?"

"Never know."

"The mayor's an attractive woman. But I don't think she can compete with Ted Thornton's fiancée."

"That fiancée," Angus said. "Thornton better watch himself with her."

"Why do you say that, Pop?"

"Because if this were a forties movie, she'd be dangerous."

Because of Pop and his noir movies, that was exactly where

McCabe's mind had gone when she met Lisa Nichols. "Yes, she does have that look, doesn't she?"

Angus's attention was back on his notes. McCabe took a sip of her mango juice and waited. She was hoping he would produce magic from his notes the way he used to pluck a quarter from behind her ear when she wanted a gum ball.

"Have you ever thought of taking up your magic again?" she said.

"What are you talking about?"

"Like when I was a kid. You used to go to the hospital and entertain the kids in the children's ward."

"Kids don't believe in magic anymore. They got three-D and holograms. They know how everything works."

"Maybe. But you ought to think about it."

"You trying to get me out of the house? Give me some way to occupy my time?"

"Yes."

"I'll find something better than magic tricks. When I'm good and ready."

"As long as you're thinking about it. And giving some thought to writing your book."

"I thought you wanted to talk about Albany in 2010."

"I do."

"Then be quiet and listen."

"What do you have?"

"I have an entry in my notes about careless doctors and risking our lives. Turns out it was related to a story we did featuring one of your players."

"Who?"

"Clarence Redfield. He'd filed a lawsuit the year before, alleging the doctor who treated his father had engaged in malpractice. After he filed his suit, several other patients or their families came forward."

"Did they have a case?"

"Hell of a case. The doctor was incompetent. His insurance

company settled and the doctor turned in his license before it was taken away."

"What happened to Clarence Redfield's father?"

"Still alive when we did the story, but in bad shape. He had only a few months left."

"Do you have anything else on Clarence Redfield for that year?"

"Nothing else showing up. Other than his lawsuit, no one was paying attention to him at the time."

"And then he left town in 2011 and didn't come back until four years ago, when his mother was ill."

Angus said, "And no one was paying much attention to him then, either, until he started writing his crime thread."

"And by then his mother had died and he'd gotten married. And then his wife and baby died."

"What'd they die of?"

McCabe paused with her glass halfway to her mouth. "In child-birth."

"I know they died in childbirth. But what happened?"

"I'm not sure what happened."

"Guess if it was anything that Redfield thought the doctor did wrong, he would have filed another lawsuit."

McCabe put her glass down on the table. "As far as we know, he didn't file a lawsuit. But mothers and babies don't normally just die during childbirth, do they?"

"Tell that to mothers and babies in—"

"I mean here in the United States, Pop. Middle-class mothers and babies under a doctor's care. And after Redfield's experience with his father's doctor, you would think he would have been especially care-ful to make sure his wife's doctor was competent."

"Then I guess you probably want to find out why Redfield's wife and baby died anyway."

"Yeah, I guess I do want to find that out." McCabe got up from the table. "Thanks."

"Always here to provide you with information."

She kissed the top of his head. "And I don't know what I'd do without you, Pop."

"Don't go getting mushy on me. Any food left?"

"On the stove," McCabe said. "I made enough for dinner and your lunch tomorrow. I've got to go send a tag to Research."

Angus was sitting on the sofa in the living room, watching a movie, when she came downstairs. This time, it was John Wayne in *Rio Bravo*.

"The Duke?" McCabe said. "Did you take your antacid?"

"Angie Dickinson's in this one. I'm ignoring his politics."

"I'm going out for a while, Pop."

"Bring back some ice cream. Rocky Road."

"You might be in bed before I get back."

"Bring it anyway. If I don't get it tonight, I'll have it for breakfast in the morning."

"Okay. See you later."

The drive across town took less than twenty minutes.

McCabe glanced at the clock on her console. It was 8:57. She got out and locked her car door.

She let herself in through the terrace doors with her key.

As she stepped into the dimly lit room, strong arms snuggled around her from behind. "Glad you could make it."

She turned and smiled, hands going to his shoulders. "So am I. I've missed you."

"Good, because I've missed you, too."

"But we need to talk. Someone may know that we've been meeting. There was a tracker on my car."

He was silent for a moment. "Who do you think put it there?"

"It could have something to do with the serial killer case. Maybe Clarence Redfield."

"Or someone else." He touched her face. "I worry about you."

"I'm not the one who thinks midnight confabs with gang members is a good idea."

"I go where I have to. Sooner or later, I'm going to get them to the table."

McCabe shook her head. "If someone's been monitoring my movements, they may know about us."

"It's been almost three weeks since the last time we saw each other. Between your caseload and my trip out of town—"

"But we don't know how long I was being tracked."

"McCabe, this . . . the two of us . . . isn't actually illegal, you know. Only a few saintly souls would even consider our rendezvous immoral."

"I know. But we agreed that before we went public, we'd be sure—"

"That we aren't just having a fling."

"Because once people begin to realize we're involved—"

"If and when that information comes out, we'll both survive."

"We'll survive, but it would be better if we could decide if and how—"

"We may not have that option. Hey, could we continue this conversation later?"

"What would you like to do right now?"

"Well, let's see. I have a bottle of wine chilling, and I've started your bubble bath running upstairs. . . ."

"That sounds like bliss."

"Then come with me, Detective McCabe."

26

Driving into work, McCabe treated herself to the sound stream from Elvis's 2000 farewell concert in Central Park.

She had been fifteen, watching the monumental event on television.

In her car, fingertips keeping beat on the steering wheel, McCabe belted out "Suspicious Minds," singing along with the King.

She knew it was a temporary lull. But she intended to enjoy her good mood until she walked through the door of the station house.

And if they were lucky, today they would find the piece that would make sense of three murders.

She was parking her car when she gave in and checked the news.

Perfect timing. The announcer was saying, "This afternoon at four, a memorial service will be held for Margaret Givens, the seventy-eight-year-old victim of a gang homicide that Albany police are currently investigating. . . ."

McCabe sighed. She would have to leave early enough to attend the memorial.

Would Clarence Redfield turn up, too, so that he could thread about it?

Even if he did, it wouldn't be the place to question him about his knowledge of the serial murders. Mrs. Givens deserved respect.

She wondered in passing if the mayor would put in an appearance. The mayor had lost no time getting to Ted Thornton's house to express her sympathy to Greer St. John. Would Mrs. Givens's family receive the same attention? If the mayor was on her political game, she'd be there. The chief would probably turn up, too.

"Morning, partner," Baxter said.

"I thought I was early. You beat me in."

"Wanted to see if Research had sent anything on the names we gave them."

"I added another query about Clarence Redfield last night," McCabe said. She dropped her jacket on her chair back and reached for her coffee mug. "I got my dad to look through his notes from 2010. It turns out Clarence Redfield made the newspaper that year."

"What'd he do?"

McCabe told him about the lawsuit. "So the question is, what happened to Redfield's wife and baby? Was it another incompetent doctor, or something else?"

"And you think that might be related to our case?"

"No idea," McCabe said. "But we won't know until we look."

The report that they received on Redfield later that morning contained all of the information that Research had been able to generate from an array of sources.

"Here's the answer to your query," Baxter said, highlighting that section on the wall. "'Wife suffered traumatic brain injury as the result of a fall. Emergency surgery left her brain-dead.'"

"'Twenty-one-week fetus in distress,'" McCabe read. "'Delivered by C-section. Did not survive.'"

"And Redfield made the decision to remove his wife from life support and allow her organs to be harvested," Baxter said. "That must have been tough."

"Yeah," McCabe said. "But I wonder how she came to fall."

"Read farther down. Says here that she fell from a stepladder in the nursery and struck her head. Redfield said she was hanging a mobile. He was asleep, heard the crash. Found her on the floor."

"Looks like it happened at around ten-thirty in the morning. Why was he still in bed? Oh, wait, here it is. He said he'd been working late at the office the night before."

"And she tried to put up the mobile by herself while he was asleep."

McCabe said, "It sounds like a tragic accident."

"But you're wondering if it wasn't?"

"Redfield makes me wonder about a lot of things. He's an odd duck, as my dad would say. Let's go through the rest of the report from Research and see if we can find justification for an interview."

"And if we do and drop by his place rather than bringing him in here—"

"We might be able to get a foot in the door and see what we can see."

"Now, this is interesting," Baxter said.

"You've found something?" McCabe asked, turning from the display of documents that she had been searching.

"Another connection to Teddy."

McCabe ducked behind her desk and sat down. "Okay, I'm ready. What connection does Clarence Redfield have to Ted Thornton?"

"Indirect and almost buried in the fine print, but someone in Research must have remembered that we'd also asked about Ted Thornton."

"What's the connection?" McCabe asked.

"After he moved back to Albany in 2015, Redfield worked as an independent consultant for a company that was a subcontractor for one of Thornton's companies."

"So, let me get this straight. The company that Redfield worked for had a contract with one of Thornton's companies."

"You've got it."

"Is Redfield still working for the company?"

"No, his contract with them ended a couple of years ago."

"About the time his wife died."

Baxter sent the document he was looking at to the wall. "See this? Redfield was working on his last contract with the company when his wife died. In fact, the company submitted a bid to Thornton the morning that Redfield's wife died."

"So that must have been why he was working late the night before."

"And then he came home and went to bed. And while he was asleep, his wife fell from a ladder—"

"And she died and so did their baby," McCabe said.

Baxter sat down on the edge of his desk. "Wanna bet Thornton isn't one of Redfield's favorite people?"

"But," McCabe said, "we still have a big gap between that and three women being murdered."

"One of the women was Vivian Jessup. She and Thornton—"

"But if Redfield were getting revenge on Thornton for . . . at least in his mind . . . being responsible for his wife's death, why not go after Thornton's current fiancée rather than a woman who might have been Thornton's lover at some point?"

Baxter said, "And there's no way to connect any of this to the summer science camp that brought Bethany and Sharon together."

"Unless . . ." McCabe stared at the bulletin board across the room, trying to think it through. "Unless Clarence Redfield is connected somehow to that summer science camp."

"How? We're pretty sure he wasn't a teacher there. And Deirdre Chase said she was the only teaching assistant."

"But we know Redfield was here in Albany in 2010, because he was suing his father's doctor for malpractice."

"Right. His first job out of the country was in November 2011. He went to Saudi Arabia. That summer of 2010, his father was in a nursing home, and Redfield was living at home with his mother. He had a job with a local company."

McCabe stood up and went to the wall work space. "Okay, let's get the time line up. Redfield attends college in Massachusetts from 2000 to 2004. He comes home for a couple of years. Then he leaves to take his first oil company job."

Baxter said, "According to Research, the company he was working for here in Albany got hit by the recession and went out of business."

McCabe nodded. "Okay. So that probably explains why he decided to take the oil company job in October 2006. Then his father is ill, and he comes home. Is here in 2010, when Bethany, Sharon, and Johnnie Mae are attending a summer science camp."

"So," said Baxter. "How does Redfield come in contact with two or maybe three little girls at a science camp?"

"If he did come in contact with them. We may really be reaching on this one."

Baxter shook his head. "I think we're onto something."

"Or maybe we just don't like the guy."

"Well, we've already spent all this time on it, so we may as well finish playing it out."

"True." McCabe picked up her mug and went over to the coffee machine. "Okay. Maybe Redfield was a relative of one of the other students."

"No brothers or sisters," Baxter said. "And his parents seem to have been only children, too."

"What about . . ." McCabe whirled around. "Remember what Deirdre Chase, the teaching assistant, told us? That she and the teacher went out looking for Johnnie Mae. And when they got back to the camp, the director told them that Johnnie Mae's sister and the sister's boyfriend had gone to pick Johnnie Mae up. What if Redfield was—"

"The sister's boyfriend?" Baxter said. "What do we have on Johnnie Mae's older sister?"

"Anything?" McCabe said, watching him check his screen.

"Research is still trying to pick up the trail after the family left Albany. But we have a name for the sister. Melanie. Melanie Jacobs. She and Johnnie Mae had different fathers."

"Do we know yet if Johnnie Mae was biracial?" McCabe asked.

"Black father. Melanie's father was white. So was the mother."

"So, next question," McCabe said. "Did Melanie Jacobs and Clarence Redfield know each other when they both lived here in Albany?"

They were twiddling their thumbs and waiting when the lieutenant passed through the bull pen. "You two got nothing to do?" he said.

"We're waiting on Research, Lou," McCabe said. "We've got this idea about Clarence Redfield."

"How he might be tied into our serial murder case," Baxter added.

The lieutenant gestured toward his office. "I want to hear this."

They were still in the lieutenant's office, going over everything they knew about Clarence Redfield, when McCabe received a tag from Research. "They're both dead," she said.

"Who?" the lieutenant asked. "We don't need any more bodies."

"Johnnie Mae Dupree and her mother. According to Research, they're both dead. When they left here, the mother and the two daughters went to Santa Fe, New Mexico. The mother opened a craft shop. The shop lost money, until she finally closed. A few weeks after that, Johnnie Mae, who had been enrolled in school, was admitted to a hospital after she passed out in class. She was diagnosed with anorexia. While she was in the hospital being treated, she came down with pneumonia. She died a few days later."

"So that left the mother and the older sister, Melanie," Baxter said.

"But the following week, the mother was picked up by the police in a disoriented state. She was taken to a treatment facility. The doctors diagnosed her as bipolar. She was given meds and released. Ten days later, her daughter, Melanie, called nine-one-one. The mother had OD'd on prescription and other drugs. She was DOA by the time they got her to the hospital."

Lieutenant Dole said, "What happened to the older sister after that? She's the one you say you're interested in."

McCabe shook her head. "Research can't find any record of her.

She walked out of the hospital after her mother died and disappeared. She didn't even go back to the house they were renting to close it up."

"Damn," Baxter said. "Nine years ago, people could still do that. Even with Homeland Security, it was possible just to walk away. Become someone else."

"Assuming she did," McCabe said. "For all we know, she may be dead, too."

"What about her possible link to Redfield?" the lieutenant said. "Anything on that?"

"Not yet. According to Research, she did have a job when the family lived here in Albany. She worked for a telecommunications company. One of the computer techs. But the company moved south back in 2014. Research is trying to contact that personnel department to find out if they can provide any information about her."

Baxter said, "Which won't help us much unless she and Redfield crossed path through their jobs."

Lieutenant Dole said, "Stay on this. The missing sister and Redfield's connection to Thornton is a lot more promising than anything else we've had. If that little shit's involved somehow—"

"Then we have to give the guy major points for chutzpah," Baxter said.

27

At noon, McCabe and Baxter decided to go out and get some lunch.

McCabe offered to pay off the bet Baxter had won at the eating place of his choice. As long as he remembered they were dining on a cop's salary.

"I could go for a really good fish sandwich," Baxter said. "Let's see if we can get a table on the barge without shoving anyone off."

"The barge" was a floating restaurant on the bank of the Hudson River. Today, when the temperature was back in the mid-eighties, with a slight breeze, it was the ideal place for lunch.

They drove along Broadway, passing the massive building that housed the SUNY administrative offices, then through the underpass and along the road that ran parallel to the river.

When Baxter turned into the parking lot, McCabe looked at all the cars. "Well, if we're lucky, maybe we've at least beaten the people who are taking the river walk over."

Baxter said, "It was bad enough when we just had state workers. Now we've got UAlbany's nanotech operation and the convention center, and getting a table anywhere at noontime is a pain in the ass."

"You get grouchy when you're hungry, don't you?" McCabe said.

Baxter grinned, looking a little sheepish. "Feed me and I'll stop complaining."

They waited fifteen minutes for a table, which wasn't bad, considering.

As soon as they were seated, Baxter asked for a basket of tortilla chips and green chili salsa.

"You're going to ruin your appetite for that fish sandwich you wanted," McCabe said, watching him munch.

"Not likely. I haven't had anything to eat since dinner last night."

"What happened to breakfast?"

"I had a choice. I didn't choose breakfast."

McCabe shook her head. "Forget I asked."

"I assume you spent the evening quietly at home."

McCabe picked up her menu. "I think I'll have the seafood basket. They have great fried oysters here."

"The clams are good, too," Baxter said. "Had a hot date, did you?"

"What would give you that idea?"

"You're looking a lot more relaxed today."

"I got up this morning and did a yoga meditation," McCabe pointed at the railroad bridge arching over the river. "Have you ever been up there?"

"Up to that little hut, you mean? No, why?"

"Because the guy who works up there is sort of like that repairman in that old washing machine commercial. A lonely guy, up there all by himself for his whole shift. But he does have something to do. He coordinates with the trains coming in and out at the station and raises and lowers the drawbridge for ships and boats."

"Not my kind of job," Baxter said. "I'm the social type." He crunched on another tortilla chip. "Not going to tell me about your hot date, huh?"

"You're assuming I had one."

McCabe was dipping an oyster into cocktail sauce when her ORB buzzed. She reached for it with her free hand. "Got something from Research."

Baxter, who was biting into his fish sandwich, nodded.

"They didn't find a work connection between Redfield and Melanie. But they did find an old link to a social network node."

McCabe clicked on the link and started down at the photograph. Then she looked at Baxter. "Bingo, Mike."

Baxter swallowed and wiped his mouth on his napkin. "What do we have?"

McCabe pushed her ORB toward him so that he could see. "Clarence and Melanie hiking the yellow brick road."

McCabe clicked through the color photos, taken by "Clarence" as he and his female companion hiked from the community garden through the woods and along the sections of the old road. It was a beautiful day in the photos: sunshine, blue sky, even some shots of the Normanskill flowing placidly between the trees on either bank.

Baxter said, "So, we've got some photos with Melanie in them. Or at least as much as we can see of her under her floppy hat. But none of Clarence."

"But how many couples named Clarence and Melanie were likely to have been in Albany in 2010?"

"Of course, this Clarence and Melanie could have come from someplace else—even some other state—and gone for a hike and posted the photos."

McCabe speared another fried oyster and took a bite. "So we need forensics to see if they can figure out the origin of the photos. Where they came from, who posted them."

"You would think if Redfield had posted them, he would have remembered to take them down."

"People used to post lots of photos on the Web. If he even remembered these, all he might remember about them is that they were of the hike along the yellow brick road."

"If they are his, we'll have proof that he had hiked in the area near where Vivian Jessup's body was dumped."

McCabe said, "Of course, a lot of people who live in Albany have hiked there."

"Okay, so what do we have? Do these photos give us anything useful?"

"I'd say it gives us enough to justify visiting Redfield and asking a few polite questions. Let's finish eating and then call the lieutenant."

28

To Baxter's disappointment, they had drawn one of the department's older sedans when they went to the garage. He drove through the cross streets leading to Redfield's house without a great deal of flair.

McCabe said, "Redfield works at home, but let's hope he hasn't gone out to run errands."

"We could have called ahead, but there would have gone our element of surprise."

"If we were driving my car and it still had the tracker, he would probably be able to see we're coming."

A battered black Jeep was in Redfield's driveway.

"He's home," Baxter said. "Unless he decided to go green and take the bus."

"Or has a bike," McCabe said. "Or walked."

McCabe rang the bell. They waited. She rang again.

"He really isn't here," she said.

Baxter said, "Maybe he's out back doing yard work and didn't hear his bell. Let's walk around there and see if we spot him."

"Keeping in mind, that we don't have a search warrant."

"Absolutely," Baxter said. "We're just assuming he must be somewhere around, since his car's in the driveway."

They walked between the house and garage to get to the gate in the backyard fence. They stood there peering over. Clearly, unless he had shrunk or become invisible, Redfield was not in his backyard.

"Keeps his grass mowed," Baxter said.

"Yes, he does," said a dry female voice behind them. "He mows mine, too."

They turned, to find that they were being observed by Redfield's sharp-eyed neighbor, who had stepped out of her own back door.

"Hello, ma'am," McCabe said to the woman, who had gray hair caught up in a knot on top of her head and was wearing an apron over her slacks and pullover sweater. "I'm Detective McCabe, and this is Detective Baxter of the APD. We saw Mr. Redfield's car in the driveway and thought he might be in back and not have heard the doorbell."

The woman's blue gaze narrowed. "You're that detective that Clarence wrote about in his thread."

"Yes, ma'am," McCabe said. "However, we're here to see Mr. Redfield about another matter. Do you know where he is or when he might be back?"

"Can't help you," Redfield's neighbor said. "I have something on the stove." She turned back to say, "And unless you have a search warrant, I suggest you stop prowling around private property."

McCabe smiled at her. "I didn't catch your name, ma'am."

"Troy. Mrs. Evelyn Troy."

"Mrs. Troy, we'll stop by later to see Mr. Redfield. I'm sure you'll remember to tell him we were here."

"Yes, I will," Mrs. Troy said, and went into her house.

She left the door open, obviously intending to observe their departure.

Baxter was about to start the car, when they saw Clarence Redfield jogging toward them. He was wearing a sleeveless sweatshirt that displayed impressive biceps, but the baggy shorts and the beat-up sneakers did nothing for him. Both look a little sad, McCabe thought.

He was chugging along as if he was going through the motions rather than jogging for maximum effect. He stopped when McCabe and Baxter stepped out of the car.

"Mr. Redfield," McCabe said. "Glad we caught you. We saw your car in the driveway, but you didn't seem to be around."

Redfield pulled off the sweatband he was wearing around his head. "As you can see, I went for a jog."

"Nice day for it," Baxter said.

"Yes, the heat finally broke. What can I do for you?"

"We don't want to take much of your time," McCabe said. "But there's someone we're trying to find, and we think you might have known her."

Redfield's gaze shifted from one of them to the other. Then he smiled. "Come on in. No point standing out here on the sidewalk."

"Thank you."

They followed him up the steps. He turned the knob and opened the door.

"It wasn't locked," he said, giving them another smile. "You could have gone on inside and made yourselves at home until I got back."

"We try not to do anything that might be misinterpreted later," McCabe said.

Baxter said, "You ought to be careful about that anyway. Lots of burglaries happen in the daytime when people leave a door or window unlocked."

Redfield smiled. "I'll keep that tip in mind, Detective Baxter."

They stepped into a black-and-white-tiled foyer. The foyer provided a view of the living room and the connecting dining room and, beyond that, the edge of a refrigerator out in the kitchen. But it was the terrarium that occupied one corner of the living room that caught McCabe's attention.

"That's impressive," she said, pointing. "It looks like a piece of furniture."

"It was once," Redfield said. "I started with an old entertainment center and added the glass and created the ecosystem inside."

"What do you have in there?" Baxter asked, moving closer.

"Anole lizards," Redfield said, following him across the room.

McCabe trailed after the two of them. "That would mean that you don't also have snakes," she said.

Redfield turned to look at her, raising an eyebrow. "You don't like snakes, Detective McCabe? No, keeping snakes in the same terrarium with lizards generally isn't a good idea. The lizards tend to end up inside the snakes."

McCabe said, "And that wouldn't work out very well."

"I used to keep a couple of snakes. But they required more care than lizards."

Baxter was peering into the terrarium. "One of them just ran up on a limb and he's looking back at me."

"That's Bill," Redfield said. "Bill has personality."

"Bill, the lizard," McCabe said. "There a lizard named Bill in *Alice in Wonderland*."

"Is there?" Redfield said. "It's been a while since I read that book."

McCabe nodded and glanced around the living room. "Nice house. But we don't want to take up too much of your time, Mr. Redfield. We know you're just getting back from your jog."

"No problem, if you don't mind looking at me sweaty. How about a glass of lemonade? I've got some out in the kitchen."

"I could go for some," Baxter said.

"Come on back with me. I always feel more comfortable entertaining people in the kitchen."

The glance that Baxter shot her as they followed Redfield echoed McCabe's perception that Redfield thought he was in control of the situation.

"By the way, I read your thread about me," she said, catching up to Redfield as he passed the dining room table. "I have to say that although I don't happen to share your opinion about my capabilities as a detective, I did find your writing style—what's the word I want?"

"*Engaging?*" Redfield said, giving her a sideway's glance.

"No . . . *engrossing*. That's the word. I couldn't stop reading. I wanted to see how you would end."

"Hope you weren't disappointed." He gestured for McCabe to go ahead of him into the kitchen. "It was nothing personal, Detective McCabe. I'm sure you're probably as good as any of the other detectives on the APD. But as a threader, it's my job to be controversial and thought-provoking."

"To feed your readers red meat, so to speak?"

"Yes, that's what they expect. I'm afraid, because you're at the center of the serial killer investigation, I had to focus on you." He smiled. "Since you have a gun, I hope no hard feelings."

"None at all, Mr. Redfield. We each have our job to do. And we do it to the best of our abilities."

"And hopefully you and your partner"—he glanced at Baxter—"and the task force, which I understand now does exist, will be able to find the killer before another woman loses her life."

"We're working on it," Baxter said. He sat down on a stool at the breakfast bar. "Mind putting some ice in my lemonade?"

"And slices of lemon," Redfield said. "I pride myself on my lemonade. Please have a seat, Detective McCabe."

"Thank you," McCabe said.

He rinsed his hands at the sink and reached for a towel. "Now, tell me what can I do for you. I hope you aren't here to ask me again about my sources."

"No, this is about something else," McCabe said. "We're looking for someone. A young woman who lived here in Albany with her mother and younger sister about nine years ago, back in 2010."

She paused, looking at him.

"I'm listening," he said. "Please, go on."

"That summer," McCabe said, "the three women, the mother and the two daughters, left Albany and ended up in Santa Fe. We know that both the mother and the younger daughter died there. We're trying to find the older daughter."

Redfield had taken a pitcher of lemonade from the refrigerator. He looked up from filling the glasses he had set on the counter. He looked interested, nothing more. "And how do I fit into this search?"

"You aren't going to believe this. But we think you might once have known her."

"Really?" Redfield set a glass in front of her.

McCabe took a sip. "This is great lemonade," she said, and meant it.

"Thank you. But you were saying that you thought I—"

"Might have known the older sister. Her name was Melanie. And when our APD Research Unit was looking for leads to her whereabouts, they checked the Web. And that's what brought us to you." She took another sip of her lemonade. "Isn't this great lemonade, Mike?"

"Terrific," Baxter said. "You ought to put a lemonade stand out front, Mr. Redfield. Or bottle the stuff and sell it at farmers' markets."

"Too much competition, I'm afraid. Everyone's pushing all-natural products these days. But you were saying about the Web search that brought you to me, Detective McCabe."

"Research found some photos that had been posted on the Web by someone. Probably years ago. They were photos of a hike that started from the community park off Delaware Avenue." She took a sip from her glass. "The thing is, the photos had a caption."

"What was it?"

"'Clarence and Melanie hiking the yellow brick road.'"

Redfield took a sip from his own glass. Then he said, "There must be more than one man named Clarence in the city of Albany."

"You're right about that," McCabe said. "But before we started looking for other men named Clarence who might have gone hiking with a young woman named Melanie back in 2010, we thought why not start with the Clarence we knew."

"Especially given your interest in the case," Baxter said.

"Are you saying that this young woman you're looking for is somehow linked to the serial murders that you're investigating?"

McCabe shook her head. "We don't know. That's why we want to talk to her."

"You mentioned her younger sister—"

"Yes. She was named Johnnie Mae. Does that ring a bell? If you can tell us anything about either of these young women—"

"I'm sorry, Detective McCabe. I'm afraid you've got the wrong man."

McCabe sighed. "Oh, well, it was a long shot, but when we saw the name Clarence . . ." She took a last sip of her lemonade. "Thank you for your courtesy, Mr. Redfield. And I agree that we should both try to be professional about this. . . . I mean about how you cover the investigation."

"I'm glad to hear you say that."

Baxter said, "We'll go and let you hit the shower." He drained his glass and stood up.

McCabe stood, as well. Her glance came to rest on the bright red label of the jar on the counter that Redfield was leaning against. "Isn't that one of the chutneys from Pluto's Planet?"

"Pluto's Planet?" Baxter said, his tone sharp.

"The design of the label is distinctive," McCabe said.

Redfield twisted around and looked down at the jar. He picked it up. "Yes, it is, isn't it? This is the apple brandy chutney. Have you tried it?"

"No," McCabe said. "I just happened to notice the display by the cash register when we were there talking to Bethany Clark's coworkers. You did know that she worked there?"

"Yes," Redfield said. "I did."

Baxter said, "You knew that? Did she ever wait on your table when you dropped by?"

"Not that I recall," Redfield said. "Of course, I may have seen her there. I tried to remember if I had after she was murdered and I heard on the news that she had worked there."

"But she didn't come to mind, huh?" Baxter said.

Redfield shrugged. "You know how the staff in restaurants is more or less invisible. Especially in a place like Pluto's Planet, where they're all young and perky."

"You're right about that," McCabe said. "Well, we'll go and get out of your way."

"Let me show you out," Redfield said.

At the door, McCabe turned. "By the way, are you going to attend the memorial for Mrs. Givens?"

Redfield nodded. "I consider it my duty to be there and report on the state of mind of the community."

McCabe said, "Then we'll see you later."

"You won't be able to miss us," Baxter said.

Redfield smiled. "I'll see you both there."

In the car, McCabe tightened her seat belt as Baxter shot forward. "We aren't in a hurry," she said.

"That asshole's lying through his teeth. He's the Clarence we're looking for."

"I think so, too. But we've got to prove it. And just because he's lying doesn't mean he's our killer."

"Wanna bet?"

"That jar of chutney on the counter . . . He invited us to go out to the kitchen."

"Maybe he forgot it was sitting there."

"Or he knew that the fact that it was didn't matter. Eating at Pluto's Planet and buying the specialty chutney is something that many law-abiding Capital District residents are guilty of having done. The place is popular. And large enough so that Redfield could have eaten there now and then and never had Bethany Clark as his server."

"But she'd been working there since the place opened in January. So the odds are that if Redfield went there more than a time or two, he at least saw her."

"Depending on the shift she was working. And, as his lawyer would say, so what? He saw her. That doesn't mean he killed her."

"Again, partner, wanna bet?"

"Nope. I want to wait and see. If he's playing games with us, maybe he'll keep pushing it until he goes too far."

They were on Central Avenue, practically back to the station house, when the dispatcher came on. "McCabe, we got a request that you see Officer Michele Lawrence. She says she might have something you're looking for."

"Copy, Dispatch. What's Officer Lawrence's present location?"

Dispatch recited the address. It was on one of the side streets off Delaware Avenue.

Baxter beeped the siren and turned against the light. "Wonder what she's got."

"She was the uniform on duty at the Jessup scene. If we're lucky, it's something useful and related to the case."

Lawrence's location was a derelict house that should have been condemned, if it already hadn't been. Lawrence herself was standing beside her cruiser. A sergeant was with her. He was holding a little girl with matted hair, shoeless, wearing a ripped and grimy pink dress. She was crying and squirming in his arms.

"What the hell?" Baxter said.

"Sergeant Perry," McCabe said, greeting the man. "This is my partner, Detective Baxter."

"Baxter," Perry said as the child, snot running from her nose, grabbed for his hat.

Officer Lawrence, who had nodded at them as they walked up, said, "Do you want me to take her, Sergeant?"

"No, I've got her," Perry said. "You bring the detectives up to speed on why you called."

Lawrence smiled. It was the infectious grin that McCabe remembered. "Thank you, Sergeant." She turned to McCabe and Baxter, looking more confident now. "We found something in the house, Detectives. I think it's one of the missing items from the Jessup case."

Perry said, "I'll keep an eye out for the grandmother. You take them in."

McCabe thought she could have gone all day without going inside that house. She hated roaches. And as soon as they climbed the rickety steps, crossed the threshold of the house, and saw the peeling wallpaper and the garbage piled in corners and the urine-soaked playpen in the middle of the living room, she knew there were roaches there.

Lawrence said, "We got a call from a neighbor. The baby was crying. The neighbor hadn't seen the grandmother in a while. She said the grandmother spends a lot of time out in the street with her shopping cart."

"And no one thought of calling before this?' Baxter said, looking disgusted.

"She was okay until a few months ago," Lawrence said. "Until then, they were just poor, like a lot of other people on this street. But she was doing her best to keep the place decent and take care of her granddaughter."

McCabe nodded. "Sometimes people just get worn-out."

"Still," Baxter said. "Why the hell did the neighbors wait until it got like this to call someone?"

Lawrence said, "The neighbor who called said she was hoping the grandmother would be able to get herself together. She said she knows that the grandmother loves her granddaughter."

McCabe glanced around and was ashamed that her first thought had been how much she hated roaches. "What was it you found, Officer Lawrence?"

"It's over here."

Lawrence led them to the far corner, where one of the heaps of garbage was piled.

McCabe saw it right away. A red rose-shaped purse sticking out from beneath cardboard and stained cloth. "Vivian Jessup's purse," she said.

"Yes, ma'am," Lawrence said. "I thought it might be."

McCabe dug into her jacket pocket for her spare pair of crime-scene gloves and reached for the expensive purse from London that had ended up in an old woman's collection of garbage. "Damn, there's nothing in it."

Outside, a woman shrieked in fury. Lawrence ran toward the door. McCabe and Baxter were close behind.

Sergeant Perry was struggling with a ragged old woman. The woman was trying to pull the baby from his arms. Baxter grabbed her by the arm. She was holding on to the baby's leg. The child began to scream.

"Stop!" McCabe said. "Mike, let her go."

Baxter backed away.

Sergeant Perry patted the little girl, whispering soothing words.

Lawrence said to the woman, "It's all right, ma'am. We were just worried because your granddaughter was alone."

The woman stood there, her chest heaving, still holding on to one of her granddaughter's legs. She began to sob.

It took another few minutes of talking to get her to let go of the baby's leg. Lawrence took the woman to sit in her cruiser. McCabe followed and knelt down beside the open door. "Ma'am, we're going to take you and your granddaughter somewhere where you'll both be safe, okay?"

The woman nodded.

"I need to ask you about the red purse we found in your house."

The woman smiled. "It's pretty. It looks like a flower."

"Yes, it does. Do you remember where you found it?"

"Where's my grandbaby? Where did that girl say my grandbaby is?"

"She's right over there. See? About the purse. Can you remember where you found it?"

The woman grabbed McCabe's hand. "I want to brush my teeth now."

"We'll get you a toothbrush and toothpaste. But first we need you to tell us about the purse. Can you remember where you found it?"

"The he/she threw it in the trash can. Thought I couldn't tell. Knew by the way he/she walked."

"You knew what?" McCabe said.

The woman nodded. "Knew he/she was one of them."

"One of who?"

The woman clutched McCabe's hand and rocked back and forth on the car seat. "The spaceship. He/she came on that spaceship. One of them." She stared into McCabe's eyes. "You ain't one of them, are you?"

McCabe patted her hand. "No, I'm not one of them. We'll take you where you can brush your teeth now."

"My grandbaby . . . where's my grandbaby?"

29

Baxter drove McCabe back to the garage to pick up her car. It was almost 3:30, and Mrs. Givens's memorial service was at four.

They had checked in with the lieutenant. He'd said Baxter could handle getting the purse to forensics. A team would search the house they had just left for the contents of Vivian Jessup's purse. But McCabe suspected the purse had been empty when the old woman retrieved it from the trash can.

The lieutenant had said McCabe needed to go to the memorial service for Mrs. Givens. Clarence Redfield would notice and thread about it if she wasn't there.

"Public relations," Baxter said.

"I wanted to go anyway," McCabe said.

The church was packed. Ushers, middle-aged women in white uniforms, were on duty to conduct late arrivals to the few remaining spaces in the rows of pews. They were also there to attend to anyone who passed out from the humidity that threatened to overwhelm the air conditioning, which seemed to be on the blink.

To McCabe's surprise, Reverend Deke was one of the six clerics on the dais. Although he had no church that she had ever heard of, he was wearing a black robe over his white suit.

The choir rose to sing the opening hymn, and McCabe settled into the seat she had managed to get on the aisle in a pew toward the back. She had dodged the usher who wanted to take her up front to fill in one of the empty spaces there. Not that she intended leaving before it was over, but her mother had taught her when she was a child that one's seat in church should be chosen with care. If the service went on too long, a seat toward the back and on either aisle would allow a swift, discreet exit.

Although her mother had appreciated what she described as the "power and passion of the black church," she had never been one to sit through endless hymns when she felt she could make better use of her time. Pop, on the other hand, would be there patting his foot and clapping his hands until the end. Even when it happened, as it often did, that he was the lone white man in the place with a little brown girl sitting beside him. Somewhere along the way, they had stopped going to church. Having introduced her to that aspect of her culture, both parents seem to feel they had done their duty.

But McCabe had encountered several of the ministers on the dais at community meetings when she was in uniform. The chief at the time had been giving lip service to community policing. McCabe and the other cops who had patrolled that zone had shown up at occasional meetings to listen to what the ministers and the other residents, who were concerned not only with crime and violence but police behavior, had to say. The chief's theory was that listening had the effect of suppressing unrest. No matter if they didn't do a lot to respond to the complaints and concerns that they heard.

Halfway through the service, one of Mrs. Givens's grandsons stood up to speak.

"This isn't my thing," he said, standing stiffly in his suit and tie. "You folks who know me know that I'm more comfortable under a car hood." He cleared his throat. "But I had to speak for my gram. She didn't deserve to die like that. My gram was good people. And you got these little kids breaking into her house and beating her. . . ." He swiped at his eyes. "My gram wouldn't have hurt anyone. She didn't like to hurt people. She shouldn't have been hurt like that. . . . It ain't right. You hear me? It ain't right."

A mumble went up from the congregation and then someone cried out, "It ain't right." Others picked up the call, chanting "It ain't right."

McCabe's gaze went upward as the woman beside her sprang to her feet. "It ain't right, and we ain't going to take it no more."

McCabe was torn between tears at the depth of the emotion there in the church and chagrin that the woman beside her had sent her mind spiraling to Peter Finch as the enraged anchorman in *Network,* yelling, "I'm as mad as hell, and I'm not going to take this anymore!"

Pop and his movies were a bad influence. McCabe dug into her shoulder bag for a tissue, remembering Mrs. Givens sitting across the table from her only a few days ago.

Around her the chant was now "Ain't going to take it no more."

Up on the dais, the mayor and the chief were looking a little uneasy.

McCabe thought, Should have sat in back near the door, guys.

Reverend Caswell, the minister of the church, got to his feet and raised his arms. "No, it ain't right," he said. "We need to do something about the violence in our community. We need the help of our friends, the chief of police and the mayor of our city, to get the services that we need in our community. We need services as good as the people in the rest of the city receive. We need to keep our young people from going to juvenile institutions and then on to prison, from going to the emergency room, and then on to the graveyard. We need to break this cycle of violence that took our beloved sister, Mrs. Margaret Givens, from us. We need to do away with both the droogie boys and the bad cops. We need to bring healing and peace to our community."

Each statement was met with a chorus of "Amen" and "Yes, Lord."

Reverend Caswell was followed by each of the other ministers on the dais, each of whom echoed the same theme with a prayer or a song.

After Reverend Deke's rendition of "Swing Low, Sweet Chariot," the mayor was invited to speak.

"I have heard your words," she said, glancing from one side of the room to the other. "I have heard your cries for justice." She spread her hands. "If I could change what has happened and raise that poor woman from her grave, believe me, I would. All I can tell you is that Chief Egan"—she glanced at the husky man with the crew cut sitting behind her—"and I will not rest until we have reduced the crime and violence in this community. We will continue to work with you. . . ."

McCabe tuned out as the mayor drifted into the standard speech from mayors about crime and violence.

She turned her attention to Clarence Redfield's profile. Sitting several rows in front of her, he was looking down. Probably at his ORB. He was probably treading live from the memorial.

As the service was ending, McCabe slipped out of the pew. She nodded to the usher in her aisle as she left.

On the church steps, she stopped to take a deep breath. Motion caught her eye. Four boys were riding down the sideway on their bikes. They stopped near the steps, looking up at the open doors.

McCabe nodded and smiled. She turned and went back into the vestibule, out of their line of vision. "Dispatcher, officer needs assistance. Possible gang activity about to occur."

She gave the location and emphasized that it was the memorial service and that the mayor and the chief were inside the church.

The dispatcher informed her that several patrol cars were nearby, responding to an acoustic readout showing shots fired and a report about a street brawl. She would send them to the church.

McCabe listened to the service ending behind her.

The boys on their bikes were still waiting. One of them was fiddling with a brown paper bag in the basket of his bike.

McCabe stepped out of the vestibule and strolled down the steps. "Hey, guys, what's up?" She held up her badge. "Can I help you with something?"

"Just hanging to watch the people come out of the church," one of them, who looked about ten and had a gold stud in his ear, said. "It's the thing for that old lady who was killed, right?"

"Right," McCabe said. "You knew her?"

They looked at one another. And then the one with the intricate pattern in his hair said, "A little. Whenever we'd see her over at the park . . ." He looked embarrassed. "She used to give us cookies."

"She used to give us homemade cookies that she'd made," one of the others said.

His friends nodded their heads. "That lady could slam down on some cookies," the one with the earring said.

They glanced at one another again and then the one with the bag in his bike basket said, "We brought her some flowers."

McCabe said, "Is that what's in the bag?"

He opened the bag and drew out a bouquet of daisies. "We thought she'd like this kind."

McCabe said, "I'm sure she loved daisies. Why didn't you guys go to the memorial service?"

The first one shook his head. "Nah, that ain't our thing. We just wanted to thank the old lady for the cookies."

The one with the intricate pattern in his hair scowled. "We would have stopped them guys from hurting her if we'd been there."

"Yeah," the others said in chorus.

The one with the bouquet in his hand held it out.

McCabe took it. "I'll see that Mrs. Givens's family gets these, okay?"

"Okay," the one with the gold stud said. "Tell them the old lady made really good cookies."

"I will. Do you guys happen to know—" McCabe broke off as she saw the first patrol car turn into the street.

Oh shit.

The boys glanced sideways at the patrol car. The inner doors of the church opened and people began to spill out.

The boys took off, zipping into the street and down the hill.

McCabe stepped out into the street and held up her badge.

The patrol car pulled up beside her. She was relieved to see two cops she recognized.

"Sorry, guys, it was a false alarm," she told them, reaching for her ORB.

"Nice flowers," one of the cops said with a smirk.

After she had canceled her call for backup, McCabe explained the daisies. The cop who had been smirking shook his head, a bemused expression on his face.

"Kids" was all he said.

"Yeah," McCabe said. "Kids. Thanks, guys."

The bouquet of daisies tucked close to her body to protect it, McCabe started back through the crowd to deliver the flowers to Mrs. Givens's family.

Some days something went right. Flowers instead of a gun.

And some days, good people who made a difference, like an old woman who passed out homemade cookies to little boys, died when they shouldn't have.

30

Not much was happening when she got back to the station. A couple of other day-shift detectives were still at their desks, filing reports or preparing for court the next day.

"He left about half an hour ago," Yin said when she asked if he had seen Baxter. "He left in a hurry. He must have had a big date."

"Yeah," McCabe said. "I guess so."

She checked her ORB to see if Baxter had left her a tag. Nothing.

Yin said, "I'm out of here, too. Thanks again for ordering the wine for our anniversary dinner. Casey was really impressed. Classy gesture, she said."

"I'd like to take the credit," McCabe said. "But it was Baxter's idea."

"The two of you are working good together, huh?"

McCabe nodded. "Like peas in a pod. Have a good evening, Walter."

"You, too."

Yin left and McCabe pulled up the master file on the case. Research was still looking for information on Melanie Jacobs and had contacted the company she used to work for when both she and the company were in Albany. Nothing useful there yet. There had been a significant turnover of staff and management when the company relocated south. The company's personnel department was searching for Jacobs's file and would forward any information that could be legally shared if it was found. The personnel manager was puzzled that the staff was having trouble finding it.

"Hmm," McCabe said to herself. "And I wonder where that file could have gotten to."

Research also had added another notation in the last ten minutes. Baxter wouldn't have seen this one before he left.

The notation was a link to a now-defunct communal posting node. And there was a photograph captioned "Clarence at the county fair with friend. Photo by Melanie."

Under a sign saying REPTILE EXHIBIT, a young man with shaggy blond hair and blue eyes smiled into the camera. He was holding a black snake with red markings. The snake had wrapped itself around his upper arm.

The young man in the photo looked a lot like Clarence Redfield might have nine years ago.

McCabe sat there staring at the photo. If Clarence Redfield had been Melanie Jacobs's boyfriend and Melanie's little sister had attended a summer science camp and been bullied by a girl named Bethany and then nine years later, Bethany and Sharon Clark, who had been caught up in the drama, were murdered . . .

Clarence Redfield was here in Albany, threading about the murders and, to all appearances, unaware that he had once had at least indirect contact with the victims.

Both Johnnie Mae and her mother were dead, and Melanie was nowhere to be found. So where was Melanie? Had she assumed another identity, become someone else? Did Clarence Redfield know where to find her?

If FIU or the State Police lab could confirm it was Redfield in the photo, they would have a wedge. An entry point for another interview, to which Redfield would undoubtedly bring his lawyer.

All right, what about the Ted Thornton connection? They knew that Redfield had worked for a company that had subcontracted for

Thornton. Redfield probably had been working late the night before his wife fell from the ladder. Had Ted Thornton been in Albany that week?

Easy enough to find out. Bruce Ashby should know. McCabe decided to call him rather than send him a tag. Almost 6:30, but he might still be on the job.

"Bruce Ashby."

She left her ORB on VOICE ONLY.

"Mr. Ashby, Hannah McCabe here. I wonder if you could help me with something. I'd rather not get into the details right now, but we're looking into the background of someone who might have tried to contact Mr. Thornton a couple of years ago."

"A couple of years ago?" Ashby said. "Who was this person?"

"Uh . . . I'm not sure what name he might have used. But I'm wondering if Mr. Thornton was in Albany during July 2017. Particularly from July tenth to twelfth."

"Hold a moment," Ashby said. Then: "Ted was here the week before and until the afternoon of July eleventh. He was waiting for a bid from a subcontractor, but he left to go down to the Tony Awards."

McCabe felt her heart jump. "The Tony Awards?"

"Vivian was nominated for her second Tony."

McCabe flashed back to the photograph in Vivian Jessup's condo. The photo of Jessup and Thornton at an event after the Tony Awards.

"The subcontractor who was making the bid . . . did they know that Mr. Thornton was waiting?"

"Of course they knew. The bid was due the next day, but I had asked them to try to get it in by the afternoon of July eleventh, because Ted wanted to see it before he left Albany."

"Did they make it?"

"No. They had all kinds of excuses, but it didn't come in until the next morning."

"I suppose their staff must have been putting in overtime."

"Not our problem. They knew three months before that the bid was due."

"Could I ask . . . did they get the contract?"

"They got it. Ted said they had made the deadline. And there was no one else who could do the job as well."

"But they might have thought that they were going to be penalized for not getting the bid in before Mr. Thornton left for the Tony Awards."

"They might have thought that," Ashby said. "I realize Ted promised to provide full cooperation, Detective McCabe, but I don't see what our business dealings with a subcontractor—"

"I hope I can explain soon, Mr. Ashby. Thank you for being so forthcoming."

McCabe said good-bye before he could ask any more questions.

Sometimes, if you just kept asking questions, you could get people to provide information before they thought about whether you should have it. She had caught Bruce Ashby when he'd sounded as if he were distracted by something else.

And that reminded her that they needed to ask Research for follow-up on the initial background checks on Bruce Ashby and Lisa Nichols.

McCabe sent her request to Research. Then she began to search the Web for the photo that she had seen in Vivian Jessup's apartment of Jessup and Thornton. Photos archived on the official node. Photos of the award winners and nominees on other nodes, as well. Best-dressed. Worst-dressed. Who was escorting whom.

Not only was the photo of Jessup and Thornton on several nodes but there was a brief interview with Jessup about her win, with a smiling Ted Thornton, her "dear friend," at her side.

Easy enough for Clarence Redfield to have seen.

He'd worked late, while Ted Thornton went down to the City for a gala event, to be there to cheer on his friend Vivian Jessup.

But if Clarence Redfield was the killer, why now? Had Vivian Jessup's arrival in Albany been too much for him? Brought back all of his anger and maybe guilt about the deaths of his wife and baby?

And what about Bethany Clark and Sharon Giovanni? Even if Clarence Redfield had felt some anger toward them because of what had happened with his girlfriend's sister, would he kill them nine years later? Kill them for something that had happened when the two girls were little more than children?

If he'd held a grudge, wanted revenge on behalf of his girlfriend, Melanie, and her sister, why had he waited?

He had been back in Albany since . . . Of course, when he first returned, his mother had been ill, and then she had died. And then for a brief period, he must have been happy. He had been married; his wife was pregnant.

And then wife and unborn child were dead. In that scenario, Vivian Jessup made some kind of sense. A target for his rage. But why go back nine years to the incident with Bethany and Sharon?

"You too, huh?"

McCabe looked up, to see Pettigrew holding out a cup of coffee. "Thanks," she said. "Me, too, what?"

"Stuck."

"Yeah, I am," McCabe said. "I can almost see it, but something's missing. You still working on the ex–baseball player case?"

"Among others. The lou says it goes into the file unless we catch a break." Pettigrew sat down in the chair beside her desk, his own coffee cup in hand. "All we know is an unidentified young woman came to visit Swede Jorgensen a couple of days before thugs jumped him and beat him senseless. He's dead. We can't find the girl or the thugs."

"But you think the girl's visit had something to do with what happened to Jorgensen."

"Probably," Pettigrew said. "Since he didn't seem to have much of a life otherwise. Okay, trivia time. Did you know that Abraham Lincoln was a baseball fan? And Abner Doubleday, who is often mistakenly credited with creating baseball, was a Union general and friend of Lincoln."

McCabe smiled. "And with that, it looks like we've found the six degrees of separation between our cases."

"So we have. Your turn. Anything interesting but not particularly useful come to mind about my case?"

McCabe took a sip of her coffee. "You know baseball isn't my game. But when I heard your player's nickname, it did remind me of something."

"What?"

"Ever see an old movie from the forties? Burt Lancaster plays a washed-up prizefighter called 'the Swede.'"

"The Swede?" Pettigrew said, sitting up straight.

"When the movie opens, he's killed by two professional hit men who come looking for him."

Pettigrew set his coffee cup down on her desk. "What's the title of this movie?"

"*The Killers.* I watched it with my dad years ago."

"In the movie, why did they come after him?"

McCabe shook her head. "I don't remember the details. Something about a holdup he had been involved in. And I think he was involved with Ava Gardner, the wife of the gangster who sent the hit men. And the insurance investigator was playing your character."

"My character?"

"The guy who was trying to figure out why Burt Lancaster—the Swede—hadn't tried to run when the killers came looking for him. Why he just let himself be killed."

"But my Swede wasn't killed. He just wasn't talking about why two thugs beat him up. Then he got an aneurysm and died."

"And if he'd been involved in a holdup, that would have turned up by now."

Pettigrew shifted in his chair, then stood up. "Still, I think, just for the heck of it, I'll go find that movie. Might give me some ideas."

"Or not," McCabe said.

"Or not. I got another one for you. Did you know there's a baseball player who was known as 'the Wizard of Oz'?"

"There is?"

"Ozzie Smith. Used to do somersaults on the field. My dad and I went to Cooperstown when Smith was inducted into the Hall of Fame. But unlikely he has anything to do with your case."

"Probably no more than Burt Lancaster has to do with yours," McCabe said. "But it's an interesting tidbit."

Pettigrew nodded. "Life is full of interesting tidbits."

He waved a hand as he headed back toward his own desk.

"You forgot your coffee, Sean."

"Toss if for me. I've had enough caffeine for one day."

McCabe tilted sideways in her chair and tossed the cup into her disposal bin. "Hey, Pettigrew, did you know that some writer had a theory that Lewis Carroll was Jack the Ripper?"

Pettigrew looked up from his ORB and gave her a bemused look. "Really? Never heard that one. You think Carroll ought to be on your suspect list?"

"Problem with that is, he'd have to be capable of time travel. That particular Ripper theory's kind of far-fetched anyway. Find your movie?"

"The synopsis and a clip."

"Feel like going for a beer when you're done?" McCabe said.

"Sure. Sometimes the answers are floating right there in the suds."

"Are they? Why didn't anyone ever tell me about that?"

31

McCabe woke up with a half-formed thought. It was gone before she could catch it. She searched for it as she was standing in the shower. Vivian Jessup's purse. Something about what the old woman had said about finding Jessup's flower purse. Or maybe about who had thrown it away.

She sat down across from her father at the kitchen table. He was wearing the biomonitor that sent his readings to his doctor once a week. He was eating oatmeal with a look of displeasure on his face. "I hate this stuff," he said.

"What do you think of when someone says 'a he/she'?" McCabe said.

"What do you mean, what do I think?" Angus said. "It's a crude way of referring to someone who is transgender."

"What if someone said she could tell someone was a he/she by the walk?"

"How was the person walking? Swishing like a girl? Stomping along like a lumberjack?"

"Our witness didn't say," McCabe said. "She drifted off into aliens from outer space. Thanks, Pop."

"You're welcome. Now, tell me what we were talking about."

"I think that the person who the witness saw might have been wearing a disguise."

Baxter was at his desk when McCabe got there. He pointed to a box of muffins. "Sorry I had to duck out before you got back yesterday."

"Something you had to do?"

"My own hot date. Her meeting was canceled. She called—"

"And you went? Nothing much was happening anyway." McCabe took a blueberry muffin from the box and sat down at her desk.

If I keep on eating my way through this case, McCabe thought, I'll need to run five miles a day for the next month.

She opened the master file instead.

"Nothing new," Baxter said. "Forensics is still sifting through the garbage from the old lady's house and nearby trash cans, but so far nothing that looks like it might have come from Jessup's purse."

"I've been thinking some more about our odds and ends. Like the flowers at the first two crime scenes. But no flower near Jessup's body. So last night, I watched *Mrs. Miniver* again."

"The movie you and Greer St. John were talking about?"

"She said that her mother had named her after Greer Garson, who played Mrs. Miniver in the movie."

"Yeah. And she said something about a scene in the movie when Mrs. Miniver was reading *Alice in Wonderland* to her children."

"They're in the family's bomb shelter. The children fall asleep, and Mrs. Miniver and her husband talk about their own childhood memories of the book. And then the bombing gets closer, and the children wake up and begin to cry," McCabe said. "But the reason I watched the movie again is because I remembered the rose. The village stationmaster names a rose after Mrs. Miniver. Vivian Jessup had a purse in the shape of a rose."

Baxter said. "So you're saying that it might mean something, that instead of leaving Jessup a flower, the killer took away her rose purse?"

"Not that knowing that is particularly helpful."

Baxter leaned back in his chair. "Here's something else that may not be particularly helpful. This morning I stopped by Pluto's Planet, where our girl Bethany worked, to sample the breakfast buffet. While I was there, I showed Redfield's photo around."

"Anyone remember him?"

"A couple of Bethany's colleagues thought they had seen him in the place now and then. But, on the other hand, they thought he might have looked familiar because they'd seen him on the news, giving Jacoby a hard time. The manager's going to run Bethany's receipts to see if she was ever Redfield's server when he ate there."

"Well, at least you've been doing something more constructive than watching old movies."

Baxter raised an eyebrow. "Don't tell me that you're getting discouraged, partner."

McCabe popped the last bite of her muffin into her mouth. "Me? Never. As long as our killer eludes, I—sorry, we—will pursue."

"'Eludes'?" Baxter's grin widened. "If only Ted Thornton could hear you now."

"He'd undoubtedly recognize a riff on Robert Browning." McCabe's hand hovered over her mug. "Pluto's Planet, Mike. Remember when they were trying to get the building permit to have a vertical garden attached to the restaurant?"

"Vaguely," Baxter said. "I wasn't that interested."

"Me, either. Other than the idea of the farm being right there beside the restaurant. But I do remember that the old couple who owned the mom-and-pop store next door didn't want to sell. They did eventually, and there was something about it on the news. Something about the investment company that was bankrolling the restaurant owner."

"And are you thinking it might be one of Ted Thornton's companies?"

McCabe said, "That kind of project took money. It's the kind of thing that Ted Thornton would have wanted to be involved in, isn't it?"

"So let's see what Research can tell us about the money behind Pluto's Planet."

"Although," McCabe said, "you would think Thornton would have told us if he had a financial investment in that restaurant, wouldn't you? Given that our first victim worked there."

"Never know what might slip a man's mind," Baxter said as he sent the query to Research. "Okay, they're on it."

"In the meantime," McCabe said, "let's have a look at what Pluto's Planet has on the Web. . . . Great. A hologram." She waved her hand and the image of the restaurant and the adjoining building spun out.

The restaurant was on two levels, a bar and casual dining on the ground floor, a formal restaurant on the second level with a balcony. A walkway linked the restaurant to the self-contained building next door, a three-story food-production plant with water-hydrated crops and the fish farm.

"According to this," Baxter said, reading the notation, "only the workers are allowed inside the vertical farm because of the risk of contamination of the crops. The walkway is only for emergency evacuation via the restaurant."

"If you read the labels, it looks like they're raising everything from artichokes to tomatoes in the farm," McCabe said.

"They must be raising enough to have a surplus. This morning, they were setting up for a farmers' market in the restaurant parking lot."

"I've bought stuff there on occasion," McCabe said. "This is an impressive operation."

McCabe closed the Pluto's Planet node and went back over to her desk to pick up her coffee mug. "I thought of something else last night when I was doing my movie watching. Mrs. Miniver has an encounter with a wounded German soldier. That reminded me that we haven't spent a lot of time on the neo-Nazi angle. Whitman brought it up during the first task force meeting, but we more or less let it drop after that."

"Because we discovered the science camp link between Bethany and Sharon and that Ted Thornton, Vivian Jessup's good friend, had financed the science camp. The only link to Nazis is the phenol as a murder weapon."

"I know. But we may as well run it through just to be sure we've covered our bases."

"Okay, we have nothing better to do while we're waiting to hear from Research."

"I have some sources that I found." McCabe sent the nodes to the wall. "Here's the article that I read about the use of phenol. These two say more or less the same thing."

"What's that one with the photographs?"

"It's a collection of photographs and interviews with survivors of Nazi prison camps," McCabe said. "I looked through it, but . . . I can't believe this. It was right there staring me in the face."

"What was?" Baxter stood up and came to stand beside her.

"Look at the first name in the second column," McCabe said.

"Aaron Jessup," McCabe said. "Playwright and—"

"That's Vivian Jessup's grandfather. I saw his name in her bio."

" 'Sent to prison camp with his parents, sister, and older brother,' " Baxter said, reading the entry.

"I looked at this before Jessup was killed. I was focused on information about the phenol not . . . Dammit."

Baxter said, "And neither of us thought of asking Research to dig into Jessup's family tree."

"But we knew about the grandfather. That he had come to England after World War Two," McCabe said. "You would think one of us would have thought of going back to look. . . ." She shook her head. "Okay, we didn't think of it. We'd better run this by the lieutenant."

Baxter's ORB buzzed. "Baxter . . . Excellent! Thanks."

"Was that Research?" McCabe asked.

"Give them the right question. It seems Teddy does own an inter-

est in that company that financed Pluto's Planet. The company is one
of his subsidiaries."

McCabe looked again at the photograph of Aaron Jessup, Nazi
prison camp survivor. "So I guess the question is what we follow up
first."

"I vote for Teddy."

"That makes sense. While we're there, we can ask if he knows
anything about Vivian Jessup's grandfather."

They met Lieutenant Dole in the hallway. He was scowling.
"Where are you two going?"

"To talk to you," McCabe said. "We found a link between Ted
Thornton and the restaurant where our first vic worked."

"That can wait. I've got an announcement."

They followed him back to the bull pen. He called for the detectives who happened to be there doing paperwork to gather around.
"We're on high alert from now through Halloween night. So if you
have any plans for the next few days, cancel them. You may be pulling a double shift and you may be out on the streets on patrol."

Groans erupted and the lieutenant held up his hand. "I'm going
to be here, too, so suck it up."

"What's the alert about, Lou?" one of the detectives said from the
back of the room.

"All we got is a credible tip received by another agency that
something may be going down here in our state capital between
now and tomorrow night."

"That's kind of vague," Baxter said.

The lieutenant turned and fixed him with his stare. "Yes, it is.
That's the way all these alerts are. Could be gangs, could be terror-
ists, could be aliens from outer space. We just keep our eyes open."

"Halloween makes everyone jumpy," another detective, French,
said. "We've had a high alert for the past three years. Last year, we
all turned out for a break-in at a middle school that a couple of patrol
units could have handled."

"Whether we like it or not," the lieutenant said, "we are on alert.
You will do your jobs. Understood?"

There was a mumbled chorus of "Yes, sirs."

"You'll be getting more information about this," Dole said as he turned to leave. He motioned to McCabe and Baxter to follow him.

In his office, they brought him up-to-date on what they had discovered about Pluto's Planet and about Vivian Jessup's grandfather.

"Okay, pay Thornton a visit. Ask politely about his interest in Pluto's Planet and see if he has anything useful about Jessup's grandfather and the death camps. If he can't tell you anything, check in with Jessup's daughter. And let me know if there is anything to take back to the task force. As the commander pointed out to me in his office this morning, Halloween isn't the best time to have people on edge about a serial killer."

"Maybe they'll stay at home with their doors locked, like Clarence Redfield has been suggesting," McCabe said.

"The older ones will. The young ones won't," Dole said. "Two of our victims were in their twenties, Detective."

"But, Lou, now we know there's some kind of connection between at least two, maybe all three of the victims. We just haven't figured out what it is."

"Yes, we have," Baxter said. "It's Ted Thornton."

Dole fixed him with his stare. "Are you ready to say Thornton is our killer, Detective?"

Baxter flushed pink. "No, Lou, I just meant he's the connection."

"Maybe. But until you can tell me we're ready to make an arrest, you keep working all of your leads. You understand me?"

"Yes, sir."

Dole rubbed his hand over his gleaming scalp. "Get moving. Let me know what happens with Thornton."

"We will, Lou," McCabe said.

"He's in a mood," Baxter said when they were out of earshot.

"He's getting pressure from the top. With the captain out on sick leave, he's got to deal directly with the commander. And the commander has to deal with—"

"And the shit rolls downhill."

"Although in this case, he was just reminding us not to jump to conclusions."

"Are you in the habit of doing that?" Baxter said, his grin back.

"When I first started out, yeah, sometimes. But he was talking about himself, too. He once made a mistake that almost got another cop killed."

"What'd he do?"

"Tell you another time," McCabe said. "Let's talk through how we're going to handle Thornton."

32

When McCabe reached Bruce Ashby, he said his boss was in Albany and in his office but that he had appointments the rest of the morning and that afternoon. When McCabe said it was important that they speak to Mr. Thornton, Ashby said they could come over, but they would have to be brief.

Thornton's office was in the corporate park that he had built when he established a base in Albany. A high-end complex with solar-paneled buildings and a park with a pond.

They took the elevator up to Thornton's suite and identified themselves to his secretary. She escorted them into his office.

Thornton, wearing a sports jacket that sagged a bit, along with blue jeans and a black T-shirt, got up from behind his desk to greet them.

"I'm afraid I don't have a lot of time today, Detectives. But Bruce tells me you said it was important." He gestured toward the seating area, where a coffee urn was already on the table. "Please sit down and have some coffee."

Baxter sat down on the sofa and reached for the urn. He glanced at McCabe.

She sat down in one of the armchairs, and Ted Thornton took the other.

"We came across something rather interesting, Mr. Thornton, and we wanted to ask you about it."

He leaned forward, elbows on his knees. "Please . . . please, go ahead. What is it that you want to know?"

"It's about Pluto's Planet. We happened to notice that you own the investment company that financed the purchase of the restaurant and the construction of the vertical farm next door."

Thornton nodded and sat up straight. "Oh, is that what you wanted to know. "Yes, as investments go, it was solid. Vertical farms are going to be an increasingly important part of twenty-first-century agriculture. They're one solution to the problem of how we feed an urban population."

"And in the case of Pluto's Planet," Baxter said, "you're feeding the restaurant's customers."

"Not me, Detective Baxter, the restaurant's owner. My company invested in the project, but that was the extent of it."

McCabe said, "Have you eaten there often yourself?"

"Now, you see, that's the irony. The vertical farm's great, fantastic. Unfortunately, the food, although served in a colorful, fun setting, is mediocre." He smiled. "Of course, I'd rather you didn't tell the owner I said that."

"Wouldn't think of it," McCabe said. "So you have eaten there?"

"Twice, as I recall. A lunch meeting and dinner. I assume you're about to get to the reason that you're asking me about one of my business investments?"

"Yes, I am, sir. Did you know that Bethany Clark, the killer's first victim, worked at Pluto's Planet? Had worked there from the time the restaurant opened."

"In what capacity? A waitress?" Sorry, they're called 'servers,' aren't they? I've always found that word rather demeaning."

"I think it's preferred because it can apply to a man or a woman. But getting back to whether you knew that Bethany Clark worked there. I gather you're saying that you didn't."

"Sorry . . . didn't I make myself clear? No, I did not know that Bethany Clark worked at Pluto's Planet. I don't remember seeing her there the two times I was a customer in the restaurant. If I had and had recognized her photograph, I would have told you that I had. Clear enough, Detective McCabe?" A glance at Baxter. "Detective Baxter?"

Baxter grinned. "Crystal clear to me. How about you, partner?"

McCabe said, "Sorry if we've upset you, Mr. Thornton."

"Not at all. I guess I'm a bit touchy about having my integrity questioned."

"Of course. That wasn't our intent. We only wondered if you might not have realized that Bethany Clark had worked at a restaurant that you invested in."

"And now you know that I didn't know that. Any other questions?"

"Actually, there is something else. We were wondering if you could tell us anything about Vivian Jessup's grandfather. Did she ever talk to you about him?"

"May I ask why you want to know?"

McCabe stared back at him, then shook her head. "I'm afraid I can't go into that right now. But please take my word for it that it's important."

Thornton flashed his trademark smile. "Taking . . . taking a woman on trust can get a man into all kinds of trouble."

"Don't think of me as a woman, Mr. Thornton. Think of me as a cop. However, I can't compel you to answer my questions—"

Thornton held up his hand. "Detective McCabe, I'm . . . I'm happy to tell you anything I know."

"About Vivian Jessup's grandfather—"

"Vivian was proud of her grandfather's place in the history of British theater and the family dynasty he had established. As I'm sure you know, Vivian's sister and brother are prominent in British theater. Their father was famous for his Shakespearean roles."

"That's a coincidence," McCabe said. "The Booth family—John Wilkes Booth himself and his brothers and father—"

"Vivian said that was probably where John Wilkes got the idea that the assassination of a leader could be honorable."

Baxter cleared his throat. "Afraid I'm not up on my Shakespeare."

"Brutus," Thornton said. "And the assassination of Caesar."

McCabe said, "Getting back to Ms. Jessup's grandfather. Did she ever talk about what it was like for him during World War Two?"

"The Nazis killed his parents and siblings. He managed to survive." Thornton shook his head. "Vivian said he spent the rest of his life trying to justify his survival."

"Was that all she said?"

"There wasn't much more to say, was there?"

"Did she ever mention an interview her grandfather had done about being a prison camp survivor? His was one of about twenty interviews and photographs in this collection."

"Did you notice the name of the photographer?"

"No, I didn't."

"Alex Snowden," Thornton said.

"Never heard of him," Baxter said.

Thornton's dark brow went up as he turned to McCabe's partner. "Haven't you, Detective?"

"Nope. Who is he?"

"Was. He died of a heart attack a few years ago. He was well into his nineties by then. Alex started out taking family portraits. He graduated to award-winning photo essays, such as the one he did on prison camp survivors. Then he turned to . . . to fashion photography, and became equally famous in that area. During his latter years, when most men would have been resting on their laurels, he took up adventure photography."

"So you knew him personally?" McCabe said.

"I did."

"And your fiancée, Ms. Nichols? She does adventure photography. Did she know Alex Snowden?"

"Actually, she did an apprenticeship with him."

"No kidding," Baxter said. "But I guess she would have been too young to have worked on the photo essay that Snowden did on the prison camp survivors."

"Much too young," Thornton said.

McCabe said, "Was it Mr. Snowden who recommended Ms. Nichols to you when your other photographer—no, you said he died of a heart attack a few years ago. So was it just a coincidence that Ms. Nichols, who had apprenticed with Mr. Snowden—"

"Forgive me, Detective McCabe, but I don't see what this has to do with Vivian or her grandfather. Am I missing something?"

McCabe gave him her best smile. "No, sorry, I was just curious." She stood up. "But we've taken up enough of your time. We should go and let you get back to work."

Baxter finished off his second cup of coffee and got to his feet. "Yeah, Ashby said you were really busy today."

"I do have another appointment. I managed to change the time when I heard you needed to see me." Thornton gestured toward the closed door. "Let me walk you out."

"Thank you," McCabe said. "No need. And thank you for fitting us in."

"Always glad to do anything I can to help. I want to find Vivian's killer, Detective."

"What happened to the sun?" Baxter said.

They stood outside Thornton's office building, looking at the sky, which had gone from blue to gray with streaks of yellow.

"The wind's picked up, too," McCabe said. "I guess that back-door cold front the weatherman was talking about arrived early."

"Brrr," Baxter said. He pulled up the collar of his thermo jacket. "It would be nice to know at least a couple of hours in advance what the weather's going to be like."

"As long as we don't get snow for Halloween. And if we've finished discussing the weather, we'd better get moving."

"What's the hurry?"

"Alex Snowden," McCabe said, leading the way toward their car. "I want to know more about the whole Lisa being his apprentice thing."

"Think there's something there?"

"Didn't you get the impression that Thornton didn't want to talk about it?"

"I got the impression that he was finding us generally annoying today."

"That, too. Your turn to drive."

With what sounded like a sigh of resignation, Baxter got behind the wheel of the vehicle they had drawn that day, another older-model sedan with no bells and whistles.

McCabe set the bag containing her black bean burger and coleslaw down on her desk. Before sitting down, she brought up the master file to see if there was anything new from Research.

She scanned through the follow-up report.

"It looks like Ted Thornton's people aren't quite as efficient as he thinks they are."

Baxter looked up from unwrapping his cheeseburger. "What did they miss?"

"Research found a discrepancy when they started to dig into Lisa Nichols's background. They aren't sure what the story is yet, but they're working with the Bureau, checking databases."

"For what?"

"It seems the child who matches our Lisa Nichols's birth record died when she was three years old. They aren't sure who our Lisa Nichols is."

Baxter chewed and swallowed. "Dang. She bought a new identity."

"Or someone gave it to her."

"Can we at least finish eating before we jump on this one?"

"Sounds good to me. I think we're going to need our strength when we tackle Ted Thornton about his fiancée."

"I wonder where she is today."

"Bruce Ashby can probably tell us."

Before calling Ashby, they gave Lieutenant Dole an update. He nodded. "Go for it. But don't screw this one up, you hear me?"

When McCabe reached Ashby on her ORB, she put him on visual.

He frowned when McCabe asked if he knew the whereabouts of his boss's fiancée.

"Lisa? She and Ted had lunch together."

McCabe said, "So Mr. Thornton took a break from his appointments to have lunch with his fiancée?"

"She came by," Ashby said. "They ate downstairs in the cafeteria. What is this about?"

"We need to speak to Ms. Nichols."

"About what?"

"We would prefer to discuss that with her."

"Then you'll have to find her. I have no idea where she is."

"Could you ask Mr. Thornton where she was going after lunch?"

"He's on a call with our London office."

"I see. When he gets off his call, would you please tell Mr. Thornton that Detective Baxter and I need to speak to him again? We're on our way back to his office."

She disconnected before Bruce Ashby could object.

33

More questions about Pluto's Planet or Vivian's grandfather?" Ted Thornton said when his secretary escorted them back into his office.

McCabe said, "No, it's about your fiancée. Didn't Mr. Ashby mention that?"

"No, he just told me that you were on your way back over." Ted Thornton waved them to the seats they had occupied earlier. "What about my fiancée?"

"We need to speak to her," McCabe said. "But Mr. Ashby tells us he isn't sure of her whereabouts right now. We hoped you might be able to help us find her."

"Why do you want to speak to Lisa?"

McCabe met his gaze. "Mr. Thornton, we have some news that you may find distressing."

"Please . . . please, go on, Detective McCabe."

"It's about Ms. Nichols. It seems she isn't who she claims to be. In fact, we aren't sure who she is."

Thornton was silent for a long moment. Then he said, "Actually, I've been waiting for her to tell me about that."

Baxter said, "So you know that she's been lying about—"

"I . . . I've known it for some time now."

McCabe said, "And you haven't confronted her?"

Thornton looked down and then glanced around his office. "You see the thing is . . . the really awkward thing is . . . I'm in love with her. Believe it or not, that's never happened to me before." He shrugged, hunching one shoulder higher than the other. "So I wanted to enjoy it as long as I could. Before Bruce makes me . . . makes me face the fact that the woman I'm in love with is . . . is probably a cheat and a liar."

"Then Mr. Ashby suspects her?" McCabe said.

"Bruce always suspects women who show an interest in me. He's convinced any woman who would have me must be after my money."

McCabe said, "Mr. Thornton, I'm sorry about this . . . but we have three dead women, and your fiancée isn't who she claims to be. It is possible that she's involved somehow in our case."

Thornton said. "So . . . so I guess we'd better find her and try to get this all cleared up."

He stood up and went over to his desk.

A moment later, his secretary opened the door. "Yes, Mr. Thornton?"

"Would you ask Bruce to step in, Sheila?"

"I'm sorry, sir. Mr. Ashby went out. He said there was something he needed to take care of and that he would check in later."

"Thank you, Sheila. That's all for now."

Thornton went back to his desk and picked up his ORB.

McCabe and Baxter waited.

Thornton turned to them. "Bruce isn't answering. Neither is Lisa."

At Ted Thornton's estate, Rosalind, the maid, responded to the summons that she had received. "What may I do for you, sir?"

Bruce Ashby turned to look into the wide eyes in the metallic face. "Do you have the access code to Ms. Nichols's room?"

"Yes, sir. I am authorized to clean her room when she's absent."

He pointed at the door. "Open it."

"I am not authorized to do that, Mr. Ashby."

"I'm authorizing you," Ashby said. "Open the damn door."

"I'm sorry, sir. I cannot do that without Ms. Nichols's authorization."

The maid turned and began to glide away.

"Damn you, you tin can! Open this door."

"My name is Rosalind, sir. And I cannot carry out your request without authorization from Ms. Nichols."

She left him standing there with his fists clenched.

Baxter kicked the locked door of Lisa Nichols's room. He cursed at the pain that shot up his leg.

Lisa Nichols looked down at the tag on her ORB. She was sitting in the red sports car, which she was using that day. It occurred to her that she might have chosen less conspicuous transportation if she had known how the day was going to go.

But she hadn't known that everything was about to unravel until she went to Ted's office. Over lunch, he had given her one of his lopsided smiles and then told her about his visit from Detectives McCabe and Baxter. They had wanted to know about his business interest in Pluto's Planet and Vivian Jessup's grandfather.

"Actually, your name came up, my love."

"It did?"

"We were talking about your mentor."

"Alex?"

Ted nodded. "They had seen the photos that Alex took of Aaron Jessup and the other prison camp survivors he interviewed."

Now Nichols stared out of her windshield. The sky was an eerie gray. She started to reach for the camera on the seat beside her and then laughed. "Not quite the time for taking pictures, Lisa."

She reached instead for her ORB.

When he came on the screen, she said, "Hello, Clarence."

"Melanie?"

"I need to see you."

"Melanie, I . . ." He pressed his hands to his eyes. "I thought you—"

"I need your help. Please, Clarence.

He nodded. "Where do you want to meet?"

"The place we used to go."

34

Snowflakes melted as they struck the windshield. Overhead, the wind whipped the traffic lights back and forth.

McCabe was on her ORB with Lieutenant Dole.

"We've got an ID on Nichols," he said.

McCabe listened and turned to her partner. "Lisa Nichols is Melanie. She's Johnnie Mae Dupree's older sister, Melanie."

Baxter cursed. "Right there under our noses."

"Lou, we're going to head to Clarence Redfield's house."

"Do that," Dole said. "I can't wait to hear what the little bastard has to say about this."

Redfield's Jeep was not in his driveway. They got out and knocked on his front door.

His neighbor did not look out of her door. Her car was gone, too.

"We could have used a nosy neighbor about now," McCabe said.

Baxter said, "Want to bet Clarence and Melanie are together somewhere?"

"That would be news to Ted Thornton," McCabe said.

. .· .

Clarence Redfield stood a few feet from the woman he had not seen in nine years . . . until he saw her on the news, stepping off of Ted Thornton's airship.

"Melanie," he said. "I'm glad you called. Are you all right?"

"Lisa," she said. "My name is Lisa now."

"You'll always be Melanie to me. My Melanie."

She smiled and shook her head. "We can't go back, Clarence. That was a long time ago. We're different people now."

"You look different. Your hair." He took a step closer. "Even your eyes. Your beautiful blue eyes—"

"There's a treatment," she said. "Blue eyes can become hazel."

"But I knew it was you. As soon as I saw you smile and touch your throat. That gesture."

"I guess it's impossible to change everything."

"If you love someone, you never forget the things—"

"Clarence, I called because I need your help. I'm in trouble. I don't have anyone else to turn to."

"What about your fiancé?"

"When he finds out who I used to be, that I don't have the pedigree that he thought I had—"

"If he loves you—"

"He loves the idea of me. Of 'beautiful, smart, talented Lisa.'"

"Melanie . . ." Redfield shook his head. "What do you need from me?"

"I—" The wind whipped her blond hair across her eyes. She brushed it back with the slender hand with the scar on the thumb. The hand that he had recognized, remembered holding in his own, stroking. "I . . ."

"You said you were in trouble," he said. "Tell me what I can do for you, Melanie."

Tears glimmered in her eyes. "You have to help me, Clarence. If you ever loved me, you have to help me."

.   .   .

The State Police helicopter that had spotted Redfield's car had reported the presence of a second car, a red sports car registered to Ted
Thornton.

Following orders from headquarters, the copter had not lingered
overhead.

Driving into the access road, McCabe and Baxter saw the two
police cruisers that had been dispatched to the scene. Baxter pulled
up behind them.

The two officers were in position, the abandoned planetarium
in sight, their presence concealed by the overgrowth of trees and
bushes.

They turned their heads to look at McCabe and Baxter. McCabe
stepped out of the car and held up her hand to indicate they needed
a moment.

She looked at Baxter, who had gotten out on the driver's side.
"We're going to assume that one of the people inside might be in
danger."

"Or," Baxter said, "we could assume they're in this together."

"Whatever is happening in there," McCabe said, "we are not going to rush in and provoke a situation."

"What are we going to do, then?" Baxter asked. "Walk up to the
door and say hello?"

"Sounds like a plan to me," McCabe said.

They were halfway up the crumbling walk when they heard
a woman scream—a piercing scream that was snatched up by the
wind.

McCabe pulled her gun from her holster as she ran. Baxter was
right behind her.

On her ORB, McCabe instructed the two officers to move up to
the door and hold their positions.

She tripped on a cracked tile inside the door, righted herself, and
moved more slowly along the corridor, where gray light came only
through the broken windows.

Baxter moved to the other wall, paralleling her movement.

They reached a doorway and saw the stairs climbing upward.

The wind howled around the building. Up above, the words being said were indistinct. A man's voice, angry, demanding. A woman's sobbing response.

The stairs creaked as they climbed, McCabe leading the way.

The door onto the roof was off its hinge. McCabe stopped, listening, allowing her eyes to adjust to the light. Then she stepped out onto the roof. Baxter followed her.

"Clarence," she said, keeping her gaze trained on the man who was holding a stunner. "Clarence, you don't want to do this."

He turned slowly toward them. "You don't understand."

"Why don't you put the stunner down and explain it to us," McCabe said.

Lisa Nichols—Melanie—had her hands to her mouth. She was sobbing.

"It isn't what you think," Redfield said. He put the stunner down carefully on the planetarium's rutted roll-away roof.

McCabe said, "Now you come toward us, Ms. Nichols."

Lisa Nichols stared at them, her gaze like that of a deer caught in a headlight. She reached down to pick up the camera case at her feet.

"Just leave that and come toward us," McCabe said.

"I can't," Nichols said. "I need this."

She reached for the case. Redfield said, "No, Melanie. No."

McCabe said, "Don't move, Mr. Redfield. Stay right where you are."

"You don't understand. She—"

Nichols screamed and lunged toward him. She was holding a hypodermic. McCabe fired her gun.

35

When the doctor came out of surgery and told them that Lisa Nichols was going to live, McCabe stood up and walked out into the hallway. She went down the hall and leaned against the wall, then slid down and sat on the floor.

Lieutenant Dole came out and looked down at her. "If she had died, it would have been a righteous shoot."

"I know that," McCabe said. "But I'm glad she's not going to die."

Lieutenant Dole said, "Redfield is ready to make his statement. You can't take part in the interview, but you probably want to hear this."

"Yes, sir, I do."

McCabe stood up and swiped at her eyes and nose.

Clarence Redfield looked up at them from his bed. The hypodermic had grazed him. Enough to pierce the skin of his arm and require observation.

His face was drained of color. The look in his eyes had nothing to do with the phenol.

He said, "I thought . . . I recognized the name of the first girl . . .

remembered Johnnie Mae. But I couldn't believe. But then . . . when the second one . . . Sharon . . ."

"Why didn't you report your suspicions?" Lieutenant Dole asked.

"I loved her," Redfield said. "I still loved her." He glanced toward the door, which was ajar, as if he knew McCabe was there listening. "And I didn't know for sure. I couldn't be sure. Someone else could have—"

"So, you decided to let it ride," Dole said. "And then Vivian Jessup was murdered."

Redfield said, "That . . . I couldn't believe that Melanie . . ."

"And you had already started to play up the idea of a serial killer stalking his victims," Dole said.

"I hoped that if she was the . . . if she had . . . I hoped she would stop."

"You hoped that, did you? Three women were dead, and you hoped—"

"Don't you understand? I didn't know what to do." Redfield rubbed his hand over his face. "I tried to contact her, but she didn't respond." He looked up at the lieutenant. "After Vivian Jessup . . . I knew Melanie . . . I knew she wasn't going to be all right. But I didn't know how to help her."

"How the hell could you ever have thought she would be all right when she was going around killing people?" Dole said.

Clarence Redfield closed his eyes and shook his head. "It wasn't her. It wasn't my Melanie, not the woman I'd known."

The next day, Dole, Baxter, and McCabe were back at the hospital, sitting in the office of the pharmacologist who had reviewed the lab analysis of the combination of drugs in Lisa Nichols's system.

McCabe had been instructed to remain silent during the interview.

"Bad combination of drugs," the pharmacologist said. "She was taking a prescribed anticonvulsant for migraine headaches. And medication she was self-prescribing for an allergy."

"An allergy?" Baxter said. "What kind of allergy?"

"A cat," the pharmacologist said. "Her fiancé said she was taking the allergy medication because she's allergic to his cat."

Horatio? McCabe thought. Had Lisa Nichols been done in by Horatio? By the maid, Rosalind, offering medication to anyone who was allergic to Ted Thornton's Maine coon cat?

And, for that matter, is Ted Thornton still Nichols's fiancé? McCabe wondered. Does he intend to stand by her?

"That was enough to make her kill three people?" Lieutenant Dole was saying. "Allergy medication?"

"I'm not saying that," the pharmacologist said. "I'm simply saying that the combination of drugs could have caused side effects that might have aggravated preexisting psychological problems. According to the physician who prescribed the migraine medication, Ms. Nichols had been experiencing a recurrence of a syndrome she had as a child."

"What syndrome?" Dole asked.

"AIWS. Alice in Wonderland Syndrome."

The three detectives in the room looked at one another and then at the pharmacologist. "Could you repeat that?" Baxter said.

"The sufferer, child or adult, perceives his or her body as distorted and experiences spatial distortions. Hence the name of the syndrome. Some people, particularly children, experience AIWS on waking. The syndrome is also fairly common among migraine sufferers."

"Do you know about Vivian Jessup?" McCabe blurted out.

The pharmacologist nodded. "A bit of a coincidence, isn't it?" He shrugged. "But AIWS isn't that uncommon. And I have been able to confirm from her old medical records that Ms. Nichols did have AIWS as a child and teenager and also experienced intense migraines."

After their interview with the pharmacologist, Dole said they'd better talk to Redfield again. McCabe took up her post outside the door while Dole and Baxter went into Redfield's room.

In response to Dole's question, Redfield said, "Yes, I knew that

Melanie had migraines. That was how we met. In a Web chat room for people who had migraines and had experienced AIWS." He frowned and gestured. "AIWS is—"

Dole said, "We've heard the term. So you and Melanie both had migraines and AIWS?"

"Yes, but my AIWS went away. I don't even get migraines that often anymore." His gaze narrowed. "Why are you asking me this? Is Melanie ill? Is that why she—"

Dole cut him off. "That's up to the experts to determine, Mr. Redfield. Thank you for talking to us."

As they walked down the hall, the lieutenant glanced at McCabe and Baxter, "Good work. But don't expect it to stick. By the time this is over, not only will Lisa Nichols probably walk but the drug company that made the allergy medicine will be the villain."

McCabe stopped short. The lieutenant and Baxter turned to look at her.

"You okay, partner?" Baxter asked.

McCabe nodded. "Just suffering from brain overload."

"That's why you're going to do that follow-up appointment with the shrink, McCabe. You need some more debriefing."

The question was, McCabe almost said, whether debriefing would get the crazy idea that had just occurred to her out of her head.

36

Friday, November 8, 2019

McCabe had been cleared to return to regular duty.

She and Baxter had tied up the loose ends.

They had confirmed that Lisa Nichols was the "collector" who had contacted Vivian Jessup. On the day that Vivian Jessup was killed, Nichols had gone to New York with Ted Thornton and then taken a fast train back to Albany. She had made an appointment to meet Jessup, had shown up dressed as a man, killed Jessup, and driven her body to the ramp in one of Thornton's cars. And then she had taken another train back down to the City. She had told Thornton that she was spending the evening with a girlfriend.

The media frenzy over billionaire Ted Thornton's beautiful "killer blonde" fiancée had gone cosmic. The district attorney was under pressure to seek the maximum penalty for Lisa Nichols from the nebulous "public" who would determine his fate when he came up for reelection. On the presidential campaign trial, Howard Miller, never one to ignore an opportunity, had taken up the cry for "justice" for the victims whose blood had been spilled by an immoral woman.

Exercising his financial clout, if not his political influence, Ted Thornton had hired the best defense attorney in the country to lead a dream team of lawyers.

But he had not been seen at the hospital since Nichols left the emergency room. He had made no statement about the status of their engagement. In fact, he was reportedly in New York City, with no immediate plans to return to Albany. And the press was not being allowed access.

McCabe looked up from her ORB and the news articles she had been scanning. Pettigrew and Yin were returning from a robbery call.

Pettigrew glanced at her, then said, "Hey, Hannah, did I tell you that old Burt Lancaster movie wasn't too far off the mark?"

McCabe said, "Are we talking about your case? The ex–baseball player?"

"The movie gave me a few ideas," Pettigrew said. "I looked back at the photos from Swede's glory days. There was one of Swede in a nightclub in Vegas with a woman."

"Only one," McCabe said. "Wasn't he known for his high-flying lifestyle?"

Pettigrew nodded. "But this photograph caught my eye. The woman Swede had his arm around looked a lot like the girl whose sketch we have. In fact, she could have been her slightly older sister. Or the woman who became her mother."

"Turns out she was," Yin said, joining the conversation. "Her mother, that is."

Pettigrew took a sip of his coffee. "The mother's name was Laurie. She married the mobster Swede sometimes hung out with when he was flying high"

Yin said, "Laurie stayed married to the mobster for almost twenty years. Until she died a couple of months ago."

"Of a drug overdose," Pettigrew said. "An accidental overdose while being treated for depression."

"We found Laurie's mother in a nursing home," Yin said. "Her mother said that her daughter had been unhappy for a long time. She started drinking heavily about the time she got married. Spent years in and out of high-priced treatment centers drying out."

"So the overdose that killed her could have been the result of combining alcohols and medication," Baxter said.

Pettigrew said, "Laurie's mother said her granddaughter, Samantha, came to see her after her mother died. She hadn't seen her granddaughter in years. Always thought of her as headstrong and spoiled."

"So she was surprised," Yin said, "when Samantha came to see her and wanted to know if her mother had ever talked about a man named 'the Swede.'"

"What did the grandmother tell her?" McCabe asked.

"Nothing," Yin said. "She didn't tell her anything because she said she was afraid for her."

"Afraid of what?" Baxter said.

"Afraid of what the man her daughter had married would do if her granddaughter asked if he was really her father."

"But you think Samantha went looking for the Swede," McCabe said. "And found him."

Pettigrew settled into his chair and picked up his ORB. "If we were cynical types, we might wonder how Laurie died. Whatever happened, her daughter left home a few days later." He paused. "Her father, or the man she had always thought was her father, expressed his concern when we spoke to him."

"What did he say about his daughter's whereabouts?" Baxter asked.

Yin replied, "The man said he has no idea where she is. But is worried sick about her. Can't imagine why she might have contacted Jorgensen. Neither he nor his late wife had seen the Swede in years. His daughter had never met him."

"That's what the man said," Pettigrew said. "when we reached him on his yacht off the coast of Spain."

"I wonder if the two thugs got anything out of Jorgensen about the girl's whereabouts," Baxter said.

Pettigrew shook his head. "I think that day when we talked to him in the hospital, he thought she was safe."

"If she's lucky, she still is," Yin said.

"What she should have done," McCabe said, "was get Lisa Nichols to give her some pointers about assuming a new identity."

The three men looked at her.

Pettigrew said, "Something about her still bothering you?"

"It's all too easy," McCabe said. "She has this syndrome. She mixes medications. She gets side effects and she kills three people. Bethany and Sharon to avenge her sister. Vivian Jessup because what?"

"Because she was afraid Jessup wanted Thornton. Or because she thought Jessup might be suspicious," Baxter said.

"Ashby was more suspicious," McCabe said. "But she went after Jessup."

"She had already killed twice," Yin said. "What's one more?"

Pettigrew said, "One more opportunity to get caught. Which might be an argument that she was no longer thinking rationally."

Baxter said, "And so she went after someone else she hated or feared."

McCabe said, "That's the narrative, isn't it? The story that her high-priced attorney is already previewing for the media. Melanie/ Lisa loved her little sister. Tried to protect her when their mother couldn't. Years later, she comes back to Albany, and one afternoon, she encounters one of her sister's tormentors in an ice-cream parlor. Hears Bethany's name and realizes she was the girl who had bullied her sister. And Melanie/Lisa decides in her irrational mental state to avenge her sister."

"And then," Baxter said, "she kills the other girl, Sharon, because she thought Sharon had been involved, too."

Pettigrew said, "It makes a crazy kind of sense. If she was suffering from the side effects—"

"If she was," McCabe said. "And if she had the drugs in her system, then she might very well have had side effects. But it was damn convenient, wasn't it?"

She reached for her ORB. "Kelsey, hi, remember when I said we didn't need that information any more about Melanie Jacobs's co-workers at the company she worked for? . . . Right. I've changed my mind. Would you see if the company can provide us with some names? . . . Thanks, Kelsey."

McCabe turned back to her three colleagues, who were looking at her with bemused expressions. "I shot the woman," she said. "That gives me the right to obsess about whether she was temporarily insane or a cold-blooded killer."

"Okay," Baxter said. "But the lou thinks we are working on—"

"We are," McCabe said. "We can go over what we have on that one while I'm waiting to hear from Research."

"They've found someone," McCabe said when Baxter came back from his lunch run. "Research has found one of Melanie Jacobs's former coworkers."

Baxter handed McCabe the sandwich she had asked for. "Good. Maybe we can wrap this up and you can stop obsessing." He grinned and held up his hands. "Your word, not mine."

"True," McCabe said, "So let's eat first."

The woman's name was Nancy Corrigan and she had not liked Melanie Jacobs (aka Lisa Nichols). That much was clear from the way her mouth puckered when she heard Jacobs's name.

Ms. Corrigan lived in North Carolina now, but she had heard about the Albany serial killer case. "I was wondering if I should call," she said. "But my husband said it wasn't important and I should stay out of it."

"What wasn't important?" McCabe said.

"The pregnancy test. A few days before she quit, I saw her in the ladies' room. She was reading a pregnancy test. She tossed it in the trash can. But I fished it out and looked. It was positive."

37

Monday, November 11, 2019

Clarence Redfield said he would come to the station that afternoon.

He arrived an hour or so later, looking thin and drawn. "Why do you want to see me?" he asked.

It was the same question he had asked McCabe when she'd contacted him.

McCabe gestured toward a chair at the table in the interview room. "Please sit down, Mr. Redfield."

He sunk into the chair. "Are you worried that I'm going to start threading again about your investigation? I wouldn't come off looking particularly good, given the outcome."

"You loved her," McCabe said.

"Is your partner listening in while we have this little chat? Should I have brought my attorney?"

"There's something I need to tell you, Mr. Redfield. I thought you might rather hear this in private."

"Hear what?'

"That Melanie was pregnant when she left Albany."

"You're lying," he said. "You're lying. She would never have gone away if she . . . She left because she couldn't let her sister go off alone with their mother. She left to take care of Johnnie Mae."

"And maybe because she didn't want you to know that she was pregnant. Didn't want to have a baby."

"No, you're wrong. She would have wanted our baby."

"I need to show you something." McCabe touched the console. "This is surveillance footage taken nine years ago at an abortion clinic in New Mexico. The FBI had the clinic under surveillance because it had received threats from a radical pro-life group."

She watched Redfield's face as he saw Lisa—Melanie—going into the clinic.

"I'm sorry," McCabe said. "But if you intend to testify for her, you should know what she—"

"Go to hell."

Redfield lurched to his feet. He opened the door and walked out of the room.

McCabe sat down at the conference table. She wasn't particularly proud of herself.

She was sitting at her desk in the bull pen when Redfield came back. He said, "I think . . . I think I know why she did it."

McCabe glanced at Baxter. "Do you want to make a statement?"

Redfield dropped down into the chair beside her desk. "I just want to tell you this before I change my mind."

"Tell us what?" McCabe asked.

"About something that happened a few days before Johnnie Mae ran away from the science camp. Melanie and I went by to pick Johnnie Mae up at the camp. But when we got there, Johnnie Mae wasn't out front. Melanie asked me to go look for her."

He paused. A muscle twitched in his cheek.

McCabe said, "Did you find Johnnie Mae?"

Redfield cleared his throat. "No, I asked one of the teachers, but . . . when I got back out front, Johnnie Mae was there. So were those two other girls."

"Bethany Clark and Sharon Giovanni?" Baxter said.

"Yes. I didn't know their names then. But it was Bethany who was smiling . . . smirking . . . at Melanie. I asked what was going on. And Bethany said, 'Your girlfriend just threw up.' Melanie glared at her. I'd never seen that look on her face before. Then she turned to me and said everything was all right. That she just had an upset stomach from something she'd eaten."

He fell silent.

McCabe said, "Was that all she said, Mr. Redfield?"

Redfield nodded. "But after our conversation today, Detective McCabe, I realize now that she was throwing up because she was pregnant." His smile looked as if it would crack. "Embarrassing, isn't it? A thirteen-year-old girl realized that, and I didn't."

McCabe said, "Did Melanie tell you what happened when she and Bethany saw each other in the ice-cream parlor that day?"

"She was in line, and Bethany was flirting with the young man behind the counter. She told him her name and wrote her tag number on a napkin. She . . . Bethany had changed a lot in nine years, grown up, but Melanie recognized her then. Before she could decide what to do, Bethany got her ice cream and left. But she came back as Melanie was leaving. They met in the doorway, and Melanie said, 'Remember me? I'm Johnnie Mae's sister.'"

"What did Bethany say to that?" Baxter asked.

"She just looked blank and said, 'Johnny who?'"

McCabe said, "I don't suppose Melanie appreciated that answer."

Redfield shook his head. "She said she couldn't get it out of her mind. She said Bethany was as much of a little bitch as she had been when she was a child. And she was alive and flirting in an ice-cream parlor, and Johnnie Mae had never had a chance to grow up."

"And, of course, Melanie had also given away her identity. Do you think that was why she killed Bethany?" McCabe asked.

Redfield looked from McCabe to Baxter. "I was the only other person who knew. The only other person who might have revealed to Ted Thornton that she had once been Melanie Jacobs. But she knew she didn't have to worry about me. She knew she could wrap me around her little finger."

"Unless," McCabe said, "you knew she'd had an abortion. And then you might not have kept her secrets. Of course, she could have told Ted Thornton the truth. She must have known he was in love with her. There was a good chance he might have forgiven her for lying about who she was once he knew the whole story."

"But he might not have," Redfield said. His Adam's apple worked as he swallowed. "And Melanie hated being poor. She hated the way she and her mother and Johnnie Mae lived."

"So she had the life she had always wanted with Thornton," Baxter said, "and she intended to keep it."

Redfield frowned. "No, I'm not explaining . . . It wasn't just about having money. Melanie was afraid a lot of the time. Even as Lisa, the glamorous photographer, she was still afraid. That day at the planetarium, she said she couldn't be alone again. She said Ted Thornton made her feel safe. She said he had money and power, and she knew that whatever happened, he would be able to take care of her and keep her safe."

"Did you tell her that you would be there for her?" McCabe asked.

"Yes. But who am I compared to Ted Thornton? She said I didn't understand. But I did." He shrugged. "Her mother was mentally unstable. Maybe Melanie inherited that. Maybe that and the side effects from the drugs were enough to push her over the edge."

"That's what her attorneys are going to argue," Baxter said.

McCabe said, "Are you still going to testify for her?"

Redfield got up from the visitor's chair beside her desk. "Or, as long as we're considering possibilities, maybe she has always been a scheming, lying little bitch. And maybe the drugs just brought out what she is. Someone who would do whatever it takes to get and keep what she wants. Her survival, and to hell with anyone else."

He turned and walked out of the bull pen. They watched him go.

"Think he's still going to testify for her?" Baxter asked.

"Guess we'll have to wait and see," McCabe said. "Want to have another look at what we have on our arson case before we call it a day?"

McCabe waved to him as she pulled out of the garage. Sitting in his car, the cooling system on full blast, Baxter waved back.

When McCabe was gone, he picked up his ORB, entered the code, and waited for a response.

"Yes?"

"Tonight?" Baxter said.

"Concerning?"

"McCabe."

"Usual." The transmission ended.

Baxter put his ORB down on the console and rubbed at the sweat on his upper lip.

The annual UFO festival in Las Vegas had been held in one-hundred-degree weather. Now the November heat wave had spread east.

Baxter reached for his water thermos.

His throat was dry, scratchy. Maybe he was coming down with something.

Or maybe he didn't like the heat as much as he'd thought he would.

McCabe let herself into the house. She dropped her thermo jacket on a chair and stretched. Even with a couple of errands along the way, she'd actually gotten home at a decent hour for once.

And she might want to leave again, McCabe realized as her father stomped into the living room holding one of his leather bedroom slippers.

"Do you see this?" Angus said. "Do you see the teeth marks?"

"Puppies will be puppies," McCabe said.

"I want that damn dog out of this house."

"We're keeping him, Pop. It's time we had another dog."

"When that fluffy ball of fur that your mother called a dog died—"

"You cried," McCabe said.

"Tears of joy," Angus said. "I am not going to walk that four-legged—"

"The Wyatt kids down the street have agreed to be our official dog walkers."

"You've got an answer for everything, haven't you?"

"Not everything. What are we having for dinner?"

"Is your nose broken?"

"Smells like lasagna. But if you're really mad at me, making your world-famous lasagna—"

"He made his world-famous lasagna for your brother."

McCabe turned at the sound of her brother's voice. Adam was standing in the dining room doorway. He was smiling.

"Hi," she said.

"Hi, sis."

"You're wearing . . . I thought you didn't like wearing the exoskeleton."

"Mai says I'm stubborn."

"So, uh, Mai's still around."

"For now. Maybe for a while."

"And the next time you come, you can bring her so that I can have a look at her," Angus said. "But I called you over here tonight to talk some sense into your sister."

Adam said, "So what are we going to name the dog, sis?"

"Spot?" McCabe said.

"Big Foot more like it," Angus said. "And we aren't going to name him anything, because you're taking him back where you got him."

"Where is he, by the way?" McCabe said.

"Asleep out on the porch," Adam said. "Interesting-looking animal. Seems to be a mix of about half a dozen different breeds."

"Great Dane on his mother's side, Dalmatian, Lab, and mutt on his father's."

"And all likely to eat us out of house and home," Angus said. "The lasagna's ready. One of you make the salad."

McCabe walked over and tucked her hand into her brother's arm. "If I haven't said it, I'm glad you're here."

Adam gave her a sideways glance and said, almost awkwardly, "Me, too."

"So, how's the research going?"

"Coming along." He looked directly at her now, one eye covered by his pirate's patch. "Someday I'm going to walk on my own two legs and feel them."

"Of course you will," McCabe said. "Mai's right. You are stubborn. Once you set your mind to something, you never give up."

Angus said, "Will you two stop yapping and—"

"Make the salad," Adam said. "We got it covered, Pop."

McCabe smiled at her brother. "Let's go get dinner on the table. I'm starving."

Sitting on his sofa, Beethoven playing in the background, a glass of bourbon within reach, Pettigrew rehearsed what he would say to his ex-wife.

She had called to say she was in town and on her way over.

"But this time, sweetheart," he said in his best tough-guy imitation, "this time, I'm not going to play the sap for you."

Pettigrew sighed. He lifted his glass in a toast. "Here's to you, Swede, from one poor sap to another."

Author's Note

This book is a traditional police procedural novel that takes place in the near future (2019) in an occasionally altered, or "parallel," universe. However, the setting will be familiar to readers who have visited Albany, New York, or will visit the city during the next few years. Therefore, I should tell you what is true in this book and what is not.

The historical facts about the city of Albany are true. Abraham Lincoln, president of the United States during the Civil War, and John Wilkes Booth, actor, Confederate zealot, and Lincoln's assassin, did both visit Albany in 1861. Lincoln was en route to his inauguration; Booth was performing at a local theater. They were in the city on the same day, and Booth may have been in the crowd that gathered to witness Lincoln's arrival. A couple of months later, Booth was again in Albany. This time he was performing with a young actress named Henrietta Irving. During a drunken lover's quarrel, Irving stabbed Booth. There is some historical disagreement about where the knife left its mark—on Booth's handsome face or on his neck. Irving went back to her room and tried to kill herself. She survived and later went on to marry and have a successful career. Four years later, Booth assassinated Lincoln at Ford's

Theater. The young major and his fiancée who had joined the Lincolns in their box at the theater that evening were from Albany. Their lives, too, were changed forever by the events of that night.

The presence of Booth and Lincoln in Albany and the incident between Booth and Irving is the subject of a fictional play by the fictional third victim in this book. My third victim is a Broadway actress whose roles have included "Alice" and, later, as an adult, the "Red Queen." Because she was obsessed with all things *Alice* and that may have played a role in her death, there is a strong *Alice in Wonderland* theme in this book. All of the statements about the *Alice* books and Lewis Carroll are based on research.

There are also references to *The Wizard of Oz* because the third victim's body is found off Delaware Avenue, not too far from Albany's own "yellow brick road." Both avenue and road do exist. The yellow-hued bricks used to construct an old, no longer used, bridge have given Albany its own version of the yellow brick road that L. Frank Baum describes in his book and that appears so famously in the Judy Garland movie.

In this book, Albany has a female mayor. At the time of this writing, all of the mayors during Albany's several-hundred-year history have been male. The reader also will notice some other tinkering with political history and popular culture. When writing a book set in the near future, a writer quickly learns that creating an "alternate universe" or "parallel world" is the only way to deal with changes that may occur in the real world. For the fiction writer, an alternate universe also allows the exploration of ideas and possibilities.

To summarize, the reader may take as fact, the historical aspects of this book. The descriptions of the geography of the city, with the exception of a minor change regarding the location of a crime scene, are generally accurate. However, although a "fast train" to Albany has often been discussed, the trip still requires about two and a half hours. The convention center referred to in the book has been proposed, but does not yet exist. The restaurant with its own attached "vertical farm" cannot be found in Albany. But vertical farming is now seen as one near-future solution to feeding an urban population.

Several scenes in this book occur on the University at Albany campus. The layout of the campus is generally as described. As portrayed here and in reality, the UAlbany mascot is a Great Dane. In the real world, the Department of Theatre Productions at UAlbany offers a minor and an interdisciplinary major. In my book, the UAlbany Theatre Department not only offers a major, but has a graduate program.

The Albany Police Department (APD) in this book bears some resemblance to the structure of the city's police department and to urban police departments in general. But the APD of this book, the officers, detectives, and senior administrators, are fictional. They were not inspired by or intended to represent real people. Even if I have inadvertently used a real-world name of someone who has served in the APD, it is a coincidence. I have done some research in a police department, but that was academic research and did not occur in the Albany PD. The events in this book also did not occur in the department where I did my research. In short, my cops are fictional and so is their Albany PD. The issues that my cops are dealing with regarding crime, police-community relations, police bureaucracy, and city budgets have some basis in the reality of policing in Albany and most American cities. But the context is 2019 and the specific crimes the detectives tackle come from my imagination, as do the personal and professional situations in which they find themselves.

The scenes involving the task force with representatives from the local Federal Bureau of Investigation (FBI) office and the New York State Police reflect common practice in major cases. However, the characters from the FBI and the State Police are fictional, not based on real people, and not to be taken as the author's commentary about either agency. Interagency cooperation is essential to solving crimes, but the cops in my book get to offer their opinions about turf.

The reader will note the contrast between some advances in technology and some problems that are less easily solved. For example, the drug referred to early in the book is inspired by recent findings regarding treatment of soldiers traumatized in battle. The medical condition discussed at the end of the book is also based on fact. But the reader will note that in this world of the near future, the surveillance technology does not always work as it should. That is because effective use of technology requires financial investment in infrastructure, maintenance, and other budgetary support. It also requires the cooperation of Mother Nature.

For more information about the setting, history, and technology in this book please go to my Web site: www.frankieybailey.com.